P9-EGM-077

# LAMENT

# LAMENT

## ALEXANDRA ADORNETTO

HARLEQUIN TEEN

Recycling programs
for this product may
not exist in your area.

ISBN-13: 978-0-373-21153-1

Lament

First published as Ghost House by Harlequin TEEN in 2014.

This edition published 2016.

This edition published by arrangement with Harlequin Books S.A.

For questions and comments about the quality of this book, please contact us
at CustomerService@Harlequin.com.

HARLEQUIN® TEEN
www.HarlequinTEEN.com

**Printed in U.S.A.**

For the ghosts of my childhood.
Without you, I might have grown up normal.

# THE UNQUIET GRAVE

"The wind doth blow today, my love,
   And a few small drops of rain;
I never had but one true-love,
   In cold grave she was lain.

"I'll do as much for my true-love
   As any young man may;
I'll sit and mourn all at her grave
   For a twelvemonth and a day."

The twelvemonth and a day being up,
   The dead began to speak:
"Oh who sits weeping on my grave,
   And will not let me sleep?"

"'Tis I, my love, sits on your grave,
   And will not let you sleep;
For I crave one kiss of your clay-cold lips,
   And that is all I seek."

"You crave one kiss of my clay-cold lips,
   But my breath smells earthy strong;
If you have one kiss of my clay-cold lips,
   Your time will not be long.

"'Tis down in yonder garden green,
   Love, where we used to walk,
The finest flower that ere was seen
   Is withered to a stalk.

"The stalk is withered dry, my love,
   So will our hearts decay;
So make yourself content, my love,
   Till God calls you away."

—ANONYMOUS

# CHAPTER ONE

I sensed the ghost before I saw her. Something in the air changed, just a fraction. I picked up a dull vibration, like the humming of bees or the crackle of leaves tossed around by the wind. At first I mistook her for one of the mourners, until I looked properly. Then, my palms grew slick and I wondered if anyone else could hear my pounding heart. The flurry of emotions that stirred in my chest was too conflicted to let me settle on just one. The ghost had crappy timing, show-ing up on the day of my mother's funeral. But then again, the ghosts I'd known had never been big on tact; they were far too self-centered.

When I was a kid, I saw them everywhere. They intruded into my life on a daily basis. It was my mom who taught me how to block them out. Now, funnily enough, the woman who protected me from the dead had gone to join them. *Don't be afraid, Chloe,* I remembered her telling me. *Just stand your ground and tell them to leave you alone.* To my surprise, it worked. They went away and until that afternoon I hadn't laid eyes on one since. Deep down I'd always known they'd come back, but why today?

I was sitting in the front row between Grandma Fee and my kid brother, Rory, watching the shiny mahogany casket being lowered into the ground. I wanted to cry, but there were no tears left. My eyes were already raw and burning. Grandma Fee gripped my hand, the only sign of emotion she allowed herself to show in public. Don't get me wrong; she wasn't unfeeling. She was just British. Her fine-featured face, still beautiful despite its lines, was set in stone. Rory looked small and sad, hunched over with his knees squeezed together. Swamped by an oversize suit, he looked younger than his twelve years. His eyes were pink rimmed and his nose was running, perhaps a combination of grief along with his plethora of allergies. I was tempted to reach out and push back the coffee-colored curls falling over his eyes, but I didn't trust myself to move even an inch. I was holding my breath and tensing every muscle into a coil. If I let go, even for just a second, I was scared I'd break into a thousand pieces. I was sort of like Humpty Dumpty. I might have been put back together, but nothing was in the right place. I would never be whole again.

The funeral service was almost over, and the reverend was sweating beneath his heavy black vestments. I watched a bead of sweat swell at his temple and meander down to disappear behind his left ear. Out of the corner of my eye I sneaked a look at my dad. Over six feet tall and lanky, he sat at an awkward angle, spilling out of his chair like he wasn't sure how to arrange his limbs. I'd never seen him look so lost. His broad hands gripped his knees so tightly, the knuckles had turned white. And every intake of breath was an effort, like he had to keep reminding himself to breathe. It made me wonder how he was going to get through the rest of the day.

But right now I had a bigger problem on my hands. The ghost stood not more than twenty feet away from me. At first I refused to acknowledge her, throwing only a cursory glance in her direction, hoping my indifference might drive her away. I held myself ramrod straight and fixed my eyes on the newly dug cavity in the ground waiting like a hungry mouth. It was strange to think that from now on this spot would hold the physical remains of my mother. The thought made me slightly dizzy, and my throat constricted to the point where I wanted to gasp for air. I found myself thinking about the casket rotting away until it finally collapsed in on itself, granting access to whatever parasites lived in the damp earth. My whole body started to tremble, and I quickly averted my eyes. Those kinds of morbid thoughts weren't going to help anyone. I needed to stay strong for Rory and Dad. If I didn't, who would take care of them?

Only when the casket was in place did my father let out a soft, shuddering breath. His face was an open book, proclaiming his loss. But who could blame him? My parents had always believed their relationship was strong enough to weather any storm, except death, I guessed.

As the reverend's voice droned on, hollow and comfortless, I watched the gray clouds gather overhead. I let my eyes flicker to where the ghost stood. From across the well-worn path that separated us, she kept her own silent vigil. It was so brazen, the way she stood there in broad daylight even though we both knew she wasn't alive. She was in the original part of the cemetery, where most of the railings were rusted and eroded, half-buried in the earth. Around her, cracked head-stones sat crookedly like bad teeth.

The woman clearly didn't belong to my world. She was dressed in black from head to toe, including the ruched bonnet framing her sallow face. Beneath it, her hair was parted severely in the center and wound in a bun so tight, the veins in her temple throbbed. The bunch of wildflowers she clutched was already beginning to wilt, as if everything in her presence quickly lost the will to live.

I didn't need a second look to know that this was not a happy ghost. Then again, the ones left behind to haunt the earth rarely are. You could always tell from the look in their eyes that they were restless and troubled. Maybe their lives ended tragically, maybe they had unfinished business or maybe they were just never able to let go. As a child, I assumed everyone could see them. It was years before I realized I was alone in my abilities. I would sometimes wonder, *Why me?* Who singled me out and decided I'd be up to the task? These were not questions anyone could answer, so I simply learned to live with my little *quirk,* hoping that one day everything would finally make sense. I was still waiting for that day to come.

The ghost commanded my attention again when the woman's eyes widened and she sank to her knees. I let out an involuntary gasp, causing more than a few heads to turn in my direction. My little brother glanced anxiously across at me. For just a second, I was filled with a flutter of hope. Was it possible that Rory could see her, too? Much as I hated the idea of him being tormented by the dead, it would mean that I wasn't so alone, that I wasn't such a freak. But as I looked back at him, I saw only concern for me reflected in his eyes.

He couldn't see anything else. I shot him a tight smile to show that everything was fine. Except that it really wasn't. Not even close.

I decided to try a new tactic. I squeezed my eyes shut and focused on willing the apparition away. The reverend's voice, softer now, reached me as if from a distance: "'Then shall the dust return to the earth as it was, and the spirit shall return unto God who gave it.'"

I opened my eyes just as the muted chorus of amens rang out. The woman was still there, right where I'd left her. Only, her eyes looked different now. They seemed mocking, as if she was amused by my efforts to dispel her.

My mother's words floated back to me once again: *Look them right in the eye. They can't hurt you.* And so I did. As I held her gaze, the scornful expression began to dissolve. The rest of her soon followed, blurring at the edges like a chalk drawing on the pavement washed away by rain. Eventually, she just wasn't there anymore.

With the final prayer concluded, everyone rose in unison and began to make their way back to the parking lot. I slipped away and headed in the opposite direction, until I was right in front of the little headstone where the woman had stood. The inscription, eroded by time and the elements, was barely visible, but I could still make out the words: *Thomas Jerome Whitley 1906–1910.* He'd been just four years old when he died.

"Chloe?" I turned to find Grandma Fee standing behind me in her tailored black suit, not one silver hair out of place. She scanned the grave site, and I could tell she wanted to ask about its significance. But now wasn't the time. Instead, she placed a gloved hand on my shoulder. "You can come back anytime you want."

"I know," I murmured. But I wouldn't be back anytime soon. I didn't need to come here to feel close to my mother. When I thought of her, I wanted to remember the things no one else would think about—like the way she used to snort sometimes when she laughed too hard, or how excited she got about birthdays, or how she'd leave little notes in my lunch box even after I was in high school. I certainly didn't want to remember her by this dismal affair.

"Come on." Gran shepherded me away. "Let's go home."

The drive back to the house seemed to pass in a blink. I'd been hoping for more time to brace myself for the congregation of mourners that showed up in our living room to pay their respects. I vaguely recognized some of the women from our church bearing casseroles and chocolate pies. It felt weird seeing all these strangers. I'd never seen them around when Mom was alive—what right did they have to show up now that she was dead? Gran found me in a corner, trying to avoid conversation or anyone who might attempt to hug me. She pushed a tray of mini quiches into my hands.

"Put these on the table," she instructed. I didn't object; I was grateful to have a job. I looked around for my friends Natalie and Samantha, but I couldn't see them. They'd been at the funeral but probably had decided to skip out on the awkward part. I wasn't surprised. If there were no tequila shooters or boys in snapbacks, they couldn't handle it.

I caught sight of Rory as he made a hasty escape upstairs. I wasn't going to drag him back. He was even more uncomfortable around strangers than I was. There was no reason we should both suffer. Dad was doing his duty, shaking hands

and thanking people for coming, even though his movements were robotic and the faraway look never left his face.
For once I was glad Gran was there to take charge. She had
that air of authority that nobody questioned. I think it was
her British accent that always made her sound bossy, even
when she was just commenting on the weather.

"I think we need more plates, Chloe," she murmured as
she walked past me. I slipped silently into the kitchen to grab
a few minutes to myself.

I'd barely had a chance to catch my breath when I was distracted by the sound of a child humming. I looked around in
confusion; I couldn't remember seeing any children among
the mourners. Then I realized it wasn't coming from inside.
I moved to the open window and peered out. In the middle
of our yard stood a majestic fir tree, a tire swing suspended
from one of its lower branches. My eye traveled slowly up
the tree that my brother and I had climbed countless times
as children. There, in the uppermost branches, sat an odd-
looking boy. For a second I thought it was one of the neigh-
bors' kids who had wandered over and climbed too high for
his own safety.

I was on the point of alerting someone when the details
sank in. The boy was wearing shorts with knee-high beige
socks and old-fashioned shiny lace-up shoes that even the
dorkiest kids in our neighborhood wouldn't be caught dead
in. That could mean only one thing. *He was dead.* Like the
woman at the cemetery, he, too, fixed his gaze on me as he
swung his legs and continued humming his doleful tune. I
wondered how it was possible for his voice to reach me so
clearly. He certainly wasn't dressed for climbing trees. His
clothes were starched and wrinkle-free, and there wasn't a

single graze on his smooth alabaster knees. I'd never set eyes on him before, yet somehow I knew his name was Adam and that in life he hadn't been allowed to climb trees.

Gran poked her head through the door.

"What's the holdup with those plates?" We both knew she wasn't really asking about the plates. She was checking up on me. More than anything, I just wanted to be left alone. My body was numb from head to toe. My own house felt alien. I saw familiar faces around me, but they seemed like strangers.

"Sorry," I mumbled without making eye contact. "Got distracted." Gran sighed and folded her arms.

"Chloe, please try to remember that everyone is here because your mother meant something to them."

"You mean they didn't come for the free food?"

She looked at me sternly. "Now is hardly the time to get stroppy."

I wasn't sure what *stroppy* was supposed to mean, so I assumed it was an English thing. Grandma Fee hailed all the way from Hampshire—Jane Austen country, as she liked to tell anyone who would listen. She'd met my American grandfather on exchange in college. They'd been inseparable, marrying soon after graduation and traveling around the States as Pop built his career as an investment banker, until he passed away from cancer a few years ago. Then, to everyone's surprise, she'd packed her bags and gone back to her roots. Maybe there were too many memories here. When I was growing up, my dad used to jokingly refer to her as Hurricane Fiona. *Board up the windows—Hurricane Fiona's about to hit,* he'd say and now I understood why. She was a woman on a mission.

"Sorry," I repeated. I really wasn't trying to be rude. I was just absent, operating on autopilot and counting the moments until I could collapse on my bedroom floor and never get up again. "I just... I don't think I can do this, Gran."

We both knew I wasn't talking about the next half hour. I was talking about the rest of my life. I couldn't picture it anymore. I'd had all these lofty ambitions. I was going to study like crazy on my SATs, get into an Ivy League school and end up as a journalist for the *New York Times*. But it all seemed like a waste of energy now, given that I didn't even know how I was going to get through the next few days.

Grandma Fee tucked a loose strand of honey-colored hair behind my ear and straightened her shoulders like she was preparing for battle.

"Yes, you can," she told me. "Do you want to know why? Because you're a Kennedy. And Kennedys were built to weather any storm. Things might knock us down, but we always get back up again. Do you hear me?"

I knew that if I tried to speak, the words would get strangled in my throat, so I just nodded mutely. Grandma Fee kissed my forehead. "That's my girl."

When she was gone, I turned back to the window for one final look. The boy was gone but his appearance had left me deeply unsettled. My strange ability had been lying dormant. I hadn't seen a ghost in almost ten years. Now two had shown up in the same day? It had to mean something. Were they back to send me a message? Was this some kind of Cole Sear–type deal, or had my mother's passing simply blurred the barrier between the living and the dead? I had no idea, and there was no one I could turn to for advice. But I knew one thing for sure. These ghosts were different than the ones that had visited me as a child. Those had simply been there, passive and unobtrusive, almost part of the furniture. But the woman in the graveyard and the little boy in our yard…they wanted something.

I knew one thing for sure. This wasn't the last I'd see of the dead.

# CHAPTER TWO

Grandma Fee decided to stay on for a while after the funeral to help get us back on our feet. To tell the truth, I was relieved. A stupor had settled over our house. It used to be filled with the sounds of lively conversation, plates clattering in the kitchen and the clamor of Rory's trumpet practice. Now there was only silence, and the days slipped by unnoticed.

I slept a lot, mainly because it meant I didn't have to think about how everything had changed, how a huge chunk of my family had been ripped away, like when a tornado sucks out the guts of a house, leaving an empty shell. I'd wake in the morning and for a few ignorant minutes everything would feel normal. Then I'd remember that my mother was dead, and suddenly I hardly knew where I was anymore. The world seemed to fall away from under me. I began to understand why people drank to drown their sorrows; I wished there was something I could do to numb the pain that felt like it was clawing at me from the inside.

The strangest part was how everything still looked the same. It was deceptive and almost mocking. The pile of clean laundry was still folded on my bed where Mom had left it. The tennis trophy she'd positioned all too prominently on my shelf seemed to stare back at me. Her leather boots were propped by my door from just last week when I couldn't find anything to go with my outfit and had ransacked her closet instead. In fact, there wasn't a single thing that didn't remind me of her, from the emerald earrings she'd given me on my sweet sixteen to the print of *Starry Night* she'd hung above my bed, hoping I'd *absorb some culture in my sleep.*

My cell phone kept buzzing with an influx of messages from people I barely knew, and I wasn't even sure how they'd found my number. Sam and Natalie were coming up with a million suggestions to try to distract me, but I couldn't bring myself to respond. Nothing mattered anymore. Nothing could begin to replace what I'd lost.

At least I still had my vault. If fear or pain ever tried to take over, I could always rely on the vault. It was a childhood invention, an image I could summon at will that never failed. My vault was impenetrable, solid steel, the perfect depository for stressful thoughts. I would picture the bad thoughts as wisps flying around in the air. I had to catch them first, like butterflies in a net; I knew they'd only come back stronger if they got away. But once they were locked away, they could only come out if and when I allowed them to.

For the most part, I kept my grief in check, apart from the odd random moment when it hit without warning. Like the time Gran was making coffee and I happened to catch sight of the mug she was reaching for.

"Don't use that!" I objected. Everyone froze, waiting for an explanation. "That's Mom's mug."

It was Rory who uncharacteristically came to the rescue.

"Here, Gran, have this one," he said, handing her a nonde-script white one from the back of the cabinet.

Or the time I accidentally strayed into my parents' bed-room in one downstairs wing of the house. I'd been avoid-ing it like the plague, but I was looking for our family dog, Darcy, a chocolate Lab named by Mom for one of her fa-vorite fictional heroes. I found him comfortably ensconced on Mom's side of the bed. Nothing appeared to have been touched since the night she died. I was pretty sure Dad had relocated to the guest room. Mom's mother-of-pearl hair-brush was still where she'd left it on the dressing table, her robe was still hanging from a hook behind the door, and the bestseller she'd been reading was sitting on the nightstand. It was like she might walk in at any moment.

The rest of my family wasn't faring much better. Rory spent the better part of each day locked in his room on his computer, surfacing only at mealtimes. Dad didn't break down in any dramatic way; he just *disconnected*. If we did manage to get his attention, even the simplest of questions puzzled him.

"Dad, how do you turn on the washer?" Rory stood in the kitchen doorway, holding a bundle of crumpled gym shorts and T-shirts. Momentarily jolted from his dazed state, my fa-ther looked at Rory like he was a complete stranger. Luckily, Gran saved the day, steering my brother diplomatically away.

"Come along, dear," I heard her say. "We'll figure it out together."

As the days passed I watched Dad drift further away from us. Some days we barely saw him, but I'd hear him late at night rummaging in the kitchen, eating cereal because he'd forgotten about lunch and dinner. For the most part, he preferred to nurse a large scotch on the back porch, looking up at the stars. Seeing him that way made my chest hurt. I waited for signs that he was coming back to us, but nothing happened. It was hard to see him unshaven, mooching aimlessly around in sweatpants. How could this be the same man who had given us pep talks about going after our dreams only a few weeks earlier? But what can you do when your whole world is shattered? How do you pick up the pieces and move on when you don't know what you're moving on for? I wished there was something I could do to ease his pain, but I was only just treading water myself.

It didn't help that the ghosts were appearing thick and fast. I was changing into my pajamas the following night when I saw the next one. A man with thinning hair sat in the rocking chair by the open window, smiling aimlessly into space. I recognized him. He'd shown up many times when I was a child, always smiling but never uttering a word. But that wasn't the scariest part. I could feel the walls I'd built to keep the ghosts out starting to crumble. They were slipping through the cracks. My grief had made me weak, and I didn't have the strength to rebuild my inner fortress. There was no room for anything other than the overwhelming ache of missing my mother.

I backed up against my desk, trying to put as much distance between us as possible.

"Go away," I told him forcefully, even though I knew he probably couldn't hear me. "You shouldn't be here."

I tried to show him I was unfazed by busying myself, rearranging my bookshelf. The smell and touch of the well-worn pages and fraying spines settled my nerves, and when I looked again, he was gone. My eye fell on the top shelf, which housed my most treasured editions. Books had always been my refuge, and I had Gran to thank for that. For as long as I could remember, every year on my birthday she'd sent me a classic novel. The first was a forest-green leather-bound edition of *Peter Pan*. I always remembered that one famous quote: "To die would be an awfully big adventure." I wondered if that was true. Did we really pass on to a dimension full of stardust and limitless possibilities? Or did nothingness await us? I sure hoped Peter knew what he was talking about.

I jumped as my bedroom door opened a crack and Grandma Fee poked her head into the room.

"Chloe? Is everything all right? I heard voices." I quickly snatched up my laptop. "I was just watching a YouTube video."

I could tell she didn't believe me as she perched on the edge of my bed, twirling her string of pearls between her fingers. She looked like she came from a different era, where women wrapped their hair in scarves and smoked cigarettes through a holder. She tucked a strand of hair behind my ear, her usual gesture of affection.

"Things will get easier," she said. "I know it doesn't feel like it right now, but trust me, I'm speaking from experience. When my mother died it really hit me for six."

The expression was unfamiliar but I knew what she meant. I figured it was a reference to cricket, which we didn't follow in America on account of it being the world's most boring sport.

"It was a long time ago now," Grandma Fee went on. "But I still remember how it felt. It's not something you ever get over. The pain doesn't really go away, but it does dull in time. Enough for you to get on with your life." I nodded, glad for once that someone wasn't sugarcoating the truth. She stood up and straightened my duvet.

"I know I'm not your mother, Chloe. But I want you to know I'm right here if you need anything at all."

I struggled to keep my throat from tightening up. Gran noticed and deftly changed the subject, squinting curiously over my shoulder at the Twitter page on the screen.

"What's this silly little sign?" she asked.

"That would be a hashtag."

"What's it for?"

"Well, um, it's sort of… It's meant to…"

"See, even you don't know!" she said triumphantly. "Honestly, I'll never understand why people feel the need to share what they're having for lunch or what the person next to them on the train is wearing. It isn't even remotely interesting."

"It's like an online diary," I tried to explain.

"So you write about your feelings?"

"Sure. So long as they're one hundred and forty characters or less."

Grandma Fee shook her head as she bent to kiss me goodnight. "Be up at eight for breakfast tomorrow."

"Gran, we don't have scheduled eating times around here."

"Just because you live in *California* doesn't mean you can't be civilized," she told me primly. "I'm making my famous Scotch Eggs."

"You do know I'm vegan, right?"

I'd been converted about six months ago after watching a PETA documentary on the meat and dairy industry. I'd shown Natalie, who'd been just as horrified and vowed to join me in the fight against animal cruelty. She'd even crusaded in the hallways of our high school until someone pointed out that her fur-lined, leather Jimmy Choo boots were a slight contradiction of ethics.

Grandma Fee gave me *the look,* brows raised, chin inclined. "Don't be so ridiculous," she scoffed. "You're not a hippie."

The next morning, I was spared the deep-fried atrocities that were Grandma Fee's Scotch Eggs when the chime of the doorbell interrupted breakfast. I ran to answer it and found a guy from the gas company standing there, twisting his lip apologetically.

"Hi," he said in a voice usually reserved for preschoolers. "Are your mom and dad home?"

"Mom's dead," I replied flatly. "And I don't know where Dad is, but you're more than welcome to look for him."

He stood there in stunned silence a few moments before clumsily handing me a sheet of paper. "I…um…have a disconnection notice for this address." I took it from him and sighed.

"Just give me a few more days, okay? I'll deal with it, I promise."

By then I was mad. I marched off in search of my dad and found him in his workshop in a pair of overalls and a mask, fine sawdust clinging to his eyebrows, temporarily transforming him into a redhead. It smelled familiar and comforting in there—a mixture of shellac, beeswax and turpentine. Dad was surrounded by furniture in various stages of repair. I leaned against an armchair whose gray stuffing had burst through the tapestry. It reminded me of our own lives, coming apart at the seams now that the weave holding us all together was gone. I had to wonder whether Dad was throwing himself into fixing broken things because he couldn't fix the damage to his heart.

Once, when I was younger, he found a discarded dresser on the side of the road that looked like a piece of junk. But as he worked away at it, something beautiful began to emerge. Something with a reddish glow and tapering legs, a bow front and soft brass handles. Seeing him restore it was like watching something come back to life before your eyes.

Dad turned off the sander when he saw me. I spotted the pile of bills gathering dust on the bench.

"Hey, Chloe, what's up?"

"I need your credit card to pay those bills." I pointed at them accusingly. He dug out his wallet and handed it over without blinking. I sighed, gathered up the invoices and went to leave. His willingness to let us shoulder all the responsibility didn't seem fair. Gran had her hands full taking care of the cooking and cleaning as well as responding to the innumerable sympathy flowers and cards we'd received. Couldn't he just handle this one thing?

"Chloe?" he called after me.

"Yeah?"

"Thanks for…y'know, dealing with things right now." He looked so vulnerable it was impossible to stay angry.

"Are you okay, Dad?"

"No," he replied. "But I will be."

Asking him *when* was on the tip of my tongue, but I stopped myself and tramped back to the house with the unopened mail tucked under my arm.

I found Gran wearing a pair of fluorescent rubber gloves, up to her elbows in the kitchen sink even though we had a perfectly functioning dishwasher. She had a deep mistrust of any *newfangled* appliance designed to save time.

"I'm worried about Dad," I told her. "I know everybody grieves differently but he just seems so…" I trailed off.

Gran took off her gloves and cupped my chin in her hands. I caught a whiff of Chanel No. 5, her trademark scent.

"Actually, I've been meaning to talk to you about that." She offered me a cryptic smile. "I know your father has been struggling. We had a little chat about it last night."

"What kind of chat?" I asked suspiciously.

"There's no need to look at me like that," she replied. "It's nothing ominous. We just came up with a little idea."

Why was everything *little* with these British people? *Little* chats and *little* ideas and *little* freaking cups of Earl Grey tea. "You just have to promise to keep an open mind. We only want what's best for you and Rory."

I felt like this was the speech that came right before we got shipped off to military school. But Gran was looking especially pleased with herself, like a cat who'd scored a saucer of cream.

"You're going to love it," she continued mysteriously.

"Love *what?*" I was seriously confused by now.

She beamed at me, her lively gray eyes crinkling at the corners. "England, of course."

# CHAPTER THREE

An emergency family meeting was called in the living room. Dad looked guilty as hell, gulping down hot coffee to avoid answering my flurry of questions. Even Rory put aside his comic books; the baffled look on his face mirrored my own.

"I can't believe you're kicking us out!"

"Please, Chloe, it's not like that," my dad said weakly.

"You can't just send us away to England!" I protested. "That's like...really far away."

"Only five thousand miles," Gran said briskly. Was that a British attempt at humor?

"But it's really cold there..." Rory added. "And they don't have In-N-Out..."

We weren't doing too well in the constructive-argument department. I'd been expecting a suggestion about grief therapy or family counseling, so this proposed trip had caught me completely off guard.

"Now, now." Grandma Fee seemed utterly nonplussed. "It's not supposed to be a punishment. Think of it as a holiday. Your father and I both feel it would do you good."

"But our whole lives are here! We don't need a holiday and I think you mean *vacation*."

"Don't be so dramatic, Chloe," she said. "Everything will be here when you get back."

"What about school?"

"Oh pish posh, there are only a few weeks left before winter break. And you can always do summer school to make up for anything you miss." *Good one, Gran.* She really knew how to entice us.

"But I don't want to go!" It came out more petulant than I intended. I couldn't leave now. I still couldn't keep the ghosts from appearing, and it was messing with my head. I wished my mom were here to back me up. If only she would send Gran a sign from the beyond, topple a vase or rattle something to voice her objection. Where was she anyway? Could she see what was happening in my life? There were so many burning questions I needed answers to, and I sure wasn't going to find them in England.

I looked pleadingly at Dad, but he was too busy trying to wipe the Benedict Arnold look off his face.

"What will we do there?" Rory wrinkled his nose.

"Oh, there's plenty to do," Gran replied. "You can go horseback riding or play in the woods. And if you're very good, I'll take you for tea and scones in the village."

"That sounds like crap!" I cried. "I don't want any scones. I just want to be treated like an adult, and that means being *asked* instead of told what to do."

"Well, Chloe, I'm afraid it's not up for discussion." Gran's voice took on that didactic sharp edge it always did when she was putting her foot down.

"Dad?"

"Please don't make this harder than it already is." He wouldn't even look me in the eye. I didn't know who to be angrier with—Gran for coming up with such a crazy plan or Dad for giving it his blessing.

"What about Darcy?" my brother asked suddenly. I was pretty sure Rory loved that dog more than he loved Dad and me.

"Your father will look after him," Grandma Fee said chirpily. "And I have a dog. You remember, Maximilian?"

"The English sheepdog?" I asked dubiously. "Isn't he, like, a hundred years old by now?"

"Well, his eyesight's not what it used to be, but he can still play a decent game of fetch."

"Super." There was no point trying to argue with Gran. She really did have an answer for everything.

"But isn't your place old and creepy?" Rory asked.

"Not anymore," Gran replied with undisguised pride. "You won't recognize Grange Hall now that the renovations are done."

The last time we saw it, Rory was six and I was almost twelve. That wasn't long after Gran bought the property, astounding everyone with such an impulsive decision. I had a vague memory of a vast gray English manor house with cracked windows and chimneys that looked ready to topple. I remembered bleak skies and thick twisted forest you couldn't pay me enough to venture into. After that, my parents kept making plans to visit again, but something always got in the way. That had been perfectly fine by me. The house had been musty and damp and made me feel like I'd fallen into a time warp. I'd kept looking outside expecting to see a horse and carriage rattle through the mud. I remembered my parents telling me that, after Pop passed away, Gran decided to fix the place up with the small fortune he had left her in his will. Initially Mom and Dad had been concerned that it wasn't a wise investment, but it had turned out that Gran had sound business acumen.

"Well, I'm not going anywhere," I said decisively. "And you can't make me."

"I respectfully disagree," Gran replied. "I'll drag you to the airport by the ear if I have to."

"That's child abuse."

"I prefer to call it tough love." She turned away and began stacking the dishes. "We're leaving tomorrow at 6:00 a.m. sharp." My eyebrows nearly hit the ceiling.

"As in twelve hours from now?"

"That's right. The tickets have already been booked."

"So you made arrangements without asking us first? Why did you even pretend we had a choice?" Gran acted as if I hadn't spoken.

"You should probably go pack," she said. "You'll need warm clothes, coats, mittens, gumboots, that sort of thing."

My closet consisted primarily of T-shirts and flip-flops. I didn't know what the hell a *gumboot* was supposed to be, and I was too darn mad to ask. The screen door slammed behind me as I stormed out onto the porch. It was a clear, still day, the dazzling California sun too bright to look at without shading your eyes. I leaned against the trunk of the gnarly old tree that had our tire swing secured by ropes in the uppermost branches and traced my fingers over the initials carved there. Mom and I had done that to commemorate my first day of school. I didn't want to picture her face, because I knew grief would hit me like a tidal wave..At the same time, I didn't want to forget what she looked like. I was scared that over time I would forget the little details, like the touch of her hands or the way she used to smell.

"Chloe." A whisper rushed out of nowhere, calling my name as if across a vast distance. My head whipped desperately around as the old swing began to rock back and forth. I knew that voice. It belonged to my mother. I shivered as a gust of wind tossed the leaves at my feet in a frenzied dance. Could she really be here? Was she trying to make contact? Or was the grief slowly making me insane? Maybe I didn't mind being insane, if it meant I got to see her one last time.

*"Chloe?"* I spun around to find only my dad standing behind me, his brow furrowed in concern. "Are you all right?"

"Yeah." I let out a long breath. "I'm fine."

"I'm sorry about before," he began. "I don't want you to think I'm trying to get rid of you."

"I don't think that."

"I'm just not sure I can deal with everything right now...."

"You're not the only one," I muttered, casting a glance at the swing still creaking in the wind.

"It was Gran's idea," he went on. "And, well, you know what she's like. But I can't stand to have you and Rory mad at me."

"I'm not mad," I told him. "I'm just... I don't know what I am. And Rory will be fine. He always is."

"I haven't told him your grandmother doesn't believe in the internet," Dad said.

"Yeah, I'd save that little bombshell for after he's on the plane."

We managed to share a laugh, and in those brief minutes

it felt like I had my father back. The conversation was cut short by my cell phone buzzing in my pocket. It was Sam and Natalie, checking up on me.

"I better let my friends know." I sighed. "They're going to freak out."

Dad nodded and went inside to give me some privacy.

"You're going *where?*" Sam's voice on the other line was shrill and demanding. I could just picture her wearing the puppy-dog pout she always wore when she wasn't happy about something. It was a face her dad had trouble resisting. Recently it had scored her both a new car and a pair of Louboutin shoes.

"No, not New Hampshire," I repeated for the second time. "Hampshire, *England*. My gran lives there, remember?" I was sure I'd mentioned this to them plenty of times before now, but information that wasn't gossip tended to pass right through them like water through a sieve.

"That's such bullshit," Nat chimed into our three-way conversation. "Why would you agree to that?"

"I didn't exactly agree."

"Wait," Sam cried. "Does that mean you'll be away for your birthday?"

"I guess so," I replied. Not that my upcoming eighteenth birthday meant much to me now.

I wasn't sure how the conversation had turned into me consoling them. Sometimes I had to wonder how they'd come to be my closest friends. I guessed it was because we'd known each other since the third grade, when all our moms were in the PTA. Sam has asked me if I'd ever kissed a boy. I'd told her boys had cooties, and we'd bonded from that moment on. We didn't have much in common anymore, but history kept us together. At least they knew me inside out and could sense my mood without me having to say a word. I appreciated the tacit agreement not to talk about my mom. I wasn't sure how I was meant to behave now that I was motherless, and pretending things were normal bought me some time.

"You guys won't even be around for my birthday," I continued. "Aren't you going to New York for winter break?"

"Yeah, and you were supposed to come with us," Sam replied. "Fifth Avenue shopping and lunch at the Plaza. What's in Hampshire except maybe some trees?"

They really weren't offering much reassurance. A simple *You'll be fine, Chloe. Just try to relax* would have sufficed. But it was typical of my friends to make a big deal out of everything. I was almost glad to be leaving the country. I couldn't face weeks of idle chitchat about the latest celebrity gossip or whether pencil skirts were in or out.

Gran allocated Rory and me one duffel bag each and told us to set our alarm clocks for the early-morning flight. I packed in record time, not caring what I threw in. After all, it wasn't like I cared what people in Hampshire were going to think of me.

Rory gave Darcy the longest hug, burying his face in the dog's neck until we had to pry them apart. Then he sulked all the way to LAX. Because we were running late, there wasn't time for protracted goodbyes. Leaving was a blur. One minute we were rushing to check in and the next we were boarding the plane. Dad looked a little teary as he waved us off from the security checkpoint. I hoped Gran was right about him needing alone time.

Heathrow was much smaller than I remembered. In fact, the whole country seemed pocket-size. To our surprise, it turned out Gran had a driver. A bearded man called Harry in a corduroy cap picked us up from the airport. The drive to the village of Wistings, where Grange Hall was located, was about two hours out of London by car. Sadly, Harry turned out to be the chatty type. Because we were American, he seemed to feel the need to act as tour guide, offering a running commentary on everything from the breed of cows grazing in the fields to various significant historic sites. Rory plugged himself into his iPad, so that left just me to keep up polite conversation.

"Does all of England look like this?" I asked after a while. The green rolling hills surrounding me couldn't have been more of a contrast to the dusty California desert we'd left behind.

"Hampshire is considered to be one of the most attractive counties to live in," Gran answered proudly. A road sign announced we were entering the village of Wistings.

"Is that an actual house?" I nudged Rory so he could catch a glimpse of a towering, ivy-clad edifice that looked like it belonged in a Disney animation.

"That's Linton House. It belongs to the Ashton-Croft family. They have twin boys heading to Oxford next year. I should have them over for tea so I can introduce you." She turned to me with a meaningful smile. That was just the sort of thing my grandmother would say, regardless of timing. She'd always been socially ambitious.

Wistings itself was quaint and tiny with houses that looked barely big enough to accommodate doll-size people. The streets were cobbled and winding. There was one bluestone church with a spire, and the main street was only a short string of shops—a post office, a pharmacy called Boots and then just a bunch of antiques stores.

I wasn't concentrating, so I almost missed Grange Hall when we arrived. A pair of tall, remote iron gates swung open, and Gran's old Mercedes turned onto a sweeping gravel drive. The grandeur of the house took me by surprise.

"Holy crap!" I exclaimed, incurring a glacial look from Gran. I guessed profanity wasn't cool in this part of the world. But Harry had the good grace to stare straight ahead and not react.

"Welcome to Grange Hall," he announced rather formally.

"Wait, *this* is Grange Hall?"

"I told you it had changed." Gran beamed, and Harry couldn't suppress a grin when he saw my slack jaw through the rearview mirror. "Rather impressive, wouldn't you say, young lady? This place used to be little more than a ruin."

But whatever it had been in the past, the house was a far cry from a ruin now. If you could even call it a house. Its proportions were far too epic for that description. Grange Hall was a perfectly preserved example of Georgian architecture painstakingly restored to its original grandeur. Even though I might be there under duress, it was hard not to be impressed by its imposing facade. Lush lawns flowed around it like a green cape, melting into the woods on either side of the property. I vaguely remembered my pop once telling me it had belonged to an aristocratic family who was forced to sell it when they fell upon hard times. I concluded that meant it had been passed down to indulged kids who squandered their inheritance and then had to find real jobs.

We stepped out of the car, and Harry disappeared with

our bags. The silence was overwhelming after the blasting horns and wailing sirens of the city I called home.

"It looks so empty. Where are the guests?" I asked Gran.

"It's off-season," she explained. I looked down to see my hands already mottled from cold. I pulled my flimsy jacket tighter and glanced up at steely skies threatening rain. The air was different here; it had a biting sting. Goodbye, mild California. I was clearly going to need warmer clothes.

In her home environment, my grandmother seemed different, more relaxed. The regal air that had made her a fish out of water in Los Angeles just seemed to work here.

"How about some tea before the grand tour?" she asked.

"Sounds good," I answered.

"I'm starving!" Rory blurted. He was still plugged into his iPad, but whatever game he was playing couldn't compete with the offer of food. Even if the food was English.

"Harry, would you please organize it?"

At the mention of his name, Harry promptly appeared out of nowhere, seeming to transform from driver to butler.

"Right away, Ms. Kennedy," he said, adding a short bow. I smothered a smile behind my hand.

A few minutes later we were escorted into a cozy parlor with a fire burning in the grate. Gran's old sheepdog must have been hard of hearing, because he was sleeping soundly by the hearth and barely stirred upon our arrival. Harry wheeled in a tiered trolley replete with warm scones and homemade jam, sticky buns as well as fresh berries and cream. There were also little triangular sandwiches with ham and cheese, cucumber or curried egg. Something told me being vegan just wasn't going to work out here. Not if I wanted to survive. As I nibbled on a cucumber sandwich and drank steaming tea out of a dainty china cup, I couldn't help but think that the whole place had the sleepy stillness of a bygone era. There were even classical statues dotting the garden. Some might have described it as tranquil, but I called it boring. No wonder so many great writers had come out of this country. What else was there to do when you were holed up inside all day?

I stared at a majestic white oak in the front garden. Its knotted base extended like a massive prehistoric foot. There was something about the tree, something eerie, as if the color around it had faded and I was looking at a black-and-white photograph.

"There's a lake just past the woods," Grandma Fee was saying. "And we have a few horses in a stable out back."

But I wasn't paying attention. Why couldn't I tear my eyes away from this ancient tree? Then, suddenly, I caught a flash of something that made me drop my fork with a clatter. For a split second I saw a thick noose hanging from the branches of the tree. From it swung the body of a heavyset man. I could see his swollen lips and his bulging eyes staring right at me. His feet, encased in heavy boots, were still twitching.

# CHAPTER FOUR

I let out a bloodcurdling scream and jumped to my feet, sending my chair crashing into a potted palm. Through the French doors, I saw Harry almost trip over his own feet. My own heart was thumping so violently I thought it was about to be dislodged and jump out of my chest. Only Gran managed to remain calm and observe me with her collected gray stare.

"Whatever is the matter, Chloe?" I looked back at the tree, but there was nothing there now but branches swaying gently in the wind.

"There was a bug," I said weakly. Everyone looked at me as if I'd lost my mind, and I felt my cheeks redden. Rory shook his head.

"Do you always have to be such a girl?" he complained. For the first time, I was grateful for his total lack of awareness.

I was so unsettled by the vision that Grandma Fee's tour of the house was a complete blur. The skin on the back of my neck was still crawling. Sure, I'd seen ghosts before, but never in their actual state of death. I couldn't get the man's blue lips and froglike eyes out of my mind. He'd been wearing a black frock coat and stiff collar, as if he were a gentleman, maybe even master of the house. Did that mean he'd once lived at Grange Hall? What had happened for him to meet such a grisly end? If I'd come all this way hoping to escape my apparitions, I was definitely not off to a great start. So much for rest and relaxation....

I followed Grandma Fee as she whisked us from one elegant room to the next. The most impressive was the ballroom on the ground floor overlooking the rolling front lawns.

"I wish Mom could have seen this." As Rory's reference to our mother slipped out, he froze.

"Me, too," Gran said and then just kept going methodically, her heels clicking on the marble floor.

"Does anyone ever use this room?" I asked, looking up at the soaring ceiling with its elaborate plasterwork.

"Not often," Grandma Fee replied. "Although Bearwood Academy is hosting its Winter Ball here in a few weeks."

"Spiffing!" I said. "Shall we telephone the Queen or just send her a text?"

"How amusing. It's a very elegant affair—you'll see."

"Can I go to the ball?" Rory piped up.

"It's just for seniors, dear." Gran patted his head. "But we'll let you sneak a peek. I could probably get *you* an invitation, Chloe, if you're interested."

"Only if Harry will be my date."

"There's no need to take that tone." I could tell I was testing her patience.

"Look, Gran," I said. "I hang out at The Soho House

and Château Marmont. So I think I'll pass on the Hogwarts high-school dance.

"*Ball,*" she corrected emphatically.

"Whatever!"

I didn't know why I was being such a brat—maybe the fact that I was cold and miserable and ready to go home after less than an hour had something to do with it. I suspected Gran would try to set me up with a polo-shirt-wearing prep-school boy who rowed in the Regatta and was descended from some lord.

"Sounds thrilling, but I didn't come here to make friends."

Grandma Fee let it drop, at least for the time being. She showed us the library next. It had a vaulted ceiling and book-cases full of leather-bound tomes. There were deep armchairs and an old writing desk with an antique typewriter plus two archaic-looking computers that probably used dial-up internet. I was already feeling cut off from the outside world.

It made me think of Sam and Natalie. I'd promised to text them as soon as I arrived. I whipped out my cell…one weak bar of reception. I waved it around uselessly.

"Are you serious?" I demanded.

"Did I mention that reception isn't great out here?" Gran said.

"How am I supposed to talk to my friends?"

"You could try writing to them," Grandma Fee replied. "Our postal service is very efficient." I bit my tongue to keep from saying something I shouldn't.

We wandered back out into the hall and Rory's eyes widened as they traveled up the imposing staircase with banisters so polished you could see your reflection in them.

"What's upstairs?"

"The guest suites are on the second floor, and the top floor is where I live. Speaking of guests, I should warn you, you might run into a couple of women from Baton Rouge calling themselves *paranormal investigators*. They visit once a year. They're perfectly harmless. Just remember to be civil if they talk to you."

"Seriously?" I couldn't stop the little flutter of excitement that stirred in my chest. What if these women knew something I didn't? Maybe they could help me understand this "gift" that had plagued me all my life.

"Yes," Grandma Fee replied. "But I don't think they've ever discovered anything. It's a load of nonsense if you ask me, but a paying guest is a paying guest."

"What's an abnormal investigator?" Rory asked as I felt my hopes deflate. How stupid of me to think the answers to my problems could be found at Grange Hall. There was nothing here besides miserable weather, poor cell reception and a dead guy in a tree. Did life get any better than that?

Farther down the hall was the sitting room with an open fireplace and a sideboard that held jars of shortbreads, tea and coffee, and a lot of mismatched china. Adjoining the lounge was a carpeted dining room with striped wallpaper and heavy sparkling chandeliers. Each table was set for tomorrow's breakfast. At the back of the house, an inviting, country-style kitchen housed old-fashioned stoves and copper pans hanging from hooks.

On the second floor I counted six double guest suites, three on each side of the hall with their own private bathrooms. One of the rooms was open with a cleaning cart parked outside the door. An emaciated woman emerged, a few wisps of thin gray hair trailing around her shriveled face.

I did a double take when I saw her sunken eyes and bony fingers, but Gran cheerfully introduced her as the housekeeper.

"Children, this is Miss Grimes. She lives here and looks after the running of the house. She may need your help from time to time, so I hope you'll be obliging."

Miss Grimes glared at me, grim faced and bent over like an old stick. She didn't look pleased to see us and gave a sharp nod. I peeked behind her into a lavishly decorated bedroom with a four-poster bed and hand-embroidered quilt. There was a rocking chair by the open window and a cedar dresser. The heady scent of roses filtered out, even though I didn't see any flowers.

We climbed the next flight of steps to Grandma Fee's private wing full of antique vases and rose-patterned furniture.

"This place is my refuge from the world," she explained, as if she needed a refuge in a house quieter than a museum. "Your rooms have been set up here." Rory's face brightened when he saw that his had a TV on the dresser. "You'll find your room at the end of the hall, Chloe," Grandma Fee added. "I thought you might appreciate the privacy."

Despite my earlier cynicism, I liked the room that was going to be mine for the next few weeks. It was spacious with a step down to a little reading nook where a rolltop desk sat under casement windows. It even had a quill and ink pot, although I assumed these were for decorative purposes only. Everything here was fresh and crisp. I was glad to be somewhere that had no connection with my regular life. This room was anonymous, steeped in character from a time that had nothing to do with my own. There was a white cast-iron bed, a traveling trunk for storage and a chair Gran called a slipper chair upholstered in floral linen. The windows were all misted over, but when I rubbed a circle on the glass I could see right out onto adjoining fields and dense woods at the fringe of the property.

As far as keepsakes went, I'd brought only one. It was a silver framed portrait of Mom and me, taken before my brother was born, when we were visiting my aunt Daisy in Oregon. For some reason Dad had chosen to have it developed in black-and-white. We were crouched on a rocky beach with the surf churning behind us. Mom's dark hair was windblown, and her white dress billowed out. But her eyes were fixed on me, and I could tell I was the most important thing in the world to her. I placed the photo at the bottom of a drawer under some cotton sweaters. I wasn't ready to have it on display yet, in case it played havoc with my emotions.

I unpacked my duffel bag, realizing how little I'd brought and how unsuitable even that was. Then I flopped down on my stomach across the bed with its quaint floral duvet and buried my face in the plump pillows. They were soft and inviting. The day of travel finally caught up with me, and I felt like I could fall asleep right then and there. I decided not to risk that, or I'd be awake all night with no TV, internet or cell phone to pass the time.

When I came downstairs I found Gran and Rory donning coats and scarves as if they were preparing for battle rather than going outside to see the stable. I politely declined Gran's offer to join them.

"I think I'd rather take a walk on my own instead…if that's all right with you."

"You can do whatever you like, Chloe. As long as you're here, you must treat Grange Hall as your home. Just remember, dinner is served in the dining room promptly at seven."

I nodded. That was easy enough to comply with. I buttoned my peacoat up to my chin and shivered.

"Best wear a scarf and gloves," Grandma Fee advised, pointing me to an old steamer trunk in the hallway. I opened the lid to find an extensive collection of shawls, smelling like mothballs, and expensive-looking leather gloves.

"Are these yours?" I asked, fishing out a fringed black shawl and trying to fashion it into something semiaccept-able to wear in the twenty-first century.

"Most of those things came with the house," Gran replied. "I don't know whom they belonged to. But it seemed wrong to just throw them out."

I left Gran and Rory and set off to do my own explor-ing of the grounds. The grass was muddy, and my feet sank into the earth with every step. I made a mental note to wear boots and not ballet flats next time I decided to go walking in the English countryside in the middle of winter. The air was heavy with the scent of rain and the biting wind pinched my cheeks, but I didn't mind. It had a reviving effect. This crisp, clean air was a far cry from the perpetual haze and smog that hung over Los Angeles.

At the end of the lawn, I looked back at the house, think-ing I should probably turn back and find a good book to read. I'd packed a few from next year's AP Lit class, figuring I'd have plenty of free time to get a head start. As I deliberated, something caught my attention—a woman, standing and looking down at me from one of the windows on the top floor, a white hand pressed up against the glass. I squinted to get a better look, but with a swish of the curtains, whoever was there vanished. It had to be Miss Grimes, I thought to myself. God, she was creepy, with her crumpled body and shadowy eyes. I knew I was being unkind; she was probably just old and tired. What did I know about her life and its hardships? But there was something in her expression… I wasn't sure whether I'd call it hungry or cruel, but I didn't like it. Grange Hall was getting stranger by the minute.

Deciding I wasn't in the mood to retreat to my room with a book, I kept walking until I came across two paths that veered sharply in opposing directions. One led deeper into the woodland and the other wound neatly around the outskirts. Not being game enough to follow the first, I opted for the second, safer path, making sure to keep the house in view. By now it was dusk. I could already hear owls hooting from the nearby trees. My nose was stinging from the cold, but I wasn't ready to turn back yet. So I trudged on, in no particular direction.

Before long I realized I wasn't alone. One of Gran's guests had had a similar idea and was walking along the same path, just a little way ahead of me. He was tall and broad shouldered, with dark gold hair tousled by the wind and a slender body. He was carrying something under one arm; by its size and shape, I recognized it as a sketchbook. There was something peculiar about him that I couldn't quite put my finger on. But on closer inspection I realized I was thrown off by his choice of clothing. He was wearing riding pants tucked into high leather boots and a billowing white shirt. It looked like an outfit from a costume store. I also noticed that he wasn't strolling like me. He was walking quickly and purposefully, as if he was going somewhere important. Suddenly he reached a bend and vanished into the woods.

Even though he was out of sight I could still hear the crunch of his boots on the gravel. I didn't know what possessed me to run after him, but the urge to know where he was going took hold, and before I knew it, I was following him. The thick trees closed in and gloom enveloped me as soon as I left the path behind. Whoever he was, he knew his way around these grounds. I could see him slipping gracefully between the trees. I was so busy trying not to lose sight of him that I didn't look where I put my feet and stumbled over a fallen log. The loud snapping of twigs underfoot got his attention. He froze instantly, shoulders tensing, his whole body seeming to stiffen. Then he turned very slowly and deliberately, as if unsure what he might find. Finally I got a good look at his face.

He looked different than anyone I'd ever seen before. He was handsome, but not in the run-of-the-mill, captain-of-the-football-team kind of way. He had a more gut-wrenching beauty, with his straight, fine features, pale skin and full lips. He looked like a prince from some faraway land you might find in a book. But his eyes were most startling, the clearest shade of cornflower blue, with just a hint of sadness that couldn't be concealed. He seemed unsettled or preoccupied as he looked fleetingly at me. Then when he saw me looking back at him, something in his face changed.

I stood up and dusted myself off. I was on the verge of introducing myself, but something stopped me. He was almost scowling at me from under his dark golden brows. If I was expecting a nod or smile of acknowledgment, I was bitterly disappointed. In fact, I was feeling more like a trespasser with every passing second. I even started to wonder whether I'd inadvertently strayed onto private property. My legs felt leaden as we stood appraising one another, waiting for someone to make the first move.

"Hi." That was the only strangled word I managed to croak out as I half raised my hand. The young man started and took a step back as if wildly offended. The expression on his face was something between horror and confusion. I didn't get it. Was it my hair? My clothes? I felt myself flush self-consciously. The way he was looking at me, I might as well have been a hideous monster. It was not exactly flattering and quite frankly a little annoying.

Without uttering a single word, he started moving toward me, his piercing eyes boring right into mine. The look on his face was so intense, it caused a dozen thoughts to flash through my brain. Could I be in danger? I didn't know this guy from Adam. He could be an escaped inmate from an asylum for all I knew. How could I have been foolish enough to venture this far alone and chase a stranger into the woods? I would have liked to stay and stand my ground. For some reason, I wanted to hear what his voice sounded like. But every instinct was screaming for me to do one thing. *Run*.

So that was exactly what I did.

# CHAPTER FIVE

Panic clouded my sense of direction; I stumbled off the path and thrashed through the shrubs, not even sure I was going the right way. The air was even more biting now. Not only could I could feel its sting on my face but also in my lungs. Even as I put distance between us, I couldn't get the image of the young man with the haunted eyes out of my head.

When I finally looked over my shoulder, no one was giving chase. The woods were just a tangle of twisted shadows. By the time I found the edge of the lawn, I'd calmed down. The lights in the house glowed like beacons, welcoming me back. A feeling of familiarity settled over me, and in that moment I couldn't have been happier to see Grange Hall, despite being sent there under protest.

The sky had changed color to a streaky mauve, scattered with stars like glittering rocks. Gazing up at them, I felt the sense of danger I'd fabricated in my mind melt away. As I hurried across the wet grass, I realized my back pocket was empty. My cell phone must have fallen out somewhere along the way, but I wasn't going back for it now. Everything would seem less threatening in daylight. For now, all I needed to concentrate on was explaining to Grandma Fee why my shoes were caked in mud and my hands were all scratched up. I was starting to feel the sting of embarrassment even before I walked back inside. Wistings was quite possibly the most uneventful place on Earth. Tearing off like a lunatic just because I'd seen a stranger now struck me as an overreaction. All the guy had done was take a few steps toward me. That didn't exactly make him a serial killer. What if he turned out to be Harry's grandson or one of Gran's employees? So what if he'd seemed standoffish? I wasn't in California anymore. People might be different out here. Maybe I needed to adjust my expectations. Perhaps this guy's behavior was just an example of that snobby reserve the English were renowned for.

Right then I had but one objective—to escape to my room and put the whole humiliating encounter behind me.

I was nearly at the front steps when I heard a polite cough and spun around. It was unnerving to see him again so soon, this time just feet away from me, leaning against a black tree trunk. His sketchbook lay abandoned at his feet, and his arms were folded, as if he'd been waiting for me the whole time. I couldn't work out how he'd managed to beat me to the house, unless there was a shortcut I didn't know about. He wasn't even out of breath; only his hair was wind ruffled and falling over his eyes.

"I think this belongs to you." He held out my phone. The suspicion in his face was gone. He looked almost apologetic now. My cell phone with its bright polka-dot cover looked out of place in his slender hands. Still confused, I made no attempt to take it. I was too transfixed by this guy, who looked like he'd just stepped off a film set. Was this standard dress code for rural England?

"I apologize if I startled you," he continued. "It's just that I wasn't expecting to see anyone." I didn't feel inclined to let him off the hook so easily.

"Well, we just got here," I replied curtly. I watched him tune in to my accent.

"You're American?" Another silence followed, which didn't seem to bother him. He was studying me so attentively that I couldn't help feeling self-conscious again. I nodded and brushed back the strands of hair sticking to my damp cheeks. "Then you must be Mrs. Kennedy's granddaughter. I see the resemblance now. You have her eyes."

"Are you staying at Grange Hall?" I asked, wanting to deflect attention from myself.

"I suppose you could say that." I waited for him to elaborate, until it was clear that he wasn't going to.

"I'm Chloe Kennedy," I said awkwardly. He gave a slight bow.

"Pleasure to make your acquaintance, Miss Kennedy. I'm Alexander Reade."

He was still holding my phone in the palm of his hand, like a peace offering. It would have been rude to let him keep standing there like that, so I took it and pocketed it quickly. "Thanks. Doesn't work too well out here anyway."

I should have excused myself and politely moved on, but I didn't. Something made me linger. There was no doubt about it—Alexander Reade was unmistakably different. And I don't mean different like the kid with Doc Martens and a pink Mohawk at my high school. He seemed to defy classification. He was in a category all his own and appeared completely comfortable with that.

I realized he was frowning at me.

"Where did you get that?" he asked. At first I thought he meant my cell phone but then I followed his line of vision and saw that his eyes were fixed on the shawl I wore around my neck. This conversation was getting weirder by the minute.

"Um… I found it in a trunk in the house. Gran said it was okay to wear. It's not yours, is it?"

He smiled. "No, it's not mine."

"It's pretty ugly, I know, but it's so friggin' cold here."

The smile continued to play around the corners of his mouth. "I'm afraid you can expect weather like this about nine months out of the year. How long are you planning to stay?"

"Not too long," I replied. "But my brother and I are here for Christmas at least. Our dad decided he needed to fly solo for a while." The words *my dad decided to abandon us* seemed more fitting, but I didn't want to be an oversharer, pouring out my life story to a total stranger. At the same time, I was sort of tempted. Maybe that was my problem in life. Always worrying what other people would think. So I shrugged my shoulders and told the truth. "My mom just died. California doesn't seem so sunny anymore." I watched his smile fade.

"I'm very sorry to hear that."

"Why? It wasn't your fault."

People say the strangest things when confronted by someone else's loss. Alexander tilted his head slightly, as if confused by me. A prickling sensation started behind my eyes. Maybe I wasn't ready to talk about my mom after all. He seemed to notice and quickly changed the subject.

"So, what is your opinion of the Grange so far?"

"It's awesome. Gran's done a great job with it."

"She has indeed restored it to its former glory." I couldn't quite decide whether his tone was ironic.

"I guess." There was no disputing that he was weird, but he was also far too interesting and attractive for that to matter. In the dwindling light, his features were blurred except for his eyes—they were bright and vivid and capable of luring you into their blue depths without any effort. My gaze fell on the sketchbook lying on a mound of dry leaves.

"Are you an artist, Alexander?" I asked.

"Please—call me Alex. And I'd say I'm more of an apprentice at this stage."

"Can I take a look?" I wasn't usually so forthright, but I figured I might as well live up to the brash Valley Girl stereotype.

He picked up the sketchbook without hesitation and began to unravel the leather cords that held it together. He handed it to me almost reverentially, as if I was an art connoisseur or someone whose opinion actually mattered.

"Be my guest."

As I turned the pages, sketches spilled out as if they'd been kept captive and were grabbing their only chance for freedom. They were mostly charcoal portraits and still lifes, executed with obvious skill. "These are really good," I said, a better adjective eluding me. I wanted to offer some keen insight or complex interpretation, but *good* seemed to be the best I could muster.

As I leafed through the pages, the subject matter began to change. Now I was looking at highly fantastical scenes, each and every one featuring a raven-haired woman against a background of churning seas or thunderous skies. Her mouth was open in a half cry, her eyes on fire and yet with a strange, childlike quality. Despite being in black-and-white, the woman was arrestingly beautiful but troubled, too. Her presence, even on paper, was so palpable I had to look away from her.

"Wow. These are—" I searched for the right word this time "—powerful."

"Thank you, but I'm rarely satisfied with my work," he replied dismissively.

"What artist ever is?"

He looked surprised, as if I'd just made the revelation of the century. Just then, a small animal scurried out of the underbrush, eyes glowing like lamps. As it ran past us and vanished into the night, Alex's whole posture went rigid and he shifted into a defensive stance.

"Relax." I laughed. "It's just a possum." His penetrating gaze flickered toward the woods.

"I am conscious of the hour," he said abruptly. There was that dark look again, the one that had frightened me the first time. He backed away as if I was giving off some foul, overpowering odor. "You had better return to the house."

"You're not coming in?" I asked.

"No."

Suddenly it felt like he couldn't get away fast enough.

"Maybe we could hang out sometime?"

"Hang out?" he repeated. I couldn't quite determine his tone. Was that contempt? Was it arrogance? Or was it just a plain old brush-off?

"Never mind…" I said awkwardly. "I guess I'll see you around."

"Perhaps," he muttered and turned his back on me.

I stood there watching him walk away until the fog swallowed him up.

Even though I'd just met the guy, the flurry of emotions he'd stirred up was impossible to ignore. This hadn't happened to me since the eighth grade, when I'd tried to work out whether a boy who was mean to me in class secretly liked me. This guy was more complex: charming and magnetic one moment, rude and dismissive the next. He was "trouble looking for a place to happen," as my pop used to say. I'd known him all of five minutes, and already I was frustrated. Why had he rushed off? And why did I care so much? The last thing I needed in my life right now was drama. So, mysterious or not, Alexander Reade became a person to avoid during my stay at Grange Hall.

Back at the house, I ducked into the guest bathroom to straighten myself up before making an appearance in the dining room. I knew by the grandfather clock in the hall that it was well after seven, but Gran didn't reprimand me for once. Rory was halfway through his dinner of something indeterminable. Was it a pie, a quiche, breakfast or dinner?

"What *is* that?"

"Toad in the hole with Yorkshire pudding," Rory told me proudly.

"Wait, the toad goes where?" I asked as Gran handed me a plate. She held out a platter of roasted vegetables, which at least bore some resemblance to food I recognized.

"Did you have a nice walk?" she asked.

"Sorry, I'm late," I said, assuming she was angling for an apology. "I lost track of the time."

"That's easy to do here. There's no need to be sorry."

"I met someone this afternoon." I tried to drop this casually into the conversation as I scooped some vegetables onto my plate.

"Who was that, dear?" Gran replied absently.

"One of your guests. Young guy. Maybe, like, twenty-three."

"There aren't any young men staying here at the moment."

"You know the one," I persisted. "Tall, longish hair, dresses like he's going on a fox hunt."

"You must mean Joe," Gran concluded. I got the sense she was only half listening. "But he's not a guest. He's a student who helps out here on weekends."

"No," I said adamantly. "This guy said his name is Alexander Reade."

"Joe's the best," Rory piped up before Gran could answer. "He's going to teach me to ride. You can learn, too, if you want, Chloe. There are four horses here." He listed them by name, counting them out on his fingers. "Aries, Sable, Betsy and Cinnamon. Betsy's my favorite."

"That's great, Rory." I turned back to Gran. "Maybe he lives in town. He seemed to know you."

"Possibly," Gran said. "But Wistings is a small place. There's no one named Reade here. At least…there hasn't been for a very long time."

"What do you mean?" I asked.

"Well, this house originally belonged to a Reade family. They built it back in 1845. A young businessman and his wife, I believe. I have all the paperwork somewhere."

"What was his name?" I swallowed back the growing lump in my throat.

"Christopher... Callum... Something like that. Are you really only going to eat vegetables?"

But I couldn't eat another mouthful because the knot in my stomach was taking up all the room. I had a nagging suspicion about Alexander Reade, but I seriously prayed I was wrong. If I turned out to be right, then things were about to reach a whole new level of weird. Even for me.

# CHAPTER SIX

That night I gave myself permission to think about my mom for the first time since the funeral. The most aching details flashed through my brain as I lay in my dainty bed, wrapped in three sweaters to keep out the chill. I thought about the way she used to hang everything in her closet inside out. It drove my order-loving dad crazy. I thought about the way she always smelled faintly like lavender. When I was sick, I would bury my face in her pillow and it never failed to make me feel better. I remembered her laugh, the freckle on her right hand, how absorbed she got working on one of her paintings and her uncanny ability to read minds, especially mine. Could she still do that now? I wondered. Maybe she was out there, reading my thoughts from beyond. Even though I couldn't see her anymore, I knew my mom wasn't just *gone*. People were too important to simply disappear. All their deepest, most complex thoughts and experiences, the love and passion they'd built up over the years…that lingered. I could feel it. If the ghosts had taught me one thing, it was that death wasn't final. I didn't know much about God, but

I liked to picture my mom hanging out with him, shooting the breeze, drinking a gin and tonic.

I couldn't help feeling abandoned by her, though. Even though I knew she hadn't left by choice, the feeling lingered regardless. I didn't know who to turn to anymore. Who would help me make sense of the world now? It wasn't that my mom had had all the answers, but whenever life became overwhelming, talking to her always left me with a renewed sense of calm. She used to know what the problem was before I even told her. She could spot boy trouble a mile off. She knew if I'd had a fight with one of my friends or if I just had PMS and needed a sugar fix.

I couldn't stop myself. I started thinking about all the things I'd never get to share with her now—graduating high school, leaving home for college, falling in love, having a family of my own. It was weird to think my kids would know their grandmother only from photographs or stories told around the dinner table. They were going to miss out on so much. I'd always imagined her being there for all the milestones in my life. But the reality was that she was never coming back, and that thought was paralyzing. Some realizations are too devastating for tears. The sadness that engulfed me then was like being caught up in a freak tidal wave. All I could do was stare at the patterned ceiling and wait for the turbulence to pass.

Finally it did, and I drifted into sleep…but only to dream about the ghosts from my childhood.

My parents thought it was cute the first time. Who didn't want a kid with an active imagination, right? It was a different story when the visions started happening on an almost-daily basis. As the arty one in the family, my mom was a

little more open-minded than my empiricist father. As an ac-
countant, he could deal only in tangibles. I tried explaining
to him my sense of a whole other world existing alongside
our own, but my dad would never stand for talk like that. He
always made a point of changing the subject or offering me
a distraction in the form of ice cream or a trip to the park.

The first time it happened, I was barely six. I was on a
stool in the bathroom brushing my teeth, because that was
the only way I could reach the faucet, when suddenly the
lights flickered and dimmed like the bulb was about to bite
the dust. In the mirror, I saw the old man standing right
behind me. His body was wasted and withered, but it was
his skin that frightened me the most. It had that waxy gray
tinge that separated him from the living. His crumpled eyelids stayed shut but his mouth was contorted in a gruesome
silent scream. My own shrieks brought my parents bursting
into the room.

As if I'd passed some initiation rite, other ghosts then
began to make an appearance. Eventually, I just got used to
sharing the space with them. For the most part, they didn't
bother me. They just drifted silently in and out of doorways
or moved objects around upstairs, sometimes making things
rattle. It was only the twins I had a problem with. They liked
to hang out in the attic, in their long nightgowns, hair loose
and hanging down their backs. They couldn't have been more
than ten when they died. I knew they didn't like me. They
would stare me down as if I was the intruder. They liked to
play games and annoy me by moving my things around the
house and hiding them. I would walk into the playroom to
find the rocking horse in full swing or all my dolls scattered
across the floor, hair mussed and clothes dusty. I always knew

when the twins had paid me a visit, because they left a smell like talcum powder behind. Their ash-streaked faces always left me wondering whether they'd died in a fire.

When all this started happening, it wasn't unusual for Mom to catch me staring fixedly into space as we sat around the dinner table.

"What are you looking at, Chloe?" she'd ask.

"That man over there" came my equable reply. I remember my dad shifting uncomfortably in his seat. Even Rory, in his high chair, would pick up on the vibe and fall silent. My dad shook his head softly, discouraging Mom from further questions. But she had another strategy in mind.

"Which one this time?"

"The man with the tie and briefcase," I said.

"And what's he doing?"

"Nothing."

"Nothing at all?"

"He's just watching."

Dad let out an exasperated sigh.

"Honey, I think it might be time to seek professional advice," he said finally.

The next thing I knew, I was sitting in a psychiatrist's office opposite the silver-haired Dr. Gellman. I noticed he wasn't wearing a white coat, which made me skeptical about his credentials. He gave me a box of crayons and asked me to draw some of the things I saw. I drew pictures for him, but my limited skills couldn't convey much. In the end the consultations didn't help. He ended up assuring my parents I'd grow out of it and suggested the best thing they could do was play along.

That was when Mom decided to take matters into her own hands.

"Maybe you should try asking them to leave," she told me one day, when I was rattled by the flash appearance of a woman hanging over a barbed-wire fence.

"*Asking* them?" My six-year-old self frowned at my mother's naïveté. How did she propose asking something to leave that didn't even use a door to come in?

"It's worth a try, right?"

"I guess," I reluctantly agreed, not wanting to let her down.

"That's my girl. You tell them they don't belong here and they have to leave right now."

I was dubious about such a simple solution but in the end it was the only thing that actually worked. It took a little while, and the ghosts resisted at first, but my willpower proved stronger than theirs. I looked at my mother with a new respect after that. But since she'd left us, the grief had eaten away at those walls I'd so carefully constructed in my mind, until there was nothing left and everything I'd been trying to keep out rushed back in with a vengeance.

I woke a few hours later, disoriented by unfamiliar surroundings until I remembered where I was. Caught in that haze between dreaming and wakefulness, I wasn't sure what was real, but, by the moon still hanging in the sky like a pale sickle, I knew it had to be the early hours of morning.

I sat up straighter as a strange odor hit me. Like fruit left out to rot in the sun, it was sweet and putrid at the same time. I got up and opened one of the casement windows, but instantly regretted it as all the warmth was sucked from the room. The wind that rushed in wrapped itself around me like icy tentacles, making me shiver from head to foot. Outside I could hear the branches of trees creaking in the wind as a soft drift of snow began to fall. I stood transfixed for a moment. Snow was not something a girl from California sees every day, so I reached out a hand and watched fragile flakes drift down to melt on my fingertips. Then I shut the window quickly and turned back to my room.

The fire had gone out, but the dying embers in the grate still cast a cozy glow, lighting up the Victorian wardrobe in the corner. It was the kind with carvings and beveled mirrors that locked with a copper key. It pretty much looked like a doorway to Narnia. I was just thinking how beautiful it was and how much my dad would appreciate it when one of the doors began to open.

My chest constricted and every muscle grew taut as I flicked on the lamp. *Don't panic,* the voice in my head told me. I'd grown up in a house full of old things. They were often faulty and rattled of their own accord. The sour smell had grown stronger, and I realized where it was coming from. In bare feet I moved closer to the wardrobe, slowly reaching a hand toward the handle.

"Chloe, don't!"

The voice came from behind me, but it was too late. I stood rooted to the spot as both doors flew open of their own volition. Even as my hand dropped like a stone, I knew there was something inside. And it was looking right at me.

The creature that stared out at me was barely recognizable, although I knew it must have been human once. Never in my life had I seen such a vision of decay. I didn't know whether to gag or scream or both. I was looking at a face that

I guessed had once belonged to a woman, but it was hard to determine gender now because her corpse was caked in mud. There was mud in the corners of her wild eyes, mud wedged between her teeth and matted in the ropelike tangles of her hair.

To make matters worse it looked like the tip of her nose had rotted away or been gnawed off by some animal. She was the epitome of despair, and yet there was something ferocious in her eyes. Now it was her long, bony fingers that reached out for me. Instinctively I kicked at the doors, managing to fling one shut. I whirled around to see a figure silhouetted against my window. It was Alex, standing arrow-straight in a long black coat. I could just make out the bold sweep of golden hair that accentuated his fine-featured profile. I let out a gasp as his crystal-blue eyes found mine in the darkness. He moved toward me in a blur.

"Stay back," he commanded. I wasn't sure what made him think I intended doing anything else. Nevertheless, I ducked behind him as he slowly peered inside the wardrobe. It was empty now.

My tongue had turned to sandpaper, and my whole body was coursing with adrenaline. I'd seen ghosts aplenty before, but there had been something different about this one. It had looked at me with loathing and hostility.

"Wh-who was that woman?" I stammered. "Why was she soaked…covered in mud? She was awful." The memory of her alone was enough to make me shudder. She was the most gruesome thing I'd ever laid eyes on.

"She's gone now," Alex said. His voice was completely level, but the crease between his eyes betrayed his concern.

"Are you sure?"

He stood aside so that I could examine the wardrobe's interior myself. He was right; it was now devoid of any malevolent presence.

"Try to calm yourself," he advised. But that was easier said than done. My heart was racing like I'd just run a marathon. Alex looked as if he wanted to do or say something to make me feel better but didn't know what. I sank down on the bed, sitting on my hands to keep them from shaking.

"I've never seen anything like that. She felt really...dangerous. Do you have any idea who she was?"

"Perhaps we should get you some water," he said, deftly avoiding answering the question.

Alex let his gaze wander out to the meadows beyond the house. I took him in from head to foot, only then realizing that he'd appeared in my room without coming through the door. Although his face was fresh and unmarred, it was far from carefree. He was weighed down by troubles beyond his years. I guessed I'd known the truth inherently since first laying eyes on him, but I hadn't wanted to accept it. The question was on the tip of my tongue. There was no point pussyfooting around, so I just spat it out.

"You're not real, are you?"

He turned to me with his usual equanimity. "Define *real*."

"Alive," I clarified, impatient for the answer.

"No." He sighed. "But you already knew that."

"Oh boy..." I leaned forward and pressed my forehead to my knees. "What the hell is happening here?"

"I've made you angry." He lowered his eyes. "I apologize for the intrusion. I merely wanted to make sure you were safe."

"Why wouldn't I be safe? That…*thing* might have been creepy, but it can't hurt me, right?"

"Not all creatures roaming this earth are as friendly as I am."

"Are you trying to scare me?" I demanded. "Because that's a dick move."

"As in Richard?" He looked confused. "Who's Richard? I don't believe I've met him."

"What?" I snapped. "No, *dick* as in… Never mind."

He observed me carefully. He looked so solid right now it was hard not to see him as a living, breathing person.

"I hope you understand that I'm trying to protect you."

"Well, I'm pretty capable of looking after myself."

He pushed a golden strand away from his eyes. "Are you always this argumentative?"

I shrugged. "Sorry if this comes as a shock to you, but women don't need a man to swoop in on horseback and save the day anymore."

"I'm sorry to have vexed you," he said, and with that turned on his heel and headed for the door. "I shall go now."

"Hey!" I called after him. "I'm not *vexed.* I just need some answers."

He stopped at the door, turning back to face me. Even though it was hardly the time, I couldn't help noticing how absurdly good-looking he was, like a fairy-tale prince, bathed in moonlight. Leaving aside his physical attractiveness, there was something guileless about him that made my former anger seem out of place. Although his expression was serious, his eyes were constantly alight. *This is crazy,* I thought. *I'm crazy.* I was conversing with a ghost, not a flesh-and-blood person, even if the veins in his neck were visible and there were still traces of dew on his collar. He seemed so real, standing just a few feet away from me, eyes looking directly into mine. It was warm because Gran kept the radiators on overnight, and I was suddenly aware that I'd peeled off my sweaters and was now dressed only in my Victoria's Secret cotton pajama shorts and a tank. I slid back into bed and modestly drew the sheets up to my chest, a gesture that made Alex avert his eyes.

"What sort of answers?"

"Like why I'm talking to a ghost, for one thing."

"Is this not a regular occurrence?"

"Oh, sure." I rolled my eyes. "It happens all the time. I had a chat with Shakespeare the other day and he told me about some new sonnets he's working on."

Alex just stared at me. Clearly, sarcasm was wasted on him. "No," I clarified, "this has never happened before. I mean, I've seen people who are…" I trailed off. For some reason I felt like the word *dead* might be politically incorrect. "People who have *passed on*. But I've never actually spoken to any of them. At least, they've never spoken back."

He positioned himself carefully on the edge of the trunk. "Are you certain?"

"I think I'd remember that." I met his gaze but found myself unable to hold it for long. I had to look past him to the charcoal sky outside that was thinning to milky gray.

"How interesting," he mused. "This hasn't happened to me, either."

"Is that why you behaved so strangely in the woods? Not because I was there, but because you could see and hear me?"

He nodded. "You clearly have a gift."

"That's not exactly the word I'd use," I replied.

"Then how would you describe it?"

I thought for a moment. "You know in *Harry Potter* how they have the Unforgivable Curses that get you sent to Azkaban…?" I broke off when I saw the confusion in his eyes. "Never mind. How long have you been at Grange Hall?"

"I'm always here."

"Yes, but since when?"

"That's hard to say." He drummed his fingers on the edge of the trunk. "Time has become so irrelevant. What year is it?"

When I told him, he looked surprised for a moment, then gave a resigned shrug.

"Is it really?" He sighed. "Then I suppose I've been here a little over a hundred and fifty years."

"You've got to be kidding me!" Was it possible that Alexander Reade hadn't communicated with a single living soul in all that time? "I guess that's kind of cool." My smile was met with a blank expression. "That means it's *interesting.*"

"Oh," he said. "Thank you for translating."

A new question popped into my head. I had a feeling that was going to happen a lot. "Alex, what makes a person hang around after they die? Why doesn't it happen to everyone?"

"I've asked myself the same thing over the years," he replied. "And the more I think about it, the more I believe it isn't a choice. The ones left behind are simply unlucky. They left the earth before they were ready and remain tied to it by unresolved emotion."

"And what about you?" I knew I was crossing the line again, but I went ahead and did it anyway.

He hesitated before answering. When he did, there was a

sadness in his eyes and a wistfulness in his voice that nearly made me tear up.

"I very much wanted to pass on," Alex said. "But I suppose I lost my way. I clung to what was familiar. Grange Hall was my home, and I couldn't bring myself to leave it. By the time I was ready, I'd missed my chance. The gateway was sealed, and I found myself trapped here in this shadow world, neither living nor ever being able to rest in peace."

My heart felt heavy for Alex, caught in the twilight zone between life and death. It sure made the problems of high school pale in comparison. I tried to think of something reassuring to say.

"Well, that sucks" was the best I could come up with. I was usually more articulate, but right then words seemed to elude me.

I didn't think he understood the modern slang, but he smiled anyway. When our eyes met, the connection was inexplicable, overwhelming and impossible to ignore. It felt like there were currents swirling in the air, binding us together. Although we barely knew each other and came from opposing dimensions, I felt strangely comfortable with him. Maybe it had something to do with the fact that whatever I said to him could never be repeated. As the milky predawn light spilled over the horizon, I noticed that Alex seemed to fade a little. His form became less substantial, like a mirage. It seemed he was reliant on darkness to give him substance.

A soft creak drew our attention back to the open wardrobe. A thick black sludge was oozing from inside, pooling on Gran's spotless wooden floor. The smell of brine hung heavy in the air.

Alex got up, worry etched across his pale face. I got the

prickly feeling that he was keeping something from me. He knew more than he was letting on. But before I could question him, he spoke.

"It's time for you to go, Chloe."

"Where?" I whispered.

"Anywhere but here...just for tonight."

"But I..."

"Hurry," he urged. "In case she comes back."

The thought made my stomach cartwheel, and I didn't need further encouragement to head for the door. "What about you?" I asked, just before I slipped into the corridor. "Will you be okay?"

The flicker of a rueful smile crossed Alex's face. "Don't worry. Anything that might happen to me already has."

# CHAPTER SEVEN

Rory's room was just a few doors down from mine. He was so deep in sleep he barely acknowledged me when I slipped into his bed. He grumbled a little when I lifted the covers and crawled in beside him, then automatically rolled over to make room. Even in his sleep my little brother was accommodating. Admittedly, we were a bit old to be sharing a bed, but he'd sneaked into my room enough times over the years after watching an unauthorized horror movie with his friends. So I felt justified in having my turn. Just this once.

Of course, there was no way I was going to sleep after what I'd seen. I just lay there, not daring to close my eyes, waiting for the sun to rise and chase the shadows from every corner. I knew I couldn't avoid my bedroom indefinitely. All my clothes were in there, and I couldn't loaf around in my pajamas all day without incurring a lecture from Gran. So I planned to get in there, dress at record speed and get the hell out again. A small part of me couldn't help feeling a little pissed off. Why was I the one forced to tiptoe around? I wasn't the interloper here. This house belonged to the living, and I shouldn't let a phantom drive me away. Besides, if I knew anything about ghosts, I was pretty sure switching rooms wouldn't help for long. There was nowhere to hide; if she wanted to haunt me, she'd find me.

I walked gingerly down the passageway to my room, pausing after each step to listen for signs of anything out of the ordinary. My bedroom door was closed, and I hesitated before nudging it open a crack. When I did, all I could see were bars of golden light falling across the buttery floor. Any sign of what had happened there last night had been completely eradicated. Standing there, with the prim rosebud wallpaper and the frilly white pillows, I could easily have tricked myself into believing the hideous apparition in the closet had never happened. There wasn't even a stain on the floor where the muck had dripped off her body. I steeled myself and mustered the courage to peek inside the wardrobe, ready to flee at a second's notice. But there were only my impractical clothes and a few musty coats hanging harmlessly from the hangers. I caught a glimpse of my face in the mirror on the door. I looked a little worse for wear after my sleepless night, but that was the only evidence that any supernatural drama had taken place.

My room wasn't big enough to include a bathroom. Instead I had to use the one at the end of the hall, with its walls covered in striped wallpaper. There was a deep old-fashioned tub with claw feet, but luckily Gran had thought to install a modern shower in the corner. The mosaic tiles were freezing, turning my feet into ice blocks. I wished I'd remembered to wear socks. It took the water a while to warm up, but it was worth it to stand under the steaming water and catch a moment to myself. Come to think of it, between family drama and ghostly visitations, I hadn't had a lot of alone time at Grange Hall.

I stepped out of the shower vaguely conscious that something in the room had changed. Then I caught sight of what it was. Across the mirror, a message was scrawled in a manic script. Someone had used the lipstick from my makeup bag to write in angry red letters: *GET OUT! GET OUT GET OUT!*

Despite being in my towel, I threw open the door, but the hallway was empty. From somewhere I could hear the distinct echo of rippling laughter, but I couldn't place where it was coming from. Without a second thought I tore off a ream of toilet paper and scrubbed furiously at the mirror before anyone else had a chance to see it. Then I threw on my clothes and hurried downstairs to breakfast. I might have appeared calm and collected, but it was a different story in my head, where questions swirled like a carousel out of control. There was no logical explanation for what was happening here and no way to forget it. Alex had been in my room last night, talking to me. I hadn't dreamed that. And what happened afterward seemed so implausible it made me doubt my own sanity.

In the dining room I fixed myself avocado and tomato on toast before sitting down next to Rory, swatting away the rasher of bacon he was waving at me.

"Want some?" he asked with his mouth full. "It's pretty good."

"Vegan, Ror," I reminded him. "We've been over this."

"Oh right, sorry!" He held up his fork. "Eggs?" I shook my head and sighed. "Why were you in my room last night? Did you have a bad dream?"

"You could say that," I replied, hoping he wouldn't ask me to elaborate.

"Don't worry," he told me earnestly. "I have them, too, sometimes."

My brother really was the sweetest, gentlest kid I knew. Most would have greeted me with a volley of complaints, but Rory only ever wanted to help. I draped an arm around his shoulder and gave him a little squeeze.

"Thanks for letting me stay."

He bumped his lips against my cheek in a clumsy kiss and went off in search of more bacon. Between the hours of eight and ten in the morning, Grange Hall served a buffet breakfast. This routine was strictly adhered to, despite the absence of guests. At 10:00 a.m. on the dot, Miss Grimes locked the dining-room doors and began to clean up. Her decisive movements reminded me of a prison warden. As Gran had instructed, Rory and I helped out by stacking the dishes and carrying them into the kitchen.

Miss Grimes didn't seem to appreciate our efforts; instead she narrowed her eyes as if she suspected we were up to no good. She was such a strange character, slipping around the house like a shadow, never uttering a single syllable. But the deep grooves etched in her grayish face told me her life couldn't have been easy—maybe she had good reason for her mistrust of people. Her quarters were off the kitchen at the back of the house, but we'd never seen inside. There was a window, but it was barred and the curtains always tightly drawn. Sometimes an old cat that looked like it had been through the wars could be seen sitting outside her door, the fur on its spine thinning in patches. I didn't particularly like cats and they didn't like me. I could swear this one flexed its claws every time I walked by. It liked Rory, though, probably because he brought it scraps from the table. Miss Grimes didn't seem to mind Rory, either. He was hard to object to. He was like a scrawny teddy bear with his curly hair and big brown eyes. I'd even seen her pat his head once or twice, but she only ever scuttled past me, looking at me as if I had an infectious disease or was about to abscond with the silver.

When breakfast was over, I navigated my way around Miss Grimes, depositing my tray on the bench beside her. She had her sinewy arms deep in the sudsy water and pretended not to see me.

"Morning, Miss Grimes!" I said, guessing my chirpiness would annoy her. "You look great. Did you do something different with your hair?" She offered me a grunt in reply.

"I'm going down to see Joe after this," Rory told me as he carelessly wiped down tables so that the crumbs fell on the burgundy carpet. "Wanna come?"

"Why not?" I was pretty keen to do anything that might block out the memory of last night, at least temporarily. I kept seeing a black-clad figure dripping with mud lurking in every corner. One thing I knew for certain: dream or not, the thing in my closet was after something. With her stretched lips and crazed eyes, she wasn't someone I wanted to encounter again. She'd literally decomposed before my very eyes. "Ready to go?" I said quickly, before my imagination had the chance to get the better of me.

"What about the chores?" Rory reminded me. I peeked through the doorway at Miss Grimes's figure hunched over the farmhouse sink.

"I think we're done, don't you?" I gave him a goading nudge. "Come on. Let's make a break for it."

I grabbed his hand, and we tore out of the dining hall into the foyer. For the first time, I felt a burst of exhilaration ripple through my body. But as Rory threw open the front door, I happened to glance back over my shoulder. Miss Grimes was nowhere to be seen, but there, lurking in the corner, was the hazy but unmistakable figure of the woman from the wardrobe.

I nearly tripped over my own feet.

"Chloe?" I felt my brother at my elbow. "You okay?"

"Yeah..." I said, refusing to look back as I followed him out the door. "Everything's great."

I could tell he didn't believe me. It was understandable. I didn't believe myself.

I'd rushed outside without thinking to grab a coat, and the cold cut right through my flimsy cotton shirt, sending my system into shock. For once, I didn't mind. It helped drive out the panic bubbling inside me. I wondered if I would eventually acclimatize to this weather. Rory didn't seem bothered by it at all. Maybe I just needed to toughen up.

Once we got to the stables I could see why Rory liked hanging out there so much. It was smaller than I expected, but a sense of calm hung over it like a protective veil. The low wooden structure adjoining a neighboring field was painted a pale pigeon-gray. Inside, dark wooden beams ran across the ceiling. In the stalls stood solemn horses with glossy coats and liquid brown eyes. A shuffling of hooves and a low whinny announced our arrival before a young man appeared from around a corner.

"Hi there, I'm Joe Parrish." The boy who greeted us had bottomless green eyes and a boyish face. "You must be Fiona

Kennedy's long-lost American granddaughter. I've heard a lot about you."

I noticed that his tousled hair was the color of milk chocolate and his smile was contagious. He was tall and loose limbed with broad shoulders, the sort of guy who was comfortable in his own skin. I thought I could see a trace of sadness in his eyes, the sort of thing only I picked up on when meeting someone for the first time.

Joe was wearing work clothes: torn jeans, scuffed boots and a flannel shirt. I caught a glimpse of a silver dog tag hanging from a chain around his neck. It had an inscription on it, but I wasn't close enough to read what it said. An acoustic guitar was propped against a wooden stool. I liked him already. He gave Rory a high five as if they were old friends.

"Joe's been teaching me about horses," my brother announced proudly. Joe put down the tack he was carrying and wiped his hand on his thigh before holding it out to me. I caught a glimpse of silver rings adorning his fingers. His handshake was warm and firm.

Rory hovered around him like an eager puppy. "Do you need help with anything today, Joe?"

Joe gave an easy smile. "There's always room for an extra pair of hands around here." He jerked his thumb over his shoulder. "Betsy over there could use a brush down. She likes you. She doesn't let just anyone touch her."

Rory's delight was obvious. He already knew where everything was kept and didn't even need to ask for directions. How had he gotten so comfortable already?

"I hope he isn't getting in your way," I whispered once Rory was out of earshot. I didn't know why I said that. It was clear that Joe didn't mind Rory being there. I wondered how much he had been told about our "situation" and whether he was letting Rory stick around out of a sense of compassion.

"He's a good kid," Joe replied, and he sounded like he meant it. We stood awkwardly for a second before I changed the subject.

"So are you in school?"

"I'm in the sixth form."

"And that means…?"

"Sorry." He smiled. "I forgot you're a Yank. It means university next year, if everything goes according to plan."

"I bet I can guess what you want to do," I said.

"Go on."

"Veterinary science?"

Joe raised an eyebrow and looked impressed. "How did you know?"

"Lucky guess."

Joe nodded. "And what about you?"

I gave a self-deprecating shrug. "Not a clue anymore."

"Well, there's no rush, is there?"

Joe was the real deal; cool without having to try. I found myself wondering what he'd say if I told him about the ghosts I'd met at Grange Hall. I'd debated telling Sam and Natalie about my ghosts on a few occasions, but had never gone through with it. They weren't receptive to anything that didn't fit into their insular little world. I could picture it now. They would both nod along and make sympathetic noises, but they'd never really understand. So consequently, there'd always been distance between us that couldn't be bridged. Joe, on the other hand, didn't seem the type to scare easy, but I still decided to hang off revealing anything that might make him question my stability. I didn't want to risk alienating my only potential friend in this forbidding place.

I could feel a dull headache starting behind my eyes that could only mean one thing—caffeine withdrawal. I'd never gone without my daily dose of Starbucks, and the watery brew that Gran served up in her dining room had proven to be undrinkable. I was used to flavored coffee and a barista who knew what you meant when you said *double tall skinny cinnamon dolce latte with drizzle.* But as it turned out, actual straight-up coffee was pretty gross.

"There wouldn't happen to be a Starbucks around here by any chance? Coffee Bean? Peet's?"

Joe frowned. "Caffeine is a highly addictive and dangerous drug. You should give it up immediately."

"Um… I don't think it's all that bad…."

"Relax, I'm just taking the piss." I assumed that meant he was joking. British humor was going to take some getting used to. "Actually, there are a couple of places close by. I'll take you later on if you like."

"Great. Thanks."

"Are you two just gonna stand around talking?" Rory sounded annoyed, maybe because I was monopolizing his new friend.

Joe and I walked over to the stall where he was brushing down a chestnut mare.

"Who rides the horses?" I asked.

Joe shrugged. "Just me, this time of the year. Sometimes over the summer you get people with kids wanting trail rides."

I tentatively reached out a hand to stroke the horse's nose

but pulled back when she snorted and tossed her head. Great, even animals didn't want to hang out with me.

"I don't think she likes me."

"Yeah, she does," Rory replied. "Betsy's just head shy around strangers."

I turned to Joe with feigned outrage. "Okay, what have you done with my brother?"

Joe grinned. "Try offering her the back of your hand first. Like this…"

I mimicked his movement, and the horse responded by sniffing me cautiously. Joe rubbed his hand along the length of her nose, and she butted her head into the palm of his hand.

"Hello, darlin'," he murmured in a soothing voice. "This is Chloe. Give her a chance. You might like her." He guided my hand to the horse's neck and moved it up and down in slow, even strokes. I felt her tension ease beneath my fingers.

"Hey, that worked." I tried not to sound too excited.

"See? Her ears are pointing forward now," Joe said. "That means she trusts you."

I noticed Joe considered his words carefully, as though they carried too much power to be thrown around casually. "Let me show you something." He picked up an apple and demonstrated how to offer it to Betsy on my palm. The horse demolished it in one clean bite, spraying my face with juice and apple fragments.

Joe laughed and turned to Rory. "How about we give the gang some exercise?" he suggested. "Feel like tagging along, Chloe?"

"Sure," I agreed readily. It wasn't like I had much else to do.

I hadn't been horseback riding since middle school when my friends and I had joined the Malibu Equestrian Club for the summer. I'd wanted to keep going, but Sam and Natalie insisted we all quit and take figure-skating lessons instead. As it turned out, the skill hadn't entirely deserted me. I was a little rusty, but the worn leather reins felt familiar in my hands and the rhythmic movement of the horse's body lulled me into a sense of peace. I'd always thought horses were majestic and powerful creatures that commanded respect. Even Rory, who was a beginner and had been assigned the smallest horse, looked comfortable following prompts from Joe. Riding through the winding country roads surrounding Grange Hall was the most fun I'd had in a long time. After a while, I didn't even notice the cold.

At one point Joe veered off the road, leading us single file along a dirt track. All sound was obliterated by the canopy of trees save for the soft thud of hooves on damp leaves. I looked up to see an expanse of droplets clinging to the branches above my head. They glittered in the watery sunshine, lending an otherworldly air to the place. As always a fine mist hung over everything, dampening my hair and clothes, but it transformed the woods into a fairy-tale kingdom, so I could hardly complain about it. For a second I thought I saw a black-clad figure ahead of us moving through the trees, but as we drew closer I realized it was only some blackened tree trunks.

By the time we got back it was already early afternoon, and I wondered how so much of the day had slipped by unnoticed.

"Ready for that coffee?" Joe asked as he helped me dismount. I couldn't answer right away because I was too distracted by my brother making heart shapes with his fingers behind Joe's back. A glimpse of the old Rory was back. Before our mom died, he'd been a prankster. Only last summer I remembered he'd sneaked down to our basement with my nail-polish remover to try to melt Styrofoam as part of a chemistry experiment. Another time, he'd set a trap for my friends by hiding his pet gecko, Plato, under the pillows on my bed. It was hard to forget the enjoyment plastered across his face at seeing the girls' hysteria.

"Sounds good to me."

"What about you, Rory?" Joe added politely. Rory looked embarrassed and shuffled his feet.

"Gran's making me go get a haircut." I noticed that his curls were growing at odd angles around his ears, like twirls of spun cotton.

"Ah, next time, then," promised Joe. He turned to me. "I need to wash up first. I'll meet you under the old oak in fifteen minutes."

I was surprised by my own enthusiasm for the outing. Maybe solitude *was* overrated. Maybe distraction was a far better antidote to pain.

I hurried back to the house with Rory dragging his feet, obviously in no hurry to accompany Gran to the local barber. In my room I changed into a clean pair of jeans and attempted to fix my windblown hair. I hesitated a fraction before opening the wardrobe, ready to spring back in case the mud woman showed up again. But everything was as it should be. I even found a coat that I decided to borrow, though it smelled like it hadn't seen the light of day in years. I gave it a few squirts of perfume to try to mask the mustiness.

I found myself wishing I'd packed more carefully. There

had to be department stores in England, right? Maybe I could ask Gran to take me shopping.

The thought triggered a wave of self-loathing for thinking about shopping at a time like this. What was the matter with me? I knew my mom well enough to know she'd want me to get on with my life, but it felt disrespectful all the same. I rummaged through the drawer of my dresser for the only wool sweater I'd bothered to pack. As I pushed things aside, I caught a glimpse of the photograph I'd hidden there. Maybe it was time to put it on display, I thought to myself. I couldn't go on living in denial forever. Besides, repressing memories of my mom wasn't exactly working for me. In fact, it almost made things harder, because when a memory did sneak through unexpectedly, it caught me completely off guard and made the pain more acute. Maybe I needed to just let it in and allow myself to feel it. But I was scared. I knew how bad it was going to hurt, and I just wasn't ready yet.

The photo was lying facedown. I turned it over and found the glass shattered. I felt sick, like someone has desecrated holy ground. It wasn't just an insignificant crack but more like the person had taken a hammer to it. A splinter of glass stabbed my finger, causing me to drop the photo altogether. How could this have happened? Could Miss Grimes be responsible? I didn't think she hated me *that* much, but she was the only person I'd ever seen come up here. Had she dropped it while nosing around and was too ashamed to fess up? Or did this have something to do with the woman in the wardrobe? Maybe she was trying to let me know I hadn't seen the last of her. I cast a glance at the carved wardrobe doors. I felt like she was watching me right now through the keyhole.

If I listened very closely, I could hear her breathing. *Stop it, Chloe,* I told myself sternly. *There's nobody there.*

From my window I could see Joe waiting in the garden in a battered leather jacket and a charcoal scarf. Behind him, to my surprise, was a thrumming motorcycle. There was no time left to ponder the mystery of the photo, so I picked it up and placed it carefully on top of the dresser, vowing to find and expose the culprit when I got home.

"Is everything okay?" Joe asked when I hurried outside, slamming the front door behind me. "You're freaked out by the bike, aren't you? I thought it was supposed to be sexy."

I couldn't help smiling a little. "Relax, I've always wanted to go for a ride."

"Good," he teased. "I can't stand girls who worry about messing up their hair. Let's hit the road."

He tossed me a helmet with bold red stripes and readjusted it without comment when I tried to put it on backward. I hoisted myself up behind him and wound my arms around his waist. He felt reassuringly strong and solid. The physical proximity was a little awkward at first, but once the bike was purring beneath me like an animal, I tightened my grip.

After heading out the front gate, Joe steered the bike onto a narrow country lane. The trees had grown thick and fast, so it felt like we were roaring through a lush and leafy tunnel.

"Don't worry!" he called over his shoulder. "I'm just taking a shortcut, not trying to abduct you."

"Who's worried?" I yelled back.

He took a slight detour to show me his school. We came to a halt outside an imposing stone building that looked more like a museum with its pointy spires and looming gates.

"Welcome to Bearwood Academy," Joe announced. "Where dreams come to die."

"Jeez, it looks like it was built for Dracula."

"It's the oldest school in the county. Founded in 1832."

"Sounds exclusive."

"It is. There's no way I'd be here if I wasn't on a scholarship."

"Does that mean you're a genius?"

"You know what Edison said about genius, don't you?" I shook my head. "It's 1 percent inspiration and 99 percent perspiration. That means we all have a shot."

"Right, and who said 'You can have anything in life if you will sacrifice everything else for it'?"

"J. M. Barrie." He glanced over his shoulder. "You know your literary greats, I see. Did you dream of being Wendy when you were growing up?"

"Actually, I dreamed of being Peter."

"Of course you did." Joe chuckled as I peered up at the cheerless windows of Bearwood Academy.

"Met any nice girls in this place or do they all fly around on broomsticks?"

"Strictly no girls allowed, I'm afraid," Joe said, making a glum face.

"No way!"

"Sad but true. The rationale being that the presence of females would interfere with the process of nurturing genius."

"Well, that's archaic." I felt a shiver ripple through me. The school was grandiose, but there was something cold and indifferent about it, too, like it shut out everyone who didn't fit inside its paradigm of success.

We rode on until we found ourselves in the midst of a

cobblestone village. Christmas decorations lent a festive air. There were fluffy trees in the shop windows and tinsel draped around the lampposts. It looked like a toy Christmas village. The houses were so perfect I thought they must be made of paper and the wind might blow them over. Best of all, the holiday smell of pine and sugar permeated the air.

The coffee shop was a converted bluestone building on a corner. Joe helped me off the bike, then sprinted to hold the door open. For a moment, I wondered if he was trying to impress me. Then I realized it was just how he'd been raised. Good manners came naturally to him. It made a comforting warmth spread through my chest. Now that taking care of the family had fallen on my shoulders, it was nice to have someone take care of me, just for an afternoon.

Joe ordered our drinks and found us a table by the window that looked out onto the street. The rain had stopped at least, washing off the dust and making everything look as vivid as a picture postcard. I peeled off my coat and noticed my phone buzzing in my pocket.

"There's reception here!" I exclaimed. "Thank God."

For the next few minutes my phone was inundated with a deluge of text messages asking how I was doing and when I was coming home and if I'd met Prince Harry yet. I shook my head and smiled before shoving my phone back into my pocket. "Sorry," I said. "My best friends want details."

"What are their names?" he asked.

"Samantha and Natalie."

"They sound like *Real Housewives* in the making."

"You shouldn't judge people on that basis," I told him, wagging a finger.

"You're right," Joe agreed. "I'm sorry. What are they like?"

"In this case you were pretty much right." I laughed. "They don't give a damn about climate change, but they do have great hair."

"I get the feeling you don't really miss them—am I right?" There he went again, exhibiting that strange intuition.

"Not as much as I thought I would," I confessed. I felt a little twinge of guilt but it was the truth. I'd hardly thought about my life back home since I arrived. Without Mom, it wasn't really home anymore. "In fact, I don't miss them at all. God, I must sound like a total bitch."

Joe cupped his chin in one hand before answering, "No. You sound like you haven't met the right people yet." He flashed me a flirty little smile. "Maybe that's about to change."

# CHAPTER EIGHT

On the street, Joe turned to me awkwardly, something obviously on his mind.

"You know…the Winter Ball is coming up in a few weeks."

"So I've heard," I answered drily. "Gran won't shut up about it."

"It should be a pretty good night." He hesitated a moment. "Why don't you come along?"

"Well, I currently live at Grange Hall, so technically I'll be there."

"Allow me to rephrase. Why don't you come *downstairs?*"

"I dunno," I hedged. "It's a long walk."

Joe grinned and rolled his eyes toward the stormy sky.

"Let me try this one more time, Chloe. Why don't you come *with me?*"

Damn it, he was asking me out. I'd been hoping to sneakily change the subject, but no such luck. It wasn't that I didn't like Joe. But the idea of any large social gathering terrified me right now. The old Chloe would have come up with a plethora of flimsy excuses not to hurt his feelings, but today I decided to give honesty a shot.

"I'm not sure I'm ready for something like that right now," I told him. "It might be a bit...much." I was surprised at myself. Usually, I was a people-pleaser, always going out of my way to avoid awkward situations. But I felt I owed Joe the truth. If he was disappointed, he hid it well.

"Of course." He nodded. "I understand. If you change your mind, just let me know."

"Sure."

Pewter clouds were scudding across the tenebrous sky as we made our way back to the bike, but the rain held off just long enough for us to pull into the driveway of Grange Hall. Then it really started pelting down. There was something about the rain that always put me in a reflective mood. Maybe it had to do with the fact that rain was pretty much nonexistent in Southern California, to the point where you woke up some days wishing the obnoxious sunshine would just give it a rest.

Joe declined my invitation to stay for dinner because he had to study for some upcoming test, but he did say "See you tomorrow," as if suggesting our relationship would be ongoing. From any other guy, I might have found that arrogant, but with him, it just worked.

I stood in the doorway, watching him pull out of the driveway until the sound of muted voices from inside drew my attention. I followed the sound into the dining hall, where I found two women I hadn't seen before. They were sitting by the fire, sipping tea and deep in feverish conversation. Both wore long, knitted cardigans and had silver hair held in place by bejeweled combs, the kind little girls might

wear when playing dress-up. Their eyes were bright and animated as they talked. In front of them, among the crumbs
and crockery, were notebooks scrawled with calculations
and elaborate symbols. They had to be the maverick sisters
Gran had spoken about.

I walked over to the table where Gran and Rory were
seated, noting that my brother looked a lot more presentable
now with his unruly curls trimmed back so they weren't obscuring his vision.

"They're professional ghost busters," Rory whispered
through a mouthful of toast covered in a dark paste that
bore a strong resemblance to tar.

"That's not a profession," I whispered back. "What the
hell are you eating?"

"Marmite," he answered enthusiastically, gesturing at a
jar of sticky brown gloop. "It's yeast extract."

"Yum?"

"So I heard you went on a little expedition today?" Gran
cut in. I narrowed my eyes at Rory. Trust him to rush home
and give a blow-by-blow description of events.

"If getting coffee can be considered an expedition," I said
lightly.

"Well, Joseph Parrish is a very decent young man. He'll
be a good friend to you while you're here."

"Thanks for the stamp of approval, Gran," I said. "Do
those women really call themselves ghost busters?"

"I told you, they prefer the term *paranormal investigators*,"
she replied. "They visit old homes around the country and
record their findings."

"Are they legit?"

"I don't know, Chloe. I don't ask to see a résumé when

someone makes a booking. A paying guest is a paying guest. Just remember you're a Kennedy, and be polite if they try to enlist your help."

"What kind of help? Do you think there's something here to investigate?"

"Don't be silly, of course not. Nobody does. But don't go telling them that."

I focused on my dinner, attempting to hide the slab of rare meat under my mashed potato. Apparently, the potato was pretty much the only vegetable recognized in England. Except for a side dish of beans boiled into a green slush. I figured the L.A. kale craze hadn't reached the village of Wistings yet.

After dinner I headed upstairs to get started on *Madame Bovary* for AP Lit. Sam and Natalie had been fairly unimpressed to learn I was taking AP Lit in the first place, but I enjoyed reading, and analysis was something that came naturally. As I left the dining hall, I walked past the paranormal investigators and felt their eyes boring into me.

When I opened my bedroom door, I jumped back in surprise. Alex was there, lying on top of my bed, legs crossed lazily at the ankles. His long hair was tied in a soft ponytail, loose locks falling over his eyes as he read an article from a magazine, wearing an expression of intense concentration. He glanced up briefly as I came in.

"What's a G-spot?"

I walked over to him and calmly took away the copy of *Cosmopolitan* that had him so engrossed.

"Nothing you need to worry about. What are you *doing* here anyway?"

It was hard to ignore how captivating he looked with the

lamplight illuminating his skin and the blue of his eyes so clear they looked almost transparent.

"Waiting for you," he answered with his usual charm.

"Glad to see you've made yourself at home."

Although I wasn't sure how, I noticed that Alex had got a fire going. I peeled off my damp coat and hung it over the back of a chair to dry.

"Did you know this was once my room?"

"Bit girlie for you, isn't it?"

He smirked. "It didn't look like this back then."

"Well, now I know why you like hanging out here so much."

"Do you mind?" How could I mind when his presence made Grange Hall come alive? The short time I'd spent with him was easily the most intriguing of my life. I had a feeling every moment we shared would be forever burned into my memory. So, no, I didn't mind. But I couldn't exactly tell him that. So I replied with a simple:

"I can share."

"That's very gracious of you."

"Just so long as you don't show up when I'm getting changed or anything."

"That goes without saying," Alex replied. "By the way, how was your rendezvous this afternoon with Joseph Parrish?"

"How did you…?" I began and then realized how redundant that question was. "It was fine, thank you."

"I noticed you went unchaperoned." It was hard to miss the note of censure.

"Excuse me?"

"A young lady must consider her reputation." In one way

his concern was touching, but the idea was so absurd it was hard not to laugh.

"You can't be serious?" Clearly he was, as his face didn't change. I thought about how best to illustrate the evolution of social norms. I dug out my cell phone and flicked through the photos until I found what I was looking for. I held it out for Alex.

"Good God." His eyes widened. "Why do you carry images of harlots on your person?" I was glad Sam and Natalie weren't around to hear that—they'd kick his ghostly butt. The picture was from the most recent Halloween festivities in Hollywood and the girls had gone all out...or all off, to be exact—there was skin and cleavage galore. If you looked closely you could even see a woman wearing nipple tassels in the background. Hey, welcome to Los Angeles.

"They're my friends," I told him. "That's what girls look like in the twenty-first century."

"But why would you choose to associate with such people?" he persisted.

I didn't think my message was getting through. "They're not prostitutes," I said emphatically. "They're ordinary middle-class girls living on the West Coast."

Alex averted his eyes. "In that case, I do not approve."

I kicked off my shoes and curled up in the armless slipper chair by the fire. "You can disapprove till the cows come home, but times have changed. Don't be a dinosaur, Alex."

"Pardon me?"

"Someone stuck in the past who won't move with the times."

"Technically I *am* stuck in the past," he replied. "Is this Joe Parrish one of your suitors?"

I gave an audible sigh. "I hate to be the one that breaks this to you, but coffee dates are no longer automatically followed by an engagement."

"And this is presumably what you wore?" His eyes traveled over my fitted sweater and tight jeans. He could have been checking me out, except for the expression of disapproval in his eyes.

"Is there something wrong with it?" I demanded.

"Not at all," he replied. "It just doesn't leave much to the imagination."

"Well, excuse me for not wearing a petticoat and floor-length gown."

Alex suppressed a smile. "Forgive me, I didn't mean to be critical. You look very alluring."

"In *this*?" I glanced down at my old jeans. "Oh man, you ain't seen nothin' yet."

His mischievous smile and the way his eyes reflected the light made it harder and harder to think of him as a phantom. In the dark he wasn't even nebulous; I could see him as clearly as my own hands.

"I've never encountered a girl like you, Chloe," he said. "You're quite remarkable."

I felt myself blushing. I'd never been good at accepting compliments, even when I was fishing for them. When a guy paid me a compliment, my usual response was to come right out and contradict him. *You have beautiful hair, Chloe. No, I don't. It's a mess. I really like that shirt on you. What, this old thing? I've had it forever. You're really pretty. It's just the light playing tricks with your eyes.* Ugh. How hard was it to just say thank you?

I felt so uncomfortable with Alex watching me that I had to change the subject.

"How's your day been?"

"Uneventful," he replied, which immediately made me feel insensitive. "My days don't vary. They usually blur into one...until now."

Was he trying to tell me something? I wasn't sure if I should trust my instincts. That was the reason Sam and Natalie never came to me for relationship advice. Characters in books never posed a problem, but my judgment was always off when it came to real life. But a new thought was spinning around in my head, like an out-of-control coin, and I needed to verbalize it.

"Were you in a relationship when you lived here?" Alex went back to studying the floor. "Come on," I prompted. "There *had* to be a girl."

"Yes, there was a woman," he said softly. "It was a long time ago."

"She's dead now, obviously," I said and mentally kicked myself for being insensitive again. I never stopped putting my foot in my mouth.

"Some people are more powerful dead than they ever were alive." I expected this to be followed by some form of explanation, but Alex remained silent, expectation hanging in the air.

"Want to talk about it?" It wasn't just idle curiosity that prompted my question. There was a note in his voice that made me wonder if he needed to get something off his chest.

I guessed wrong. He gave a slight, distant shake of his head. "I have no wish to discuss her."

"That's fine. I'm sorry," I said. "It's not like we really know each other, after all." I tried to hide my disappointment that he had chosen not to confide in me, when I was ready to share every last detail of my life.

"It's not that I don't trust you, Chloe." His voice dropped an octave. There he went again, turning my name into a melody. It spun around the room like a magic charm, sending ripples down my spine. I had a sudden impulse to reach out and touch him. But I talked myself out of it. I was behaving like a child. Besides, was it even possible for me to touch him...and would he want me to?

"What is it, then?" I asked.

"It's not a story I'm proud of."

"It won't change my opinion of you, if that's what you're worried about." I got up and went to sit at the end of the bed, close enough for the toe of his boot to touch my leg if he moved just an inch.

"This house has a history," Alex confided, his gaze traveling to the window. "A dark history."

"Well, whatever happened couldn't have been your fault."

"What makes you so sure?"

"I can tell," I replied confidently. "You're a ghost and I'm not afraid of you, so you can't be all bad."

"Why don't you tell me about you?" he suggested suddenly.

"I'm not that interesting." He tilted his head, and I marveled at the regal planes of his face. It felt as if a young lord from a forgotten portrait was staring back at me.

"I beg to differ."

"You don't know anything about me."

"I know there's a story to tell. I have finely tuned instincts."

"What do you want to know?"

"How old are you?"

"Going on eighteen. You?"

"I was twenty-three when I died."

"That's so young."

"I certainly don't feel young," he replied. "Perhaps because I've had a century and a half to dwell on my mistakes."

I shrugged. "We've all done stuff we'd like to forget."

"You're too young to say things like that. What regrets could you possibly have?"

I hesitated just a moment. "Um... I wish I'd told my mom I loved her more when she was around. Instead of fighting over stupid stuff like curfews and diets."

"What makes you think you can't tell her now?"

"Well, she's not here, is she? That's one minor problem."

"Are you sure about that?" Alex's entrancing blue eyes held mine. I struggled to look away, but his gaze was too intense. "Do you think the people we love ever really leave us?"

"I've wondered about that," I whispered. "I don't know. But if she's around, why can't I see her the way I see you?" Alex sat up a little straighter and looked at me intently.

"I'm fairly certain your mother has crossed over."

"Then she isn't here, is she?"

"Once you cross over, you can no longer reach the living," he explained. "But that doesn't mean you can't watch over them. Your mother sees you, Chloe. Every tear and every smile."

I turned my face away. His words, although intended to offer comfort, were like opening a wound that had just started to close over. I felt like I was wading into uncharted waters without a life raft.

"How can you know that if you're still here?"

Alex sprang up and walked to the window, where he stood with his back to me, his hands holding the sill. "I hear whispers from the other side."

I didn't know what else to say. My grief was back, threatening to drag me under. I didn't want him to see that. I wasn't ready to share that part of me with him yet.

"Isobel," he said out of the blue.

"Excuse me?"

"The woman. Her name was Isobel."

"Oh."

I wasn't sure if he was trying to distract me, but it worked. I tried to imagine this woman from the past. Of course, she would have a captivating name like that. *Isobel.* It was the name of someone you wouldn't want to mess with. It even sounded ominous, like the tolling of a bell. It conjured images of a cloaked woman riding bareback across windswept moors. Someone named Isobel would take risks and command attention. I already didn't like her.

Alexander moved to my dresser, where he idly picked up a bottle of perfume I'd packed. He turned it over in his hands.

"Was she your wife?"

"Isobel *was* married, but not to me."

That caught me off guard. What was he hinting at? Had she been an unrequited love? That was hard to believe. I was pretty sure Alex could charm the pants off any woman he wanted. If he had this much lure in death, I could only imagine what he'd been like in life. He was captivating, witty and intelligent, and there was something in his eyes that made you want to melt. I was tempted to ask for details but couldn't bring myself to. I was too busy feeling humiliated for thinking he might have been interested in me. Whatever his feelings were for this Isobel, they were clearly unresolved. And everyone knew you couldn't compete with a memory. Memories were perfect and reality was flawed.

"She made a bad decision," Alex continued without prompting. "And she was forced to live with the consequences. Women didn't have the choices they enjoy today."

"What kind of bad decision?" I urged, even though I wasn't sure I wanted to hear more.

"A marriage not founded upon love and respect is bound to end in disaster, wouldn't you agree?"

"Why would she marry someone she didn't love?"

"Many reasons," he said. "Financial stability, social position, breeding, to name a few. Her family encouraged the union."

"And you two fell in love even though she was off-limits?"

"Isobel was part enchantress. It was impossible not to desire her. She had that effect on everyone she came into contact with, men and women alike. I used to watch people around her. No one could refuse her anything."

I wished I hadn't pushed for information that would leave my ego in tatters. How could I have been so naive? Alex liked me because I was a good listener. He had a story he needed to tell, and I was the only audience available. Anything more was the product of my imagination. Immediately, I felt my defenses go up. I couldn't put myself in a position where I might get hurt. Not right now.

"She sounds amazing," I said flatly.

"She was. I'd never met a woman I was so drawn to," Alex continued. "Our bond was magnetic. But then life ruined her—it made her bitter and ugly inside. I tried but I couldn't save her. So I gave up." He looked out at the silver moon hanging in the velvet sky. I could almost see its reflection in his sorrowful eyes. "And then you came into this house like a breath of fresh air, Chloe Kennedy."

What was that weird ripple I felt in my chest? I'd never experienced the literal sensation of falling for someone before. When he talked like that, it felt like the floor was about to give way beneath my feet. I knew he wasn't exactly declaring his love; it was merely a suggestion of what might be. But it made me feel lighter inside, like I weighed next to nothing.

"Well, I try," I said as indifferently as I could manage. But Alex saw through my charade, and his lip twitched in a smile.

As I drank in the details of his face, I could feel the distance between us closing. It might be imprudent and it might be irrational, but something was happening here, even if I couldn't find a label for it. Time and space dissolved around me, and I felt like I'd been waiting all my life for Alexander Reade to show up.

# CHAPTER NINE

I heard someone at the door and felt my heart lurch in my chest, but it was only Rory bursting in with his usual disregard for privacy.

"Rory! You have to knock. How many times do I have to tell you?"

"But the door was open." He seemed surprised by my flustered manner.

"That's not the point."

"Who were you talking to?" my brother asked curiously. He was looking at me like he wasn't sure my mental faculties were intact.

"What do you mean?" I growled, trying to buy myself time as I thought up a plausible excuse.

"I heard you. Just now."

"No one. I was rehearsing a speech." I grabbed *Madame Bovary* from the bedside table and waved it at him. "School project, okay? What do you want?"

"Relax. Gran and I are going to see a movie. I was just seeing if you wanted to come."

"No."

"Well, sorry for trying to be nice." Rory's face as he backed away made me immediately contrite.

"I'm sorry." I held up my hands. "I didn't mean to snap at you. I'm just tired. I'll come next time, okay?"

"Sure." He nodded. My brother was never one for holding a grudge. He knew way before his years that life was too short for that. "'Night, Chloe. Love you."

"I love you, too," I called after him. "Have fun!"

I looked around for Alex, who had vanished the moment Rory appeared.

"Alex?" I made sure to keep my voice down. "Are you still here?" The curtains shimmered as if they were about to catch fire before he simply materialized from within their folds.

"You don't think he saw anything, do you?" I asked. Alex seemed unfazed.

"I hid for your benefit. I thought you might be uncomfortable. But unlike you, your brother isn't able to access the dimension I reside in. I could have been standing right in front of him and he would have been none the wiser."

I breathed a sigh of relief. I was protective of Rory; he'd been through enough in recent times and didn't need to contend with the supernatural, as well. Alex studied my face.

"Get some rest. You look tired."

"Where are you going?" I'd grown accustomed to having him around; I wasn't sure I wanted him to leave.

"I won't be far."

"Right, so you can protect me." I gave a playful smirk.

"You shouldn't jest about things you don't understand."

"Maybe I wouldn't *jest* if someone enlightened me," I replied pertly. But he was already gone, leaving only a faded outline in the space he'd just occupied. I flopped down in the window seat and cleared a circle on the misty glass with the sleeve of my sweater. I gazed out at the frosted treetops, wondering where Alex was and what he was thinking. The room felt impersonal and empty without him.

I showered and changed into my sweats but I wasn't ready for sleep. So I settled down to read my nineteenth-century French classic, which was equally difficult because I kept getting distracted thinking about Alex. Where was he right now? Could he see me? Where did ghosts hang out when they weren't manifesting—on the roof, in the treetops or inside the walls? I liked to imagine him perched on the roof wrapped in a cloak, impervious to the weather. By now I'd read the same sentence at least eight times and decided to put the book down. I left the lamp on for security and closed my eyes.

I felt like I'd only been asleep a few minutes when I heard it.

My whole body tensed at the sound of voices floating from what seemed to be outside my door. At first I assumed it was Alex, keeping vigil, but listening more closely, I realized there were two voices, one musical and lilting, the other deeper and more resonant. Even though I couldn't make out what was being said, the overall tone sounded urgent. I wondered what they were doing here—the upper floor was Gran's private quarters and off-limits to guests.

I checked my watch and saw that it was close to midnight. Barefoot, I tiptoed to my door and opened it a crack. The landing was deserted and silent. I crept down the hall and stuck my head into Rory's room. He was fast asleep, snoring softly under a mound of covers. The hum of voices started up again, louder this time as though the people were right behind me.

I found myself drifting down the staircase, the wall sconces lighting my way. Once I was in the foyer I realized the voices were now coming from the library. The man sounded stern and I thought the woman might be crying. The door was already open, so it didn't even feel like spying as I inched my way closer.

"Chloe!" I whirled around to see Alex at the top of the staircase. His ponytail had come loose as if he'd been in a great hurry to get to me. There was an odd, imploring look on his face. His hand was half-raised, as if he was trying to pull me back. What was up? I trusted him and wanted to listen, but the compulsion pulling me toward the room was too strong to ignore.

I turned my back on him and walked toward the door. Something happened to me then that was entirely new. My world fell away, collapsing like a house of cards. I knew the ghost of Alex was still behind me. I even had the feeling that he was still talking to me, but I couldn't hear him. The scene playing out before my eyes was so riveting I couldn't have torn myself away even if I'd wanted to. And I didn't want to. I knew as clearly as I knew my own name that I'd gone back through time....

*In the lavishly decorated library the most ravishing woman I've ever laid eyes on stands in an embroidered dressing gown that trails the floor. Unaware of my entrance, she gazes intently into the face of a young man in riding boots and a loose cambric shirt.*

*The man is Alexander Reade.*

*The library and its occupants are bathed in a golden light. I hover* at the door, merely an onlooker. But I can no longer move. It's as if someone demands I see this. If I try to move, a searing pain in my head cripples me and roots me to the spot. Being here feels wrong, and if I could find my voice I'd apologize for the intrusion.

The woman's gown is made of rich silk brocade in a deep jade color that sets off her loose coal-black curls. Her skin is the color of moonstones, and the nails on her long fingers are polished gems. The arch of her brow is so perfect it could have been painted on. There's something both earthy and exotic in the composition of her features, something regal and wild at the same time. I recognize her from somewhere, but at first I can't work out where. Then it hits me. Although her hair isn't matted now and her dress is immaculate, this is the woman from the wardrobe. She couldn't look further removed from the decaying apparition I last encountered. Everything is different, except for her eyes. They are the same eyes that stared back at me from the dark recesses of the wardrobe, almond-shaped and the color of liquid amber.

She is so poised now; her trembling lip is the only indicator that she might be on the brink of tears. Alexander stands in front of her, calm and composed. But I can see he's struggling, despite the sternness in his eyes.

Instinctively, I know this meeting is risky. It shouldn't be happening. What are they doing there alone at this hour? The tension in the air is palpable and I find myself worried for them, the way you are for the protagonists in your favorite TV drama.

The household has retired for the night, but they could still be discovered at any moment. I know somehow that Isobel's husband is away on business. But what if he returns unexpectedly? What if one of the servants stumbles unwittingly on them? They haven't even had the sense to draw the curtains. They'll be in full view should someone drive up at this moment. They're like teenagers made reckless by passion and throwing caution to the wind.

A silver candelabrum on top of the grand piano lights up the room. I realize as I stand there that this isn't the same room Gran showed us on her tour. The computers are gone and the furniture is heavier, covered in rich fabrics. Ancestral portraits hang from the walls. There's one of Isobel, in a flowing white gown, above the mantel. Pearls are woven through her hair and her eyes, bold and haughty, look out at the spectator. But now, slumped on the sofa, she seems vulnerable. She doesn't speak for several protracted minutes.

Alex attempts to leave but she reaches out and pulls him toward her. He doesn't resist and they sit together side by side, desolate and desperate. He lowers his head into his hands with a groan.

"Alexander," she murmurs fondly, trailing her fingertips down the back of his neck.

"No, Isobel, we cannot continue like this any longer."

She shakes her head, refusing to listen. "You don't mean that."

He sits up straighter and clasps her chin in his hand, forcing her to look at him. "I'm deadly serious."

"I won't listen to talk like that. You can't make me!" She wrenches herself free and begins pacing the room in growing agitation.

"We knew this day would come," Alex continues more gently. "We have to be strong now."

"Strong?" The look on her face changes from desperate to mocking; all traces of her earlier vulnerability are gone. The mood shift is unsettling to watch.

"So turning your back on me is being strong? It's strong to return me to a life of misery?"

"God knows how long I've agonized over this decision," Alex mutters through a clenched jaw. "Do you think I want to abandon you?"

The fact that she succeeds in eroding his composure fuels Isobel's strength. "Then don't!"

Alex drags his hands through his hair in frustration. "We can't be discreet. To continue is madness."

"Then let's choose madness!"

"You're not thinking rationally or you wouldn't say such things."

"I can speak for myself."

"But you cannot speak for me."

His comment, barely audible, sparks an unexpected burst of anger.

"Then go if that's what you want! I won't hold you. Leave me to my suffering. Do you think if I had known who he really was I would have married him? I was young and naive with an uncertain future. Judge me if you will."

"I don't judge you, but we must all live with the choices we make."

"So I must be punished for my mistake until the day I die?" Her eyes are awash with tears until they fall, streaming down her flawless skin.

Alex dissolves at the sight. When he speaks, I can hear the defeat in his voice. "I'm not trying to punish you, my love. I'm only trying to save us. Do you care so little for the welfare of your soul?"

She brushes away tears and defiantly meets his gaze. "What do I care about my soul when I'm already in hell? But I see you think only of yourself."

"It's you I'm thinking about!" Alex's whole body reflects his frustration. "If we are discovered, the world will dismiss my actions as folly, but your life will be ruined."

"Stop preaching! If I wanted sermons I'd go to church."

He looks at her with an expression of deep regret. "I take full responsibility for what happened between us. I succumbed to weakness. Forgive me, Isobel, and erase me from your mind."

"How can I? Give me a less impossible task." She drops her head and bursts into ragged sobs.

In an instant he is by her side. "Don't cry. I can't bear it."

He pulls her hands away from her face and presses each of her fingertips to his lips. There's something so powerful in the gesture that it stops her midsob. She bites her lip and gazes at him with eyes that even the most resolute man would find hard to resist. Their breathing quickens. A moment later, his face is buried in her neck, and she's clutching fistfuls of his hair. They're so lost in each other that their faces blur when they kiss.

"I can't go back to the way things were," Isobel moans, when they finally break apart. "I don't have the strength!"

Alex kisses her reverently on the forehead and stands with a new resolve. "Then we have but one choice, my love. But it requires courage."

"What do you mean?"

"We must tell Carter the truth and leave Grange Hall forever. We can start afresh, somewhere far from here. We'll go to New York, where no one will know us. We can apply for an annulment—God knows you have the grounds. If you truly cannot live without me, then come away with me."

I watch in terror as hope, confusion and finally panic cross Isobel's face.

"Tell Carter?" she echoes.

"It's the only way."

"Have you taken leave of your senses? Have you not seen his treatment of the servants? He's hardly the forgiving type."

"We aren't his servants."

"We may as well be. This is too rash, Alexander. Let's sleep on things and talk again tomorrow." Her measured response can't help but be disheartening.

"Of course," he says. "Take as much time as you need."

She heads to the window and looks out into the dark night. "How would we live?"

The question offers him a glimmer of hope and he answers readily, "Modestly at first, until I can establish myself. But we will be together. Isn't that all that matters?"

"He'll never permit it."

"The world is big, my love," Alex replies, "and not all places as narrow as here."

"I can't be expected to live like a gypsy," Isobel cries. "Shunned by polite society."

Alex walks over to the grate and kicks it with the toe of his boot. A shower of sparks is released into the air.

"Then what would you have me do?"

"Just stay."

She's not easy to resist with her luminous skin and glittering eyes. Alex exhales so loudly I think his lungs might collapse. He presses his lips in a tight line.

"I can't."

"Why not?" she cries, sounding as plaintive as a child.

"Because I want to be better than that."

Isobel opens her mouth but this time words elude her. What more is there to say? I feel my blood frost over as she glides past me, the fabric of her gown rustling on the floor.

I watch as she sweeps up the staircase without once looking back.

# CHAPTER TEN

I found myself lying on my back on Gran's Oriental rug staring vacantly at the ceiling. Alex was there, by my side. I could hear his voice ringing in my head as the real world crystallized slowly around me.

"Chloe, can you hear me?" Cool fingers trailed against my cheek. Was it my imagination or was he really touching me?

I wanted to ask, but my throat was too parched to form words. Instead, I tried sitting up, which wasn't such a great idea. Black splotches exploded across my field of vision and my legs felt as if they were made of jelly. I sank back down against Alex. Even through my daze, I was aware of his scent, like the woods after a rainstorm, when everything has been washed clean. He smelled of new beginnings.

"Slow down, Chloe." How was it possible for someone's voice to carry so much power?

"Everything's blurry," I mumbled.

"It'll pass in a moment. Hold on to me."

To my surprise, my hand closed around his wrist. I blinked slowly as the mass of shapes around me came into focus. The first thing I saw was Alex's face, so radiantly beautiful, it was hard not to feel like the wind had been knocked out of me all over again. But as soon as my head cleared and my pulse returned to normal, his hand seemed to disintegrate around mine. He was still there, but now my fingers passed right through him.

"What just happened?" I croaked. His blue eyes were wide and watchful.

"I can't be sure," he replied. "But I think you broke through."

"Broke through what?"

"Time..." He paused. "And space."

"That's ridiculous." My knowledge of time travel came from Harry Potter, and I was pretty sure I didn't have a time turner.

"More ridiculous than this conversation?"

He had a point there. If someone had told me a few weeks ago that I would strike up a friendship with an absurdly good-looking nineteenth-century ghost who lived halfway across the world, I would have assumed they were either tripping or certifiable.

"Well, no." I gave a goofy smile, which I immediately tried to smother.

"You fainted." His whole face was pinched with worry. His phrasing made it sound almost romantic and transported me back to a time when women swooned over men on horseback. It definitely sounded better than *you fell over like an uncoordinated idiot,* which was what I would have said. I'd never fainted before in my entire life, although I'd seen it happen to Natalie after doing too many Jäger bombs on an empty stomach. Afterward we'd had to sit with her all night while she hugged the rim of the bathtub. "How much do you remember?"

"Everything."

"Can you be more specific?"

I took a breath. I wasn't sure I wanted to share what I'd seen, but it was Alex's life I'd been intruding on, so he probably had a right to know. Besides, he was the only one who could help me make sense of this new and bizarre situation.

"I saw you and Isobel here in this room," I began slowly. "She was crying because she wanted you to stay with her and you wouldn't. You said you were better than that."

It was the abridged version, but it was the best I could manage right now.

"You saw that?" His voice was slightly strained and he averted his eyes. "I'm so ashamed."

"You don't need to be," I said. "Not with me."

"You don't think ill of me?"

"Why would I judge you over something that happened a hundred years ago? That would be a little unfair. People make mistakes."

"You're the first person ever to say that," Alex murmured. "But still, I can't imagine why you saw what you did."

"Well, that makes two of us. But can we talk about it tomorrow?" My world was starting to spin again. "I think I need to go back to bed."

"Of course, forgive me." Alex looked apologetic. "Let me escort you back to your room."

"You don't have to," I said. "I'll be fine."

Alex lifted his chin, almost as if he'd taken offense. "I will not leave you in this condition."

For some reason, I felt an overwhelming urge to be alone.

Maybe I didn't want him to see me so weak when *she* had been so in charge. Even though she was gone, the room was still charged with her lingering presence. I needed a few minutes alone to digest what had just happened, and Alex had a habit of knocking all the thoughts right out of my head.

"I'm just going to get some water," I said, heading for the door.

"I'll come with you."

"No, don't," I said, and he stopped short. "Just meet me in my room later, okay? We can talk things over then."

"As you wish." His voice had a slight stiffness to it now, as if he felt dismissed. I knew he only wanted to help, but I wasn't sure he could. Maybe we were both in over our heads. I watched as he faded away before my eyes, like an image in an old tapestry.

I found my way to the kitchen and poured myself a glass of water. Then I sat down at the scrubbed farmhouse table and let each ice-cold sip sober me and clear my thoughts. I didn't try to make sense of anything yet. All I knew was that the specters had retreated and there were no more voices in my head…at least for now. One thing I knew for sure, Alexander and Isobel had been wildly in love, a dangerous, illicit love that was doomed from the start. But why were their ghosts still trapped at Grange Hall? Was their connection so strong even death couldn't sever it? What had happened after the exchange I witnessed? Did they run away together? Somehow, I doubted it. Had Alexander left Grange Hall or stayed behind to remain with her? The dark history he spoke of was coming to life before my eyes. Only, this time, I wasn't afraid. Whatever secrets lay hidden within these walls, I was determined to know them.

I drained my glass and stood to leave when a cacophony of sound filled the kitchen as the appliances suddenly began to go haywire. The kettle on the stove rattled and blue flames licked its sides, the turntable in the microwave spun out of control and the toaster kept popping up even though I could see that the cord was unplugged. At the same time the overhead lights started swinging, filling the room with strange, elongated shadows. My nails instinctively dug into my palms and my ears started to ring. The noise seemed magnified, assaulting me from all angles. Even the crockery on the table was clattering as though we were in the middle of an earthquake. I desperately racked my brains for a plausible explanation, but deep down I knew there wasn't one. So I sat back down with bated breath, gripping the sides of the table and hoping the noise would rouse Gran or Miss Grimes or anyone really so I wouldn't have to ride it out alone. But no one came.

Then, as suddenly as it had started, the clamor stopped. The silence that replaced it felt even stranger.

I knew I needed to get out of there. I couldn't waste another second. But when I tried the swinging door that led from the kitchen to the hall, it wouldn't budge. Not even when I threw all my weight against it. A shiver snaked down my spine, and I knew intuitively that someone was behind me. My body felt glued to the spot. I turned slowly to see Isobel's ghost sitting at the head of the table.

She was more vaporous than Alex and gave off some sort of electrical charge, like she might literally shock me if I got too close. She sat completely motionless, watching me with a mixture of curiosity and scorn. The Isobel of the afterlife was different than the woman I'd seen in the library. She was still beautiful, although death had ravaged her. I really wished her head wasn't cocked at such an odd angle. It was unsettling, as if all the bones in her neck had been removed, making her as pliant as rubber. Her hair was long enough for coils of it to spool on the table like yarn. Her lips were bloodred, like a wound in her face, revealing small white teeth and overly sharp incisors.

"Hello, *Chloe*." She enunciated my name slowly, breaking it into syllables as if it was a foreign word she needed to grow accustomed to. Static filled the room when she spoke, and her voice sounded mechanical from lack of use.

There was something almost coquettish about her manner, but there was nothing playful about her eyes, which looked like two bottomless dark wells. There was no misreading the enmity in them. She hadn't exactly been subtle about her objective: Isobel wanted me gone. For whatever reason, I posed a threat and my arrival had upset a delicate balance.

"What do you want from me?" I asked, sure my voice betrayed the panic I felt. I hoped she couldn't see how hard my back was pushed up against the door, to put as much distance between us as possible. Then I remembered my mother's advice. It was important to stand my ground and not to show fear. That was easier said than done when the apparition looked as fierce as this one.

"Stay away." The words were hissed at me rather than spoken, and her head jerked rapidly back and forth like a snake. I didn't know what else to do, so I nodded weakly. I wasn't about to ask for clarification. *Hey, maybe we can sit down and talk this out?*

Isobel's ivory skin was glowing an almost extraterrestrial

blue. She interpreted my silence as agreement, but she wasn't quite finished with me yet.

"Do you find him beautiful?" That was a loaded question if I'd ever heard one; no answer was going to be acceptable, so I stayed silent. Despite her arresting beauty, there was something untamed about her, and I couldn't predict what she might do next.

"P-please open the door," I stammered. The sound of my voice reignited her wrath.

"You shouldn't be here." It was a low growl, emitted from the back of her throat.

Those words seemed to strike a chord with me, and I was seized by an unexpected bravado. I lifted my chin and straightened my shoulders. This was *my* world she was encroaching on. It was an incontrovertible fact; my right to be there outweighed hers. That was how it worked. There were universal laws that couldn't be overturned; the dead couldn't command the living.

"Actually, if anyone shouldn't be here, it's you," I said.

At first she looked taken aback by my words, then a tinkling laugh slipped from her mouth.

"Foolish, foolish girl." The way she said it sounded like an incantation, spelling out my doom. But it was too late to take it back now.

"Grange Hall belongs to my grandmother," I said. "She owns it, and I have every right to be here."

"You shall do my bidding," Isobel snarled.

"I wouldn't bet on that."

Maybe that wasn't the smartest thing to say under the circumstances. Isobel wasn't expecting to be challenged and I watched as rage contorted her features. Her lips curled and the shadows under her eyes became more pronounced, turning them into cavities. The hairs on my arms stood on end as a creeping chill permeated the room.

I'd always held firm to the belief that ghosts, no matter how diabolical they might appear, were powerless to harm. That had gotten me thorough what would otherwise have been some terrifying experiences. But suddenly I wasn't so sure. The ghost of Isobel frightened me in a way no other had before.

The overhead light shook violently as she rose from her position, upending the chair she'd been sitting on. She was taller than I'd realized, and her presence filled the space. She looked like an animal waiting to pounce, and before I knew what was happening, she walked straight through the length of the table, removing the barrier between us. Confident that her prey was cornered, Isobel allowed herself time to savor the moment.

The only other way out of the kitchen was on the opposite side that led out into the back garden of Grange Hall. It must have once been a service entrance for the help, but nobody used it these days. I decided to make a break for it. Without looking back, I sprinted over the overturned chair and fumbled clumsily with the barrel bolt that held the door shut. I managed to slide it free and bolted into the damp night, jamming my shoulder painfully against the frame in the process.

Outside, I had no idea what my next move should be. I thought of running back to the front steps and alerting everyone by frantically ringing the doorbell. But then I thought of Gran and Rory, asleep upstairs. I didn't want to draw them into danger, so that plan was quickly abandoned. Being in the open air felt safer than the confined space of the kitchen.

I couldn't bring myself to look back or even watch where I was putting my feet. I almost lost my footing several times on the damp grass. When I hit the driveway, the stones stabbed painfully into my bare soles but I didn't give it more than a passing thought.

I glanced over my shoulder to see the wraithlike figure of Isobel in slow pursuit. The farther I got from the house, the more I began to think I'd done something seriously stupid. Why had I chosen to isolate myself like this? I could scream blue murder out here and not a single soul would hear me. *Good one, Chloe,* a voice in my head reprimanded. *What are you going to do now?*

So I did the only thing I could think of. I screamed into the night, perhaps the very words that might spell my doom.

"Alex, I need you!"

# CHAPTER ELEVEN

I waited for a moment but nothing happened. Isobel was still drifting toward me, hair streaming like a shawl, her eyes bright with anticipation. Her feet barely grazed the ground. Blind panic stopped me from seeing the rock that sent me crashing headlong into a garden bed. I hauled myself up, ready to bolt again, even though I knew I would run out of steam before Isobel did. I figured she had to be toying with me for her own amusement. She could have easily caught me by now, but she was playing her own little game of cat and mouse.

As if reading my thoughts, I felt her glacial hands grip my shoulders from behind. Her fingers created a sensation like a thousand spiders burrowing under my skin. She spun me around so fast I felt my insides lurch. I stared up at the ghoulish woman before me, her gown billowing, her nails digging into my flesh like needles. Her hot breath formed a suffocating fog between us. She was like a leech, draining me of energy. Already, my strength was beginning to wane. I didn't stand a chance against such a formidable opponent.

My feet were lifted clean off the ground as her fingers tightened their grip around my throat. I kicked and flailed but felt my legs pass straight through her. She didn't have a physical body, so how was she able to choke the life out of me? I knew I was in trouble when my chest started to seize up. The world dimmed as my burning lungs struggled for air.

Then she let out a shriek and loosened her grip.

"Isobel!" Alex's commanding voice cut through the night. "What madness is this?" Isobel's face reflected her surprise as she found herself being hauled off me. I stumbled onto the grass where I knelt, spluttering, desperately trying to suck down air. Isobel lunged for me again, but Alex was too fast for her and blocked her path, pinning her against a tree. I watched them move in a blur of entwined, translucent limbs.

"Chloe?" He looked for me wildly over his shoulder. "Are you hurt?"

"I'm okay," I said, my voice still husky from the assault. I could tell Alex wanted to come to my aid, but he couldn't risk letting Isobel go in her current state. Having her plans unexpectedly thwarted spurred another burst of violence. She gnashed her teeth and thrashed from side to side. I almost felt uncomfortable bearing witness to this madness.

"The girl has nothing to do with us," Alex said. His hair had fallen over his eyes and his shirt came loose from the struggle. "Leave her out of it."

"I'm not the one who dragged her into it!"

"Promise me," he insisted. "Promise you won't harm her."

A defiant look came over Isobel. "Why? So you can keep her all to yourself?" she said, eyes blazing.

Alex ignored the taunt. "If she comes to harm, you will never see me again. Do you understand?" He spoke in an even voice, and it was the threat that worked to subdue her. She looked stunned, and it took her a moment to recover. But once she did she was ready to bargain.

"I will do as you ask if you answer me one thing," she said. Her eyes were now wide and pleading, all former virtue seemingly restored. It was disconcerting to watch. Alex held her gaze, and the pause that followed seemed to last forever. "Do you still love me?"

Alex stiffened before giving an almost imperceptible nod. I couldn't ignore the sensation of being stabbed in the chest with a shard of ice. I could hardly bear to look at them. I got to my feet and began to back away from them.

"What about the girl?" she persisted, not yet satisfied.

Alex made a shushing sound as he reached across and put a finger to her lips. "She means nothing."

His touch was enough to change her whole demeanor. Her rage vanished, the panting stopped and she was once again the composed, commanding beauty I'd recently admired in the library portrait.

As for me, I'd heard enough. I ran back toward the house with Alex's words ringing in my ears. *She means nothing.* It stung more than I cared to admit, whether or not he was telling the truth. What did I really mean to him? Our friendship seemed real to me, but perhaps I was nothing more than a passing distraction. After all, I would leave Grange Hall in the near future. Isobel and Alexander would remain here forever. On a rational level, I knew I shouldn't have *any* feelings for him. What could the future possibly hold for us? I reminded myself once again that he was dead. As in deceased, gone, expired. His heart didn't beat anymore, and blood didn't pump through his veins. What would it take for that fact to sink in?

I looked back at the misty figures on the lawn. Alex had released his hold, and Isobel seemed oblivious to any presence other than his. She held out her hand, and I watched him take it. Together they walked away toward the cover of trees. My last image of them was of her transparent gown trailing on the ground before they became two milky wisps in the night sky. Even then I stood waiting pathetically for some kind of sign from Alex. I half hoped he would turn around just to make sure I was safe or give some indication that I was still on his mind. But he didn't, and I hated myself for wanting it so much.

Back inside I made my way to the sitting room and collapsed into the nearest armchair. My hands instinctively traveled to my neck. It was hard to forget Isobel's fingers obstructing my breathing. No matter what promises she had made, how would I ever feel comfortable here again?

It made sense now why Alex had been so on edge whenever we'd been together, why he'd overreacted to the slightest sound. He must have known something like this might happen. But if that were true, he could at least have given me a heads-up. If I'd known what Isobel was capable of, I might have handled things differently. Maybe instead of winding her up, like an idiot, I'd have promised her the world just to get away from her.

But something about this still didn't sit right. Ghosts existed; I'd wrapped my head around that a long time ago. But they weren't supposed to be able to hurt you. That was the one rule I'd always lived by. That was what my mom had taught me. And yet, Isobel could and would have killed me.

What was the point of psychic abilities if you didn't have a manual to tell you how to use them? As I saw it, I had two choices here. I could find some excuse to pack up and leave, ignore everything that was happening to me, resume my old life and try to find peace in whatever way I could. Much as that idea appealed right now, something in me rejected it. I'd never been one to run from a challenge. Besides, I had a feeling that whatever was unfolding here was no accident. I was meant to witness it. I felt inextricably linked to the story of Grange Hall, even if I didn't quite understand my part in it.

A wave of exhaustion overcame me. It felt as if a lifetime has passed since my arrival instead of mere days. I'd learned an important lesson, though, about the living and the dead. Trying to bridge the two worlds was only going to end in disaster. Every fleeting moment I shared with Alex, Isobel would make me suffer for. You couldn't hide from the dead, and you couldn't keep secrets from them. They saw everything.

I closed my stinging eyes for a moment, and when I opened them Alex was sitting on the ottoman in front of me. He moved closer, his pale yet vivid eyes studying me the way they always did.

"Chloe," he began, "please allow me to express my deepest regret…"

I shook my head and interrupted him. "It's okay. I get it. It's not your fault."

"It is entirely," he said. "I should never have put you in a position that might allow you to get hurt. But you showed great courage tonight, defying Isobel that way."

"I wouldn't call it courage so much as stupidity," I replied.

Before he could answer, his attention was drawn to my battered feet.

"You're hurt," he said, almost accusatory, although I knew it wasn't directed at me. I lifted an ankle, to see angry lacerations where the rocks had broken the skin.

To my surprise, Alex reached out and trailed a finger tenderly along the sole. His touch produced a cool sensation that reminded me of being at the shoreline with waves lapping at my feet. The burning subsided at his touch.

"That feels better." I sighed.

"Good," he murmured, without moving his hand. The moment was charged. It felt like anything could happen. Then he broke the spell.

"You should probably soak them in warm salt water."

"Why would I do that?"

"It's a natural antiseptic, of course."

I gave him a dubious look. "I might have to ask Siri about that."

"Siri being some kind of medical manual?"

"Um…not exactly. She's a voice…on my phone… Never mind. You'll learn."

He smiled sheepishly for a moment until his expression clouded again. "I want you to know that my behavior earlier with Isobel… I thought it was for the best."

I waved my hands dismissively. "I get it. It's fine."

"It's anything but fine. You almost died tonight. Everything that's happened is my fault. It seems I'm still paying the price for the poor judgment shown a long time ago."

"Don't you think it's time you stopped punishing yourself over the past? Look, I'm not saying what you did was right, but this hold Isobel has over you…it's not healthy. You need to let it go…let her go."

"I've tried. It's no use."

"Why?"

"Because it wasn't just an affair." He turned away so I couldn't see his face as he dropped his bombshell. "Carter, her husband, was my own brother." I didn't reply right away. What could I say? "So, you see," Alex continued, "you have misjudged me. I am neither decent nor good."

"I don't know," I said eventually. "You did just save my life back there."

He raised his head, and I saw the spark was back in his translucent blue eyes. "Why do you refuse to think ill of me, Miss Kennedy?"

"Maybe I see who you *are* rather than what you *did*."

"So you think there's hope for me yet?"

"Indeed, I do."

As our eyes met, the heat that traveled through my body was impossible to ignore. I quickly cleared my throat and changed the subject.

"There's one thing I don't get. If Isobel isn't real…how was she able to hurt me?"

Alex looked reluctant to answer at first, as if he'd been anticipating this moment but hoping it wouldn't happen. "Isobel is no ordinary ghost," he admitted finally.

"How do you mean?"

"I mean she's a vengeful spirit. That's why she was able to touch you."

"But you touched me just a moment ago," I said. "Does that make you a vengeful spirit, too?"

"Of course not," he replied. "Sometimes, an emotion will

allow a ghost to break through and connect with the living. It might be passion or anger or concern—the sentiment must simply be intense. The moments of connection are unpredictable and fleeting. As for Isobel, she's an entirely different kettle of fish."

"Different how?"

Alex paused again before replying, "It's not that easy to explain. I think it lies with our intentions. Ghosts as a rule are unhappy creatures—we're trapped, isolated, confused, unable to depart the earth and yet no longer part of it. We may prove to be a nuisance, sometimes even tricksters, moving things about in the night. But vengeful spirits can generate an energy of their own. They almost always died before their time and in a violent, painful manner. So they are driven by darker emotions. And when those emotions are stirred, their power can be enough to inflict damage on those around them. In short, they're not afraid to wreak havoc in the world of the living."

"Yeah, I kinda got that. So you're saying Isobel doesn't *want* to leave Grange Hall. She wouldn't cross over, even if somebody was there to help her."

"Honestly, I'm not sure," Alex replied. "But I don't think so."

"And she hates me because she thinks I'm trying to come between you?"

"Exactly."

"That means she'll be back...."

"Undoubtedly, yes. But I don't want you to worry—I'll be here when she does."

I looked past him, out the window at the silky night. "You know, this is dumb, but I almost feel sorry for her."

"Don't," Alex answered forcefully. "Make no mistake. Isobel is a predator, not someone who can be won over by kindness."

"A predator who's still madly in love with you."

Alex shook his head. "I seriously doubt that. Isobel lost everything she held dear in the world. It left her an empty vessel. She has no shred of humanity left, only bitterness and despair. I'm sorry you have been dragged into our sordid drama. That was not my intention. But I shall keep a close eye on you from now on. I give you my word."

"I keep telling you I can take care of myself," I said.

"I've no doubt that's true under normal circumstances," Alex replied.

"You can't follow me around everywhere."

"Just make sure you don't go wandering off on your own. Isobel is unlikely to come after you in the presence of others."

"Well, that's something," I said with relief.

"And now I think it's time you were in bed, don't you?"

"I doubt I'll be getting much rest tonight."

"Perhaps you will allow me to stay with you until you fall asleep?"

"Perhaps." I smiled and then another thought occurred to me. "And, Alex…"

"Yes?" He looked up expectantly.

"I'm sorry about…the way Isobel's turned out," I said awkwardly. "I'm sure it's hard for you to watch."

"You know something," he replied thoughtfully, "I believed my connection with Isobel to be something that happens only once in a lifetime, an experience never to be replicated." I felt my heart sink into my stomach, but I nodded anyway. "Until you showed up." His words hung in the air like a magic spell.

"What?"

Alex gave a lazy smile. "Although, technically I was right about the connection being once in a lifetime. But perhaps you get a second chance in the afterlife."

Without another word, he headed upstairs, beckoning me to follow. Despite everything, I couldn't wipe the smile off my face as I quickly brushed my teeth and slid in between the covers. I felt safe enough to allow myself to relax and empty my mind. I could feel Alex's presence at the foot of the bed as I drifted into a deep, fathomless sleep.

# CHAPTER TWELVE

Sometime in the course of the night, I dreamed of Alex with his cryptic smile, hair falling softly to frame his striking features. When morning came I woke, expecting to find him unmoved at the foot of my bed. Instead, Gran marched into my room like a drill sergeant, pulling open the curtains and flooding the room with feeble sunlight. Then she stood over me with her arms folded, clicking her tongue in the most galling way that made me drag a pillow over my head.

"Are you sick, Chloe?"

*Lovesick maybe,* I thought. What was the remedy for that?

"No, Gran."

"Are you sure?"

"I'm sure," I groaned.

"Then there's no excuse to still be in bed. Half the day's gone."

"What time is it?"

"Time you were up and about. You know what they say, don't you?" I didn't know, and I didn't have the slightest interest in hearing it, but I knew she was going to tell me anyway. "Early to bed and early to rise makes children healthy, wealthy and wise."

"Nobody says that, Gran." I burrowed deeper under the covers to block out the light.

"They do around here. Now, up and at 'em!"

"Nobody says that, either."

Without Alex watching over me, I felt unsettled again once Gran left. I was still reeling from the events of last night. It might have helped if I could talk to someone about it, but it wasn't the easiest thing to bring up in casual conversation. The third floor was deathly quiet, and my frayed nerves reacted to every creak and groan of the floorboards. I flew into the shower, soaping myself as fast as was humanly possible. But nothing out of the ordinary happened until halfway down the stairs I heard the sound of a woman laughing. It wasn't the first time I'd heard it, that tinkling laugh like a chord on a piano. It seemed to brush right past me, and a moment later, it was gone. I figured it must be Isobel's way of letting me know she was still around, keeping me on edge without breaking her promise to Alex.

I tried my best not to dwell on it and headed to the dining room. The daily buffet breakfast had been cleared away, so I slipped into the kitchen to pour myself a bowl of cereal. Sadly, all I could find was something called Weetabix, which looked like little bars of tree bark. Where were the Froot Loops and Lucky Charms? My presence there incurred the wrathful glare of Miss Grimes, who watched me like she thought I was on the verge of committing a crime. *What the hell is your problem?* I wanted to ask. Instead, I flashed her a cheesy grin and chomped as noisily as I could on my Weetabix, which tasted exactly as I suspected. Then I made my way to the sitting room, where I found the two ghost busters hunched over a table, making extensive notes. A burlap bag lay open on a chair and I could just make out what looked like a compass and a miniature tripod along with other bizarre measuring equipment I couldn't identify.

If I hadn't known what they were there to do, they might not have gotten my attention. They could have been members of the local bush-walking club in their anoraks and rain boots. Underneath I caught a glimpse of plaid skirts and cable-knit sweaters. One of them was even wearing a crochet hat covered in lime-green daisies, as if that were an acceptable thing to do in civilized society. But if you looked more closely, you could detect a certain air about them, as if they belonged to some kind of secret club. They kept tilting their heads and frowning, as if listening in on something unseen.

They looked up in tandem, cutting off their conversation midsentence when I entered. I quickly planned a hasty escape, figuring I was encroaching on their secret paranormal business, until I saw them beckoning me over. To be honest, they seemed a little loopy. Not because they believed paranormal activity existed, but because they were actively seeking it out. What was wrong with them?

Not that I was in a position to judge, now that I went up to my room every night excited by the idea of finding a ghost waiting for me.

As I approached, I picked up the scent of lilac and talcum powder in the air. One of them pulled up a chair, while the other studied me intently through her tortoiseshell glasses.

"Chloe, isn't it? Please sit down." I was surprised to discover they knew my name. Had Grandma Fee told everyone I was coming?

"It's a pleasure to meet you at last," the one in the beret said. "We're the Hunt sisters. My name is Mavis, and this here is May."

"Hi," I said, thinking how much they reminded me of fortune-tellers at a fair. I remembered Grandma Fee's instructions about politeness just in time. "I hope you're both enjoying your stay."

May peered at me with a laser-beam gaze. "You're up late, dear," she remarked casually. "Rough night?"

Mavis shot her a disapproving look. "It isn't polite to pry, sister."

"I'm just making conversation."

"Then talk about the weather!"

"What? The weather is the last refuge of conversationalists."

"I didn't get much sleep." I jumped in before Mavis could offer a retort. I had a feeling this tennis match of a conversation might go on for a while.

"Neither did we," May replied. "Usually we're dressed and out the door by the crack of dawn."

"Um…why?" I asked bluntly, then quickly cleared my throat and tried a more people-friendly approach. "I mean, how interesting. Why is that?"

Mavis was more than willing to proffer an answer. She leaned in, conspiratorial. "Having too many people around can interfere with our line of work."

The way she said it made it sound like they worked for the CIA. I smiled and nodded as if I knew exactly what she was talking about.

"May I tell her?" asked May, her knees jittering like an excited schoolgirl. Mavis showed no sign of objecting. It was enough encouragement for May to continue, "We've just had a significant breakthrough! You're the first to know."

"We don't know for sure yet," her sister corrected. "But we have a good feeling."

"That's great." I tried to look honored to be chosen as a confidante.

"As you know, evidence is difficult to gather in our field," May prattled on.

"Sometimes impossible," added Mavis. "Did your grandmother tell you what we do?"

"A little bit," I replied.

"Well, it's not easy to get people to take us seriously. They sometimes refer to our work as a pseudoscience! I think that shows great ignorance, don't you?"

I nodded in tacit agreement.

"Well, you can't exactly sit down and interview a ghost," Mavis said and chuckled heartily at her own joke.

"Have you ever actually, you know, *seen* a ghost?" I ventured to ask. The women exchanged frowning glances.

"No, not as yet, but we're very close," May said.

"How do you know?" I asked.

"All the signs are there," she replied. "We haven't told your grandmother, because we didn't want to worry her, but this house has more cold spots than any we've visited in the country."

"Is that why Gran runs the heating overnight?" My feeble attempt at humor eluded them.

"And the electromagnetic readings are off the charts in certain places."

I wanted to ask what electromagnetic readings were, but May continued before I got the chance.

"Would you believe, a family came to stay here about a month ago with their German shepherd and the dog simply refused to set foot inside the house. He just sat in the driveway howling until they had to take him home. Animals are very intuitive. If that's not a sign, I don't know what is."

I couldn't argue with them there.

"So what's the breakthrough?" I asked, attempting to refocus the discussion.

May's eyes lit up. "We discovered that there has been an actual sighting right here at Grange Hall!" Her voice trilled a little too loudly and echoed in the corridor outside.

"Keep your voice down!" chided Mavis, even though we were the only people in the room. "We're not ready to broadcast our news to the world."

Was it the guests or the ghosts she didn't want to overhear? Maybe both. May nodded and covered her mouth with her hand as if she'd shared too much.

"Wait, someone actually saw something?" Maybe these women knew more than I was giving them credit for. Maybe I'd finally found people who could help me understand my "gift," as Alex called it.

"That's right." May nodded enthusiastically. "Back in '61."

"Nineteen sixty-one?" I repeated dully. "That's a long time ago."

"It doesn't matter," Mavis whispered. "Evidence is evidence." She flipped through a scrapbook and pulled out a newspaper clipping, which she smoothed out on the table in front of us. "Look here."

She pushed the yellowing page toward me. I peered closely to see that it was from a local paper, dated August 15, 1961. There was a grainy black-and-white photograph of a little boy with a solemn face and a traditional short back and sides haircut. The accompanying article was brief and clipped, as if the story was hardly worth reporting at all.

MISSING: A seven-year-old boy (Peter Beckett) has disappeared from the Grange Hall Women's Home after being left unattended for a short time. He reportedly spoke of visiting the lake at the rear of the property with a woman whose identity remains unknown. It is unclear whether she is connected to the disappearance. If you have seen this child, please contact the local police.

"What happened to him?" I asked. "Was he ever found?"

"Yes," Mavis whispered. "Three days later, washed up in the reeds without a scratch on him."

"So? It was probably just an accident," I muttered. "This doesn't prove anything."

"What more proof could you want?" May cried, her head bobbing like a flower. "A little boy speaks of seeing a strange woman and then mysteriously drowns."

"It doesn't say she was strange," I replied. "How do you know she wasn't just some random person from the village?"

"Because nobody else could see her," Mavis replied. "We read the archives at the police station. In the weeks before his death, Peter Beckett insisted a woman came to him in the night, wanting to be his friend. But nobody ever found out who she was. There's no evidence to suggest she existed at all. And according to the report, he knew how to swim. So it raises the question—what really happened out there?"

Even though it happened years before I was born, the story

still gave me the chills. I looked down at the photograph again. There was something in the boy's eyes that unnerved me. They weren't like the eyes of a seven-year-old. They'd seen too much. They knew too much. I pushed the clipping back toward Mavis. They were still looking at me as if they'd just made the discovery of the decade.

"We're on our way to the lake now to do some fieldwork of our own," Mavis said.

"What could you possibly find after all these years?"

"Not *what*, my dear." May's eyes glittered. "*Whom.* You're welcome to join us."

I racked my brain for a good excuse, but one wasn't forthcoming. "I have a pretty busy day, but thanks for the invite."

"Of course." They nodded. "We'll keep you posted."

I watched them pack up and leave with their collection of utensils. It was too soon to tell if their abilities were genuine. I honestly hoped they were. Then I could confide in someone who could finally shed some light on my situation. But I hadn't seen them at work, and there was still a chance they were just two kooks messing around with forces they didn't understand. If that was the case, it was only a matter of time before it blew up in their faces. And I wasn't about to get caught in the explosion.

The image of Peter Beckett lingered with me for hours after I'd left the sisters behind. I couldn't get his face out of my head. Like me, had he perhaps seen something he wasn't meant to? Was Isobel the woman accompanying him? Even if it had been her, was she really capable of murdering a child? What did she hope to gain from it? It was just too far-fetched to make sense.

Part of me wished I had accepted the invitation to go down to the lake. Maybe I could have been useful, although Alex had warned me to fly under the radar. Actively seeking out Isobel wouldn't be the smartest move. And yet, deep down, I wanted to do something to show her I wasn't afraid and that I wasn't backing down. Not yet, anyway.

But I couldn't go alone. I wanted to make a point, not get myself killed. So I headed to the stables to see if I could convince Joe to come with me. I found him sitting on a bale of hay, sipping from a chipped mug and intermittently strumming his guitar. He acknowledged my arrival with a broad smile.

"What color is this?" he asked as soon as I walked in. I liked the way he greeted me as if we were old friends. His fingers deftly stroked the strings, and a lazy chord hummed in the air.

"Green," I replied without even having to think about it.

"Very good!" He grinned. "But that was an obvious one. This one will be harder." A metallic twang reverberated around the stable. It was slow and melancholy but not in the ordinary way. Like it had a problem nobody else could understand.

"That's purple," I said, and he nodded. Then he put aside the instrument and stood up.

"Please don't stop on my account."

He gave a self-deprecating shrug. "My playing isn't worthy of an audience yet."

"They seem to like it." I gestured toward the horses.

"Well, stalled horses get bored," he replied. "Just like us."

"I never really thought about it, but I guess that makes sense." Joe was in tune with things most people missed, like the way an animal might be feeling. I liked that about him. Nothing seemed to escape his notice. Even my best fake smile didn't fool him.

"It's good to see you, Chloe," he said. "Even if you do look like crap."

"Aww, thanks, what every girl wants to hear." His green orb eyes searched my face.

"Is something wrong?"

"Nope, I just came by to see if you wanted to go for a walk."

"Sure, why not?" He stood immediately. "I get the feeling you have a destination in mind."

"I wouldn't mind checking out this famous lake. Is it far?"

"'Bout half a mile from here. We can take a paddleboat out when we get there, if you feel like it." He poked his head out the door and squinted at the sky. "Looks like rain, though."

"What else is new?" I sighed.

"Maybe if we get a move on we can make it there and back before it starts."

I followed Joe down a winding path choked with bracken, our breaths making clouds of frost in the air. I liked the way we could walk in comfortable silence, neither one feeling the need to talk. Eventually we hit a clearing and the lake just sprang into view. It was much prettier than I'd imagined, with grassy banks that flanked a body of still, dark water. Drooping branches of weeping willows trailed into the reeds. There was even a rickety white footbridge to cross from one end of the lake to the other. I spotted the paddleboats Joe mentioned moored at a pier, rocking gently on the water.

Mavis and May were there, some distance away. I pulled Joe behind a tree before they had time to notice us. May was recording information into a handheld tape recorder while Mavis pointed some black gadget that looked like a TV remote. I watched her get down on her hands and knees and aim her mystery device at the water.

"Why are we hiding?" Joe whispered.

"Shush!" I flapped my hands and stole a furtive glance out from behind the tree trunk. "What do you think they're doing over there?"

Joe shrugged like it was no big deal. "They're taking readings with their trusty EMF. It's a device for measuring electromagnetic fields."

"It looks like the buzzer that goes off when your table's ready at the Cheesecake Factory."

Joe laughed. "The theory behind it is that all matter emits a level of energy. So fluctuations can suggest the presence of paranormal activity."

"How do you know all that?" I asked.

He gave a rueful smile. "Let's just say I've been roped into helping out a few times."

"Do you think that EMF really works?"

"I highly doubt it. If it did we'd know a lot more than we do, right?"

One of the women squinted and glanced in our direction.

"Please don't let them see us," I hissed. "If they do, we'll never get away."

Joe grabbed my hand. His grip was warm and solid, and for a moment it took me by surprise. "Follow me."

Together we sprinted down the sodden path away from the lake. We didn't stop until we reached an abandoned building sitting among a nest of straggly weeds. The windows were smashed, the paint was peeling and a nervous energy engulfed me the moment I laid eyes on it. I took a step back, out of breath from the run.

"Where are we?"

"This used to be part of the original property," Joe answered. "I think it was a guesthouse back in the day. Guess it hasn't been used in a while, huh?" He finally noticed the look on my face. "Chloe? What's up?"

I couldn't bring myself to tell him the truth. He was my only flesh-and-blood friend in this whole place and I didn't want to risk pushing him away. But there was a distinct, dark shadow hanging over the old guesthouse. I was glad I wasn't the one holding the EMF, because I was sure it would have been going crazy right about now.

# CHAPTER THIRTEEN

The vibrations coming from the building were so strong I could feel them under my feet like tiny electric currents. Often, when a ghost was near, I could feel static in the air, but this was stronger than anything I'd encountered before. Whatever lay inside that guesthouse was powerful…possibly dangerous, and it scared the life out of me. How could Joe not feel it? It literally felt like the core of the earth itself was in revolt, and every ripple sent my stomach shooting into my throat.

For a moment, I was seized by a crazy impulse to just spill the beans and tell Joe everything that had happened to me since arriving at Grange Hall. But how well did I really know him? Where would I even start? Would he think I needed psychological help and tell Grandma Fee? Even relaying a fragment of my story would be enough to send any sane guy running for the hills. I didn't want Joe to run anywhere. I liked him, and more than that, I needed him as an ally.

A weighty silence, the usual precursor to a storm, hung in the air until a distant rumble of thunder shattered it. Soon the trees were bowing in the wind and the clouds looked ready to burst. I felt the first fat drops of rain on my cheeks, followed by a crack of lightning that sounded like the snap of an elastic band magnified about a hundred times.

"Okay, I may have miscalculated when the storm would hit," Joe said. He made an apologetic face.

I shivered. The cold had crept through my knitted gloves, paralyzing my fingers, and I hadn't been able to feel my toes for the past half hour. I wanted to make sure they were still there.

"We should head back, right?" I suggested eagerly.

Joe glanced at the pewter sky. "Too late for that. We'll have to wait it out."

My heart took a dive.

"Where?" I asked, feeling like an idiot because the answer was patently obvious. We weren't exactly overwhelmed with choices. Joe jerked a thumb at the guesthouse, sitting like a burned-out husk, daring us to venture inside. I would have preferred to take my chances outside and risk getting struck by lightning.

"We can take shelter here until it passes."

I shook my head firmly. "There's no way I'm going in there."

"It's perfectly safe, Chloe," he said casually. "There's nothing to be scared of, except maybe the odd spider, and I promise to fight off any that have the nerve to show up."

"You don't understand," I hedged. "I'm just not comfortable." A dull throb had in fact begun behind my temples.

"You're not claustrophobic, are you?"

"No."

"Well, c'mon, then! Where's your sense of adventure?"

The decision was made for us when the heavens opened. We instinctively turned up our collars and sprinted for cover toward the only place that offered it. We huddled under the eaves, pressing our backs flat against the front door that I imagined had been a lustrous red once, but time had faded it to its current dirty oxblood. The windows were too encrusted with dirt for me to see anything inside.

Water poured from the trees in sheets and was starting to pool in the clogged gutters. I noticed the reverberations in the earth had slowed now, to a dull, erratic heartbeat. Joe angled his body to shield me from the rain and kicked away the creepers that were blocking our way. He ran his fingers along the top of the sagging door frame and triumphantly produced a rusty key. But the timbers had shifted over time and even with the key, it took some effort and a few shoves from Joe's shoulder before the door finally gave way.

Inside, the smell of damp enveloped us immediately.

"Some guesthouse," I said. "Looks more like a shed."

"It was probably beautiful once," Joe replied. "I bet your gran has plans to restore it."

"I'm sure she does."

"My money's on beauty center. What d'you think?" The conversation was helping to distract me. Joe's British accent made everything sound playful. I liked the way he clipped his vowels, although there were times I had to strain to catch what he said.

"No way!" I laughed. "Gran thinks getting a French manicure is excessive." I did my best snooty impression of her. *"We must always strive to enhance the mind!"*

"She doesn't really say stuff like that?"

"Sadly, she does."

Now that I was joking around with Joe, my previous fears seemed unfounded. The place was harmless enough, just full of dusty boxes and old furniture.

The dark clouds outside made it difficult to see, and we stumbled around, bumping into things shrouded in sheets. Joe found and tried the light switch, but the power was either out or had long been disconnected. Cobwebs trailed from the rafters and I squealed when a lone cockroach scuttled past my foot. True to his word, Joe stomped it with his boot. The pulsing in my head competed now with the sound of rain hammering the tin roof. We slipped off our soaked coats and gave ourselves a moment to acclimatize. I wondered how Mavis and May were faring out there in the downpour. They didn't look the type to be easily dissuaded, so maybe they were crazy enough to work through it.

There was nothing to do but explore the cottage while we waited for the weather to clear. If it weren't for the layers of dust, we could have been in a thrift shop full of collectibles. I realized the place was comprised of only one long room separated into two areas by a few creaking steps. The upper level was the designated bedroom, which still housed an old brass bed behind a Japanese lacquered screen. There was a pine dresser with a rose-patterned wash jug and basin, although the jug was cracked down the center and the rim was chipped. Someone had pushed a dressmaker's dummy into a corner, and battered old hatboxes and suitcases were stacked beside it.

The lower level must have been the living room. Small paned windows stretched across an entire wall, allowing the watery light to filter in. Under it a moth-eaten chaise longue was positioned to catch the light. A rug had been rolled up and leaned against it like a sagging pillar. The place was literally packed to the rafters with junk. All of this couldn't be Gran's stuff; some of it had to belong to her predecessors at Grange Hall.

"Do you think the dead try to communicate with us?" I asked out of the blue. I hadn't intended broaching the subject, but I guessed I wanted to test the waters.

Joe pondered my question in respectful silence. I could see I'd put him on the spot. He didn't want to offend by disputing the idea, yet it was too out of left field for him to support. Or maybe, like most people, he hadn't thought enough about it. I could almost see the wheels turning in his head. He was probably wondering whether he'd met his daily time quota with Miss Screwball U.S.A. "I don't know," he said eventually. "But I don't think so."

"So you don't believe in the concept of an afterlife?"

"I didn't say that. Is everything okay? You're acting weird."

"If you had any idea how weird I am, you'd stop hanging out with me."

"Chloe!" He smiled broadly, even though I failed to see any humor in my revelation. "Let's get one thing straight. I like you far too much to stop hanging out with you."

That was tough to wrap my head around. I was that strange, secretive girl who permanently looked like she'd just seen a ghost. What on earth did he see in me? I wouldn't want to date me, and yet I couldn't seem to do anything to put Joe off. I decided not to say anything self-deprecating. It would just sound like I was in need of reassurance, like that girl at the gym with the toothpick legs who tells everyone she needs to lose five pounds. But I was genuinely curious.

"You really like me?"

"Really truly."

"But why?" I couldn't resist asking.

"Well, for starters, I like that you're weird." I laughed outright. Joe had a way of taking the awkwardness out of things. "But seriously, I like you for loads of reasons. You're cute and smart and feisty. But most important, you're probably one of the most genuine people I've ever met. You say what you feel and don't try to impress anyone. I guess what I'm saying is, you're not afraid to be you." I basked in the compliments. I got the feeling Joe Parrish's good opinion was not easily earned, so I must have done something right.

"Actually, being me is scary as hell, but thanks."

We continued to pick our way around the rooms. Every time we disturbed something, it raised a cloud of dust. Some of the cardboard boxes on the table weren't sealed, so I rifled through and picked up the first thing that came to hand—a leather-bound volume of Tennyson's poems, the pages gilt-edged. There was a curling inscription written in faded ink inside the cover. *To my dearest Isobel, Happy Birthday. December 1853.* That was all the gift-giver had written, ensuring his or her identity remained anonymous. As I stared down at the message with its long, sloping letters, I heard the sound of labored breathing. I looked around for Joe, but he'd moved to the loft area and was skimming through a box of old vinyl records. Just for a moment, I could actually feel warm breath on my neck. It was enough to make my hairs stand on end and a prickling sensation course down my spine.

A gust of wind tore open the front door and rushed inside like a stampede. The book was snatched greedily from my hands and flung across the room with unprecedented force. It bounced off a wall and landed facedown with a thud, sending dust swirling through the air. Joe jumped down the steps and had to use his whole body to shut the door against the gale-force wind. Then he bent to pick up the volume from the floor, looking at me with flushed cheeks and ruffled hair.

"I take it you're not a Tennyson fan?" he asked drily.

"Joe, that wasn't me," I replied, dead serious.

"Very funny, Chloe."

Why couldn't he sense something was wrong? He might not share my abilities, but didn't he have any intuition?

"Actually, it's not funny at all."

"What are you talking about?" He seemed puzzled by my sudden mood change.

I walked over and grabbed him by the shoulders, too alarmed now not to share the truth. "There's something here. That's why I didn't want to come in," I said hurriedly. "I think we should leave."

"Wow. Don't tell me the old girls have got to you!" I held his gaze, refusing to return his smile. "You're serious, aren't you?"

"Joe, I think there's a reason we ended up in here."

"There is. It's because it's pissing down outside and we don't want to catch pneumonia."

"I mean other than the weather."

"Okay, I'm officially confused. Are you saying you're…" He petered out, looking unsure how to continue. Had there been more time, I might have been subtler, eased him in more gently. But he was going to struggle with what I was about to tell him no matter how delicately I put it.

"Psychic? Yes, that's exactly what I'm saying."

I didn't know what prompted the decision. Maybe it was

the fact that I didn't know what might happen and I didn't want to have to go through it alone. Not this time.

"How long have you known?" Had he just gone from skepticism to acceptance in a matter of seconds? Joe didn't think I was crazy. Instead, he was asking for details. I had to be impressed by that. The only other person who'd ever reacted that way to my so-called *gift* had been my mom. I felt the old familiar sting behind my eyes and quickly blinked it away.

"Awhile. Joe, I'd rather you didn't mention this conversation to anyone."

"My friends don't call me The Vault for nothing."

"Thanks for understanding."

"Well," he said, his lip curling in a slight smile, "I'd be lying if I said I understood. I don't understand at all. But I do believe you."

"Well, that's something."

Joe walked over and folded me up in a hug, his chin resting on the top of my head. It was a small gesture, but it settled me. I wasn't sure how to react at first; it had been a while since I'd been this physically close to someone. But I managed to relax into it and felt myself leaning against his broad chest. I could feel his warmth seeping through his shirt. I hadn't felt anything this comforting in a while.

"You know, if you ever need to talk to anyone about this stuff, you can talk to me," Joe said.

"I know." Then I returned to the present and ducked from beneath his grasp.

"Can we please go now?" It was impossible to miss the note of urgency in my voice. Joe cleared a patch on the window with his sleeve and peered outside.

"Looks like the rain's easing up…. We could probably head back now before your gran sends out a search party. Unless you'd rather stick around and try to find out what's going on here?"

I rolled my eyes. "Rule Number One, Joe. You don't actively go looking for trouble."

He laughed. "Well, I don't scare easy. Here, I'll show you. After all, if there *is* something here, it would be rude of us not to say hello!"

"What?" It was hard to fathom why he did what he did next. He was either testing me or trying to allay my fears. Either way, he had no idea what he was fooling around with, and I was too slow to stop him. He spread his arms wide and turned in a full circle. "Hey there, goulies and ghosties and long-legged beasties and things that go bump in the night!"

"Joe, that's not funny…."

"Come out, come out, wherever you are!"

His last words seemed to break down a barrier. As his singsong invitation ricocheted around the room, whispered voices rustled through the air in response. I could pinpoint the exact spot they were coming from. I started. "Don't tell me you can't hear that!"

Joe scratched his head and looked at me blankly. Heart pounding, I turned to face our invisible company, sitting on the chaise, engaged in hushed conversation. "There are people sitting on the sofa talking right now."

Looking genuinely worried about me now, Joe started steering me back through the clutter toward the door. It was when I got there that I made the most serious mistake of the day. I couldn't resist. I took one last look over my shoulder at the abandoned guesthouse and a second later wished I hadn't. The now-familiar wave of nausea hit me just before I saw her....

A woman in a black silk mourning dress stood in the corner. A veil covered her face, blurring her features. As I stood, transfixed, she slowly raised a gloved hand to peel back her veil. The face beneath was in such an advanced stage of decomposition that it was barely recognizable, barely even human. I felt my whole body sag forward, and I clutched Joe's arm. I heard him say something, but the words were lost, as if he was trying to reach me from the end of a long tunnel.

I couldn't take my eyes off the woman. Her skin was cracked like old pottery. One eyelid sagged, pulling her face into a scowl. But the corners of her mouth were twisted up in an unnatural smile, as if she were a puppet on a string. As she leered at me, a single engorged maggot wriggled from between her dead lips and fell onto the dusty floor.

# CHAPTER FOURTEEN

"Hey!" Joe snapped his fingers in front of my face, obscuring my line of vision. "Chloe, what's happening?" I looked past him to find the room now empty. Already my mouth had gone dry and my hands were trembling.

"It's okay. She's gone."

Joe's puzzled gaze swept the room. "Let's get you outside." Did I detect a flicker of nervousness? He was holding the door open for me. Tempted as I was, I knew I couldn't leave. Not now. There was that compulsion to know again. Something lay hidden in this ruin of a place, and it was my job to uncover it.

"Not yet," I said determinedly.

"I thought you wanted to get out of here?"

"Just five more minutes."

Joe nodded reluctantly. "Okay, but you're starting to scare me."

The air felt charged. A pulsing energy like a heartbeat filled the space. I shut my eyes and tuned in to the sensation building in my chest. It was tugging me forward, like being pulled along by an invisible string. I followed it until I reached something concealed beneath a sheet, propped against the far wall. Without thinking I reached out and pulled the sheet down. It made a sound like birds taking flight and released swirling dust motes into the air. I heard my own sharp intake of breath when I saw what lay beneath.

The life-size portrait of Isobel I'd seen in my first vision stood before me. In real life, it was even more overwhelming. Her chin was lifted slightly and her dark, formidable eyes stared back at me. Her scarlet lips were lifted in a haughty sneer. Had the portrait been smiling when I'd last seen it? I couldn't remember now. All I knew was that Isobel was here in the room, and I almost believed that, had she wanted to, she could have stepped right out of that frame.

Suddenly the pages from Alex's sketchbook flooded back to me. They had been preliminary sketches, but it was the same image. So it was he who had painted Isobel. Of course, the finished product was very different: every shade considered and every brushstroke painstakingly executed. The work, an homage to beauty, should have been hanging in a gallery somewhere, not hidden from the world under a yellowing sheet.

The woman immortalized in the painting filled the room, mocking the passage of time. Her beauty was so unnerving you had to look away to avoid being confronted by your own mediocrity. But there was something else, too. The artist had managed to capture her strange mix of power and vulnerability.

"Wow!" Joe's voice breathed behind me. I had completely forgotten he was there. He studied the portrait from over my shoulder. "Looks like she was someone's muse. Any idea who she was?"

"Her name was Isobel Reade." I whispered her name, laden with danger. "She lived here a long time ago."

"How do you know that?" I didn't enlighten him. There was no simple answer to that question.

"I wonder if your grandmother knows this is here," he continued. "I'm sure she'd want it on display in the house."

"No!" I answered quickly. "This is where it belongs. Help me cover it back up."

We both lifted the sheet to drape back over the portrait. I couldn't stand to look at her a moment longer. But as my fingers made contact with the ornate frame of the canvas, a shiver rolled down my spine and it happened again…the same inexplicable occurrence that had taken place in the library.

This was how I used to imagine Alice feeling as she plummeted headlong down the rabbit hole. Once the journey had begun, there was no going back. The only difference was that this time I recognized the signals: the light-headedness, the shifting of physical planes and the sensation of lapsing into a dream. I couldn't move, because my feet had turned to lead. I knew Joe couldn't help me. He probably had no idea what was going on. I could hear him talking, but his voice came out distorted, like a song played at a warp speed. As I was sucked further and further into the void, I couldn't remember his face or the color of his hair. I couldn't remember what day it was. I couldn't even remember my own name.

There was nothing to do but grip the edge of the nearby table and wait for the world to change. If time really was a dimension, then mine had been left behind. The contents of the room blurred, and when they reassembled, I wasn't in an abandoned guesthouse anymore....

*The room is painted a canary-yellow and bathed in light. The shutters on the windows are open. I know it's summer by the heady scent of blooms that wafts in from outside. There's still a Japanese screen separating the bedroom from the workspace. Behind it the sheets on the bed are rumpled. On the dressing table the washbasin and jug are vibrant and new. The chaise longue isn't worn but upholstered in lustrous pale blue velvet.*

*The lower level is dominated by a long table covered with an assortment of brushes in jars and tubes of paint squeezed and twisted into various shapes. There are canvases everywhere, occupying every available space. I know that in time, each one will make something come to life. On a side table is an arrangement for a still life: a decanter of red wine with pewter goblets and a dish of tawny summer fruit.*

*The fluty tone of a young woman's voice punctures the lazy silence.*

*"Alexander, how much longer?"*

*Isobel Reade half sits, half reclines on the chaise, a red camellia positioned artfully behind her ear and a black lace mantilla draped over her shoulders. She looks like a Spanish noblewoman. Her long hair is scooped into a pile at the top of her head but some coils have escaped to fall over her butter-smooth shoulders.*

*"Isobel, please!" Alex scolds, but he doesn't sound angry. "You've been sitting less than an hour."*

*She pouts. "But I'm getting a stiff neck."*

*"Just stay still and try to stop fidgeting."*

*"If I'd known how tiresome this was going to be I would never have agreed!"*

"*Think of it as a sacrifice in the name of art.*"

*Isobel exhales in frustration.* "*I loathe art.*"

"*Be that as it may, you made me a promise and I intend to hold you to it. If you can manage one more hour, we shall go riding together. Let that be your incentive.*"

"*Do you promise?*"

"*Solemnly. Now, no more talking.*"

"*You mean I must be silent as well as still? That's too cruel.*"

*Alex puts a finger to his lips and his attention is absorbed once again by the canvas.*

*They haven't really been arguing so much as playing a game only the two of them are in on. He bargains with her as if she's a child, and her protests are thinly disguised flirtation.*

"*Alexander?*"

"*Yes?*"

"*Am I beautiful?*"

"*Obviously.*"

*Her eyes widen coyly.* "*How so?*"

"*Like an angel,*" *he replies.*

"*I'm not an angel, though, am I?*"

"*No, you're more of a sorceress.*"

"*It's sad how youth and beauty never last, isn't it?*" *She sighs.* "*I don't want to change.*"

"*I can't arrest the passage of time, but in this painting you shall always be perfect.*"

*They both laugh, and when their eyes lock, neither one can tear their gaze away. The seconds seem impossibly long. Eventually, Isobel sighs again.*

"*I've ruined the pose, haven't I?*"

"*No matter. I can fix it.*" *Alexander puts down his brush and kneels before her. He adjusts the folds of her shawl, his hands brush-*

*ing along her collarbone. The attraction between them is so strong, the ripples echo in my own body.*

*The sound of boots crunching on the gravel outside breaks the mood. A resounding voice carries into the studio.*

*"Isobel! Where the devil are you?"*

*For a moment, panic crosses her face, but Alex composes himself in an instant and moves to the open window.*

*"We're in here, brother!" His voice doesn't betray the slightest hint of wrongdoing. "I'm working."*

*"Ha! Is that what you call it?"*

*He ignores the gibe as Carter Reade strides into the room with the air of a patrician, although he can't be more than thirty. The brothers share similarities, and yet they are entirely different. Carter is heavier for a start and has a ruddier face, possibly from drinking. Where Alex's hands are slender, his are fleshy. They share the same moonlight-pale eyes, although Carter's gaze is sharper, more focused. Alex is lost in his own world.*

*"I'm here to reclaim my wife," Carter says. "I think you've monopolized her long enough."*

*Isobel looks at him archly, her composure restored. "Need I remind you that this was your idea, darling?"*

*"Was it? I don't remember that!" Carter demurs as Isobel shakes her head as a form of reprimand.*

*"Well we're almost finished here, aren't we, Alexander?"*

*"We would have been finished a lot sooner if you were more cooperative."*

*Isobel throws him a petulant look, but Carter only laughs indulgently.*

*"Isobel cooperative? That'll be the day. Now, tell me, how is this pièce de résistance progressing?" He takes a step toward the easel, but Alex raises a protective hand.*

"It's not ready."

"Far be it from me to upset the artist." Carter backs away, but his tone shows how little regard he has for the profession.

The vibe has changed distinctly upon his arrival, and an over-bearing masculinity fills the room. He swaggers over to Isobel and his lips stretch into a broad grin of appreciation. Finally he extends an arm to help her down from the platform where she's been standing. Alex averts his gaze with a pained look.

"Come now, don't sulk!" Carter bellows. "I'll let you borrow her again tomorrow. Although, perhaps, Isobel, we should not encourage my little brother in these frivolous pursuits."

Irritation flickers in Alex's eyes. "Is that what you think art is?"

"I'm sure I haven't the faintest idea what art is," Carter replies nonchalantly. "But I know it doesn't put food on the table. Let's hope this isn't just another passing fancy."

"What are you suggesting?" Alex is suddenly indignant.

"Please, brother," Carter scoffs. "First it was the ministry, then poetry, now painting. What next, I wonder?"

For a moment they stand locked in a silent power struggle.

When Alex speaks, his voice is formal and stiff. "If you wish for me to leave, you need only say so."

Like a mediator Isobel pushes her way between them. "Now look what you've done, Carter!" she cries. "Why must you two always quarrel?"

"Oh, calm yourself, Isobel," Carter says. "My brother isn't going anywhere. Who would be left to entertain you if he did?"

Isobel turns to Alex, imploring. "Don't take anything he says to heart. You wouldn't leave, would you? I would be inconsolable if you did."

Alex gives an imperceptible shake of his head and Isobel quickly falls silent.

"There! See?" Carter's voice is gratingly loud. "Now that you have your bosom friend back, would you be so kind as to return with me to the house?"

As he turns away, he steps on a canvas and kicks it carelessly aside.

"Why are you angry?" Isobel looks confused.

"I'm not angry. I just ask that you perform your duties as mistress of this house from time to time."

"Have I neglected them?" she asks drily.

"The servants cannot be expected to make decisions alone. They need direction from you."

"What do I care whether they buy fish or beef for supper?"

Carter's whole face jumps with a twitch. "You are my wife, and you will make that your priority. After that, you may fill your days as you please."

"You mustn't blame her," Alex interjects carefully. "This is my fault. I've demanded too much of her time."

Carter grunts gruffly in reply but seems placated. He turns to his wife. "I'm expecting company tonight," he says. "See to it that everything is in order."

"Whom are you expecting?"

He glares at her, daring further questions. "Some business associates of mine."

"A night of drinking and cards, I assume?" Isobel's voice is sharp.

"Don't be so inhospitable!" Carter booms. "And remember, I answer to no one." He takes a deep breath and lowers his voice. "Every man must be allowed a vice or two. Isn't that right, Alex?"

Sullen, Alex makes no reply. Carter pushes past him toward the door.

"Isobel, I want you back at the house." He looks over his shoulder, and his bloodshot eyes are almost wild. "Do not cross me on this."

*He pushes open the door and the frame shudders from the force. Isobel watches his retreating back from the window.*

*"He's insufferable. I can't tell you how much I hate him!" she proclaims, once he's out of earshot.*

*"He was not always so…rough around the edges," Alex replies as he begins to put away his tools.*

*Isobel tosses her head. "I don't care what Carter says. I only worry that he'll do or say something to drive you away."*

*Alex stops, his blue eyes startling in the sunlight, strands pushed away from his noble forehead like a mane of gold.*

*"Does Carter ever frighten you?"*

*Isobel considers his question a moment. "Sometimes when he's been drinking. But I've learned how to manage him."*

*"I wish you didn't have to manage him."*

*"We all have our crosses to bear."*

*"He doesn't deserve you!" Alex squeezes his eyes shut. "If I were so fortunate as to marry a woman like you I would…" He falters, as if realizing he's said too much.*

*"What would you do?" Isobel asks, breathless.*

*He takes a moment to steady himself before continuing, "I would worship her and ensure she never wanted for anything."*

*"I think you must be the sweetest man in all the world!" Isobel cries.*

*Alex crosses the room and takes her by the shoulders. "Promise me something?"*

*"Anything."*

*"If Carter were ever to direct his rage at you, I want to know about it."*

*"Very well." She tilts her swanlike neck and presses her lips lightly against his cheek. "Now I had better go back. His temper will only worsen."*

*Alex gives a tight nod and waits for her to leave. He watches her retreating figure with an expression of longing I've never seen on a person before. The moment she's no longer in view, he picks up a jar of dirty brushes and flings it against a wall.*

The sound of breaking glass propelled me back to the present. My head felt like it was stuffed full of cotton wool, but through the haze an image flashed repeatedly like a neon sign.

"I know where I've seen Carter before," I said aloud.

"Who's Carter?" Joe was still beside me, looking baffled.

"Let's just get out of here," I said. "I'll explain later."

Joe nodded his assent. "I think we could both use a nice cup of tea, don't you?"

"Good idea." I was already familiar with this English antidote to all of life's challenges.

Without protest, I allowed Joe to walk back with me. I was glad he didn't ask any more questions. He had good instincts and knew when he shouldn't push too hard. As the house with its ancient oak came into view, I remembered my first day when I'd seen a man swinging from a thick branch, his face swollen in death.

Now I knew his name. Carter Reade.

# CHAPTER FIFTEEN

I spent the rest of the day on tenterhooks waiting for Alex to appear so I could tell him about the episode in the guest-house. But he didn't show up. The whole of the following day, too, passed without any sign of him. I told myself it didn't matter, but the knot in my stomach told a different story. The worst part was having no means of contacting him. I was so accustomed to people being a call or a text or a Facebook message away. But I just had to accept his absence without any means of questioning it.

At the same time Alex decided to decamp, Isobel's presence seemed to intensify. Every night I could hear her in the halls, sometimes laughing, other times crying. Sometimes I would be woken in the night by an earsplitting shriek. One day Harry drove me into town to get supplies from the pharmacy, and on the way home, I saw her by the lake, twirling in a gossamer gown to a silent melody. It made Gran's ownership of Grange Hall feel fraudulent, as if Isobel was still the real mistress of the house. It made me feel like I was trespassing, too, but I figured that was exactly how she hoped I'd feel.

I didn't get it, though. Isobel's hatred for me seemed disproportionate. What did she think was going to happen between Alex and me? What *could* happen? Maybe I was missing something. I resolved to ask him about it if he ever deigned to make an appearance again. He was the only one who could possibly answer my growing list of questions. Why was I having these visions? What did they mean? Was Isobel controlling them, or were there other forces at work? And just to address the elephant in the room, where the hell *was* Alex? What was he playing at? Had he been unsuccessful in his attempt to sever Isobel's hold over him? Was he staying away in some twisted attempt to protect me? Could he be jealous over my burgeoning friendship with Joe? I couldn't deny that I liked Joe, but I *needed* Alex…and not just for protection. I felt like he was a key I needed to unlock a vital part of myself. His absence was making me uneasy, in a *lull before the storm* kind of way. I spent my nights tossing and turning and constantly looked a little worse for wear as a result. Gran looked at me curiously as she neatly tapped the top off a boiled egg at breakfast.

"You look tired, dear. Didn't you sleep well?"

"Not really," I admitted.

"Perhaps you ought to try meditation."

*Sure, Gran,* I thought, bitterly. *That'll solve all my problems.*

"Or a long bath," she went on. "That always helps clear my head." As an astute reader of people, she knew something was up. But she'd never be able to guess what. Besides, she wasn't the type to believe in anything weird or wacky. If there was no concrete evidence, she'd just dismiss it. Except for Jesus. He was the only one who didn't need to prove himself.

I had real-life drama unfolding before me with every passing day. I didn't need my books for that. By the time we'd finished breakfast, my frustration needed some kind of outlet. I threw on a coat and mittens and bolted out into the wintry morning. I could feel Alex's presence, as if he was close by watching me but refusing to make an appearance.

I broke into a jog and kept going until I reached the clearing in the woods, a safe distance from the house. I ran so hard I began to sweat under all my layers of clothing. I peeled off the coat and tossed it onto a pile of dead leaves. Then I spread my arms wide and tilted my face up to the sky.

"Alex!" I yelled as loudly as I could. "Where are you?"

I turned in a full circle, mistaking every shadow or scuffle in the underbrush for his presence. But he wasn't there, and with every passing second, I grew angrier and angrier. He was messing everything up. I had one cardinal rule when it came to dating—never chase a guy, dead or alive.

"Fine, be a jerk!" I shouted, kicking at the dirt. "But I just want you to know, this is *very* uncool. Friends don't bail on friends when things get tough.

"You know, I'm glad you're not here. I don't even want to see you anymore!" I was winding down. There was just one thing left to say, whether he could hear me or not. "My bad for thinking you were one of the good guys."

I ran full pelt back to the house, barely stopping to draw breath. I went straight up to my room, blowing off Rory when I passed him on the stairs. The moment I slammed the bedroom door behind me, I saw it. The window was open a fraction, even though I was sure I'd left it firmly shut when I'd left earlier that morning. There, sitting on the windowsill, was a single sprig of winter jasmine. A cascading bush of it was growing at the bottom of the porch steps. I only knew it by name because Harry had pointed it out to me once, trying to educate me on local flora. I twirled the stem between my fingers. I knew it was from Alex; a peace offering of sorts, his way of letting me know that, despite his absence, I hadn't been forgotten. It had a pacifying effect.

I placed the flower on my pillow and lay down beside it. Even though it was only midday, I found myself drifting into a restless sleep.

I sat up to find Alex in my room. I knew I was dreaming, because everything wore that silver sheen that can never be replicated in real life. Plus the moon outside was so big and low in the sky, I thought it might swallow up the house. He was sitting in a chair by the window, wearing a loose white shirt and riding boots, as if he'd just jumped off a horse. He was staring out the window toward the woods as if the answer to all of life's mysteries could be found there. His wheat-gold hair was tousled and took on a pale sheen in the moonlight.

I felt a rush of blood to my head and hastily tucked my hair behind my ears, before remembering I was supposed to be mad at him. Funny how my anger evaporated the moment I laid eyes on him. I slid out of bed, conscious of my heart-print flannel pajamas, and folded my arms accusingly.

"And where exactly have you been?" I demanded, even though part of me simply wanted to enjoy his unexpected return.

"Not far," he answered softly, turning his head to look at me.

"And how was I supposed to know that? I thought you'd bailed."

"Bailed?"

"Y'know…gone for good."

"I'm never really gone." There was a twinge of sadness in his voice. "I've told you that."

"Well, you could have at least given me a sign." I found myself mimicking his voice. "Perhaps as a matter of courtesy?"

"I'm sorry, Chloe. I didn't mean to upset you," he answered. "But I did try to give you a sign."

I looked around for my flower. It wasn't resting on my pillow anymore. Someone had moved it to the dresser. It looked fragile now, like the petals were already wilting.

"I don't like when you're not around." I tried to pull off Isobel's flirtatious charm, but my voice just came out sounding infantile.

"I came back," Alex replied. "Doesn't that count for something?"

"But this isn't even real…." I paused, not entirely certain anymore. "Is it?"

He shrugged. "Does it matter? Waking or sleeping, I'm still not real."

I shook my head. I wasn't about to let him off this easy. "You can't pull a no-show all week and then invade my dreams."

The newfound attitude in my tone seemed to amuse him.

"Do you see it as an invasion?" he asked with a wry smile.

"You bet I do!" I wasn't ready to give up my moral high ground just yet.

Alex cupped his chin in his hand. "That's interesting."

"What's interesting about it?"

"You invited me in." His brilliant blue eyes danced over

my face in a way that made what I was about to say fall right out of my head.

"Wait, what?"

"I was your last thought before you went to sleep."

I opened my mouth to protest but then remembered that I couldn't actually deny that.

He waved a dismissive hand. "Don't worry, it wasn't intentional. We are not in control of our subconscious."

"Exactly," I said gruffly. Then added as an afterthought, "How does that even work?"

"In sleep, our defenses are down and it becomes easier for the living and the dead to communicate. That's why so many dream of loved ones immediately after their passing. Sometimes it's their way of saying goodbye."

I remembered having the most vivid dream about my mom the night we left the hospital. There had been a feeling of calm in the dream, and I'd known she was trying to tell me she was okay. Of course, the next morning, things were no better. I wanted her to be at peace but wasn't anywhere near ready to let her go.

A worrying thought crossed my mind. "Is that what you're doing now?"

"Of course not. This is about me not being able to stand the idea of you getting hurt."

"For the record, disappearing from someone's life without explanation could be construed as hurtful, too."

"Is that your way of saying you've missed me?"

"Of course I have." I sighed. "But I don't want to just see you in dreams. How do I know that I didn't make the whole thing up?"

"You didn't," he assured me. "But we must be patient for a while...until things calm down. Can you do that for me?"

His use of that inclusive *we* went a long way toward making me feel better. I nodded in agreement.

"Good. Would you like to wake up now? Your grandmother would certainly disapprove of long daytime naps. She's probably on her way up here right now."

"Who cares," I said. "Can't we talk a little longer?"

Alex inclined his head. "We may talk as long as you wish."

"So..." It took a moment to build up my nerve. "Did you miss me?"

A slow smile crept over his face, reminding me of the sun coming up over a hill. "More than you can imagine."

"Really?" It was hard to hide my pleasure. I felt sufficiently encouraged by his admission to go down a bolder track. "Alex, if this is my dream, does that mean I can make anything happen?"

"You're in charge," he replied.

"If I'm in charge, what are you doing all the way over there?"

If I'd said that in real life, my cheeks would have been blazing. Who was I kidding? I never would have said it in the first place. But this was a dream. I spent so much of my waking life trying to keep it together, making sure I didn't say the wrong thing. But what were dreams for, if you couldn't finally let yourself go a little? I didn't even feel like Chloe anymore. I felt as if some seductive and superconfident alter ego had taken me over.

Alex was watching me with a curious expression. "Where, pray tell, would you like me to be, Miss Kennedy?"

I raised an eyebrow. "Do you really need to ask, Mr. Reade?"

It worked. A moment later, he wasn't in the chair anymore but lying next to me on my bed in all his princely beauty. I felt something stir inside me that I hadn't felt before. It was intoxicating and nerve-racking at the same time. His scent enveloped me, but there was an undertone I struggled to place. Could it be sandalwood or was it cinnamon? Maybe it wasn't anything that could be labeled by any earthly object. But to me, it was the smell of riding bareback through the woods in the rain. I'd never been the sort of girl who liked to share her personal space, but being this close to Alex only made me want to get closer. But any closer would mean... Well, it wasn't something I'd ever done before.

Truth be told, the furthest I'd ever gone with a guy was making out and a bit of heavy petting in his car, what we'd referred to as first base in school. I knew Sam and Natalie would be shocked if they uncovered that little secret. Between the two of them, my friends could write a book of *sexcapades* to rival that of many thirty-year-olds. I'd lied to them about it for fear of being labeled frigid, one of the more indelible of high-school stains.

I wasn't a prude. It wasn't like I needed a ring on my finger or anything, but I'd always wanted the circumstances to be just right. The only opportunities that had been presented to me involved frat boys encountered at college parties we'd gate-crashed, obscene hip-hop music and an overwhelming smell of tequila. And the boys had always had single-syllable names like Chad or Brad or Chuck. You'd think they'd be easy to remember, but they were surprisingly difficult. I was holding out for the right time, the right place and the right guy. I wanted it to be a special memory, not something I would later want to block out.

My mom's voice floated back to me: *Don't do it if you'd be ashamed to tell your children about it.* I had taken her advice and always believed that when the right moment came along, I'd just know.

I realized that dream-sex with a ghost might be slightly nontraditional, but maybe this was my perfect circumstance. It was different for everyone, right? For the first time in my life, I knew what it felt like to *want* someone. I wanted to feel Alex's hands on my skin. I wanted to drag my fingers through his hair like I'd seen Isobel do. I wanted to press my forehead against his and feel the thrum of our entwined bodies. So this was what passion felt like! This was what prompted lovers to take wild risks. I understood now how invincible Romeo and Juliet had felt. *"With love's light wings did I o'erperch these walls."*

The best part was seeing my desire reflected in Alex's eyes. All my self-doubt crumbled to dust. As he lay beside me, his breath warm on my neck, I wondered how I'd ever be able to look at a living, breathing boy the same way again. How could anyone else ever again stand a chance?

The next thing I knew, I was fumbling with my pajama top, trying to look irresistible at the same time. Alex watched me intently, his eyes traveling over my body in a way that made me shiver from head to foot. I could feel my leg pressed against his. Then he did something unexpected. He put his hand over mine and stopped me.

*Wait. That wasn't supposed to happen.*

"Is something wrong?" I asked.

He bowed his head and pressed my fingers to his lips.

Then, to my disappointment, he slid away from me, returning to his post by the window.

"I don't understand," I said, self-conscious at last.

"We're not ready, Chloe," he answered. "We should wait."

"Wait for what? This isn't even real—you said so yourself."

Alex's features were pinched as he tried to find the right
words. "I wouldn't want you doing anything you might regret…even in a dream."

"I thought you said my dream, my rules?" I reminded him.

"Not this time."


I sat bolt upright and rubbed my eyes. The day was so
gloomy, it was hard to tell what time it was. Alex was there,
fully clothed and standing like a sentinel at my window,
watching the winter sun struggle to make an appearance
from behind a curtain of cloud.

"Sleep well?"

"Am I awake?" I pinched myself to make sure.

"You are now."

"I just had the weirdest dream."

"I know. I was there."

"Great. I was hoping I'd made that part up." I grabbed a
pillow and hid my face in it. I'd never been so humiliated.
Getting rejected in real life was bad enough. "I'm sorry. I
don't normally behave like that, I swear."

"There's no need to apologize, Chloe. I got to see a new
side of you, one, you may rest assured, that was not easy to
resist."

"Yeah, but you managed," I said, voice muffled by the
pillow.

"Only because I've had decades to work on my self-control."

I threw my pillow aside. "What are you saying? That I'm just a horny seventeen-year-old with no sense of boundaries?"

"Please don't remind me that you're only seventeen."

"Seventeen is the new twenty-one," I told him. "And just for the record, could what happened…or rather didn't happen just now…ever, you know, happen for real?" It was potentially the clumsiest sentence I'd ever spoken, but I think he got the gist.

"I've never exactly tried it." His eyes twinkled as he gave me his most beguiling smile. "Maybe one day we'll find out."

At that moment, as if in response to his words, my door handle began to rattle violently as if someone outside were trying to wrench it from its hinges. We both heard the growl, deep and guttural, as if a wild animal was stalking the halls. I opened my mouth to speak, but a second later Alex was by my side, pressing cool, slender fingers over my mouth.

"Don't make a sound," he whispered. Then he slowly unclamped his fingers and positioned himself in front of me. Goose bumps covered my arms as someone outside turned the handle very slowly and deliberately. Alex passed his fingers over his eyes, indicating for me to feign sleep.

*Trust me,* he mouthed before fading out of sight.

I rolled onto my side, my heart seeming to pound right out of my chest. It was so loud I was sure it would betray me. When the door opened, the cold air that rushed in transformed the room into an icebox. I realized my hands were balled into fists, clutching the sheets. I relaxed them and tried to focus on regulating my breathing. I prayed Alex knew what he was doing. I trusted him, I reassured myself. I trusted him with my life.

I heard the rustle of silk as Isobel approached the bed. There was a strange rattling sound I couldn't place until I realized it was her breathing with lungs full of water. Her damp hair brushed against my cheek as she leaned over me. I imagined her trying to suck my soul from my body. I could feel my skin crawling. I wasn't sure how long I could keep this up, so I repeated Alex's name over and over in my head, focusing hard on each syllable. Finally satisfied that I was indeed asleep, Isobel moved away. I heard objects on my dresser being moved around and dared to open my eyes a fraction to see her standing like a shadow, her back to me. She picked up each item in turn and studied it as if it might offer clues to a mystery. That mystery was me.

Isobel stiffened as her eye fell on the sprig of jasmine Alex had left for me. She picked it up and twirled the stem in front of her face, inhaling the heady scent. Then her shoulders went completely rigid as she randomly crushed the fragile flower between her long, bony fingers.

# CHAPTER SIXTEEN

Despite his promise, I knew Joe had ratted me out by the look on Gran's face over breakfast. She didn't bother trying to hide it; she just fixed her stern gaze on me and frowned over the rim of her teacup.

"When were you going to tell me about what happened yesterday?"

I tossed aside the remnants of my toast and decided to play dumb. "What happened yesterday?" Gran fixed me with an impatient stare. "Joe said something, didn't he?"

"If he did it's only because he's a responsible friend who happens to be concerned about you."

"There's nothing to be concerned about."

Gran turned to my brother, who was looking back and forth at us like a boxing match was about to ensue.

"Rory, if you've finished with your breakfast, I think Miss Grimes could use a hand in the kitchen."

I could tell he wanted to stay and watch the show, but when Grandma Fee pursed her lips and arched her eyebrows like that, it was better to just do what she told you. He pushed his chair back and shuffled away reluctantly.

"Joe's overreacting," I said as dismissively as I could.

"Joe Parrish doesn't overreact," she replied, like his word was scripture. "That's why I'm worried."

"What exactly did he say?"

"He seems to think you've been having seizures."

*Oh, awesome, great way to underplay things, Joe.* I tried laughing it off, but it came out sounding strained.

"That's ridiculous," I told her. "I think I'd know if I was epileptic, Gran. They're more like…like…"

"Yes?" she said. "What would you call it, Chloe?"

"I don't know! Little dizzy spells, maybe? They only last a few seconds."

"Well, Joe seems to think it's more than that. He said something about hallucinations, and I've no doubt it's caused by a deficient diet. I'd like you to see my doctor and get some tests done."

I gritted my teeth and made a mental note to punch Joe in the face next time I saw him. He had one job, and that was to keep his mouth shut. Instead, he went running to my grandmother the first opportunity he got. As if I didn't have enough stresses without her breathing down my neck.

"It was nothing. I just need to get more sleep." Grandma Fee narrowed her eyes, and a terse little "hmm" escaped her lips. "If it happens again, I'll make an appointment with the doc myself."

"We'll see," she said. The way she said it, I knew I hadn't heard the end of this. Not by a long shot.

As soon as I was dismissed, I gave in to my overwhelming urge to find Joe and blast him for his betrayal. I marched off in the direction of the stables, where I found him mucking out the stalls in his old worn boots and a plaid shirt.

"What the hell is wrong with you?" I demanded.

He jumped at my entrance and dropped the rake. One look at my face told him everything he needed to know.

"Uh-oh."

"That's right. I can't believe you did that. Didn't you say people call you The Vault? What exactly is your definition of a vault?"

"Listen, Chloe…" He took a step toward me.

"I wouldn't do that if I were you." I pointed a warning finger. "For your own protection."

"Okay, okay. I'm sorry. But I was worried about you. Really worried. Think about what happened, then ask yourself what you would have done."

He had a point there, but it wasn't enough for me to relinquish my rage. "I don't know, but I sure as hell wouldn't have told Gran I was having *seizures.*"

"Well…that's sort of what it looked like from where I was standing." He rolled his eyes back in his head and let his tongue loll out to one side. "Kind of like this." He was only trying to lighten the mood, but it wasn't going to work. Well, it was working a little.

"Do you have any idea how much trouble you've gotten me into? Gran likes to interfere even when she doesn't have a reason. Now she's going to be sticking her nose into my business every day. Ask Rory if you don't believe me. Where is Rory anyway? Is he here with you?"

"No, down at the lake, I think. With our resident ghost busters."

"What?" That took my attention off myself. My anger

ebbed like water down a drain. "What the hell's he doing there?"

Joe shrugged, but I could see my reaction surprised him. "Just helping out, I guess. That's cool, right?"

"Not really!" I couldn't control how shrill my voice sounded. The face of the little boy from the newspaper clipping flashed in my mind. He had innocently wandered down to the lake and never come back. I didn't know for sure how he'd met his fate, but the idea of Rory being so close to Isobel's haunt made my stomach churn. "Who told him he could go out unsupervised?"

Joe laughed at my dramatic reaction. "I'm sure Rory can take care of himself. Besides, he's not unsupervised—he's with two middle-aged adults."

"Two middle-aged nut jobs, you mean!"

"That's a little harsh. What are you so stressed about? Does this have anything to do with what happened yesterday?"

I didn't bother answering him. Instead, I turned on my heel and ran out of the stables. "Wait!" I heard Joe call behind me, but I wasn't waiting for anyone.

I pelted through the scrub at breakneck speed. All I could think of was the look on Isobel's face when I'd last seen her. It was the same hungry look a wolf gets when it spies a deer ripe for the slaughter. Alex might have extracted a promise from her not to harm me, but their agreement hadn't stipulated anything about family or friends.

By the time the lake came into view, my sides were aching and I was out of breath. I spotted Rory right away, laughing and chatting with Mavis and May. It made me feel like a bit of an idiot for making a scene. The three of them were sitting in a wooden rowboat with chipped paint. Rory looked thrilled to be acting as oarsman while the sisters took their routine measurements.

This time they'd brought along some new additions: what looked like a digital camera and something else I didn't recognize dangling from a narrow pole. May was aiming a long flashlight between the reeds into the water. If it weren't for the obvious age difference between them, they would have passed for three kids out in search of adventure. I was a little reassured by the fact that they'd been sensible enough to strap on life jackets, even though you couldn't find a more placid-looking scene.

The lake had a surreal quality that day. It was shrouded in mist, and the trees leaned gracefully over the water like dancers. Everything seemed fine on the surface, but I still didn't want Rory involved in anything connected with the supernatural.

"Hey, Rory!" I called out. "What are you doing? You need to get back here right now!"

"I can't," he called back happily. "I'm the captain of this expedition."

Mavis and May both waved energetically as I shook my head. They were even more juvenile than my brother, only they didn't have his age as an excuse.

"We're almost done here." May's reedy voice carried over to me. "Our new captain has been an enormous help."

"That's great!" I called back as casually as possible, not wanting to alarm them. "But we have to go out." Lying seemed easier than trying to explain my irrational fears. But my brother was having too much fun to let me interrupt it.

"Right now?" he asked.

"Yes. *Now.*"

"Where we going?" I ransacked my mind for something guaranteed to eclipse his current euphoria.

"Pizza," I announced triumphantly.

"Since when does Gran let us have pizza?"

"As a special treat," I yelled. "But if you're not back at the house in ten minutes, you have to eat sushi."

I wasn't sure if it was the lure of pizza or the threat of sushi, but I watched Rory do a double take and start steering the boat back toward the pier. Joe appeared at my side, hair tousled, but not even breathless from the run.

"See." He motioned to my little brother. "He's perfectly fine. There's nothing to worry about."

No sooner were the words spoken than a sound reached us: a woman singing a doleful lullaby. I knew everyone heard it, because we all stopped to listen. Rory dropped his oar and May's flashlight dropped into the lake with a soft *plunk*. We all stood, motionless.

I saw something move under the water. The lake was already a murky brown color, like tea that had been brewed too long, so the thing was camouflaged at first. But as it rose slowly to the surface, I could make out a black hump covered in what looked like sludge. From where I stood, it looked like a giant rodent snaking its way closer to the boat. Still, no one seemed to register what was happening but me.

"Rory!" His name caught in my throat. "Row faster!"

But he wasn't moving. He was mesmerized by the hypnotic melody throbbing through the air. His hand that had been clutching the oar had gone limp.

The hump stretched out, seeming to elongate as it drifted alongside them, now close enough to knock against the side of the boat. It waited for a moment, as if playing a strange game, before rocking the boat. It was a gentle movement at first, the way you'd rock a cradle, but then it built in momentum. Mavis and May both scrambled back as a thick mist crept over from the reeds, obscuring their vision. The tendrils engulfed the little vessel like hoary fingers.

I realized how far down the bank I'd ventured when icy water flooded my shoes. I hadn't even noticed, because from my new vantage point I could see that the seaweed wasn't seaweed after all, but ribbons of long, black hair. And the lump was no animal, as I'd first thought. It was a woman in a black lace dress, floating faceup in the water.

I'd never known a fear so intense that it could wipe out thought. Tension filled my body as I watched Isobel's corpse drift on the water, her heavy dress billowing like a parachute. I knew she was just waiting for the right moment to pounce. Ordinarily, in instances like this, my first instinct would have been to run. But I couldn't. There was no way I was turning my back on my little brother, not even to run for help.

Clouds rolled overhead, and thunder sent a clear warning for us to take cover before the skies opened and let fire.

"Rory! Get away from there!" My voice reverberated around the lake, sounding like that of a stranger. Through the mist that had fallen over the lake like a gauzy curtain, I saw my brother pick up his oar. The Hunt sisters were gazing around with a mixture of fear and anticipation. I wanted to tell them they were idiots, playing with fire and just waiting to get burned. Third-degree burns. They didn't know about Isobel. They were nothing but pawns in her demented chess game, and she could obliterate them all without batting an eye.

Only one thought offered me hope, and that was that her

appearance was meant only to frighten me. But I wasn't naive enough to believe that. I'd seen enough to know that Isobel didn't play fair, so I made a decision on the spot. As soon as I got Rory out of danger, I was going to come clean about everything to Grandma Fee, even if she dragged me to the closest psych ward by the ear. I wasn't equipped to handle this, and I wasn't too proud to admit it. Besides, how would I live with myself if anything happened to Rory because I failed to speak up?

I suddenly realized that Rory was rowing with all his might but getting nowhere. Something was wrong. Why weren't they moving? An unseen force was holding them in place. The scene was surreal, like looking at a painting of a lake with a rowboat frozen on the water. I was certain of one thing. Alex was the only one capable of exerting any influence over Isobel now. But where was he? He should have been able to sense we were in trouble.

"Come on!" I cried, my throat raw from shouting. "Rory, look at me!"

"It's okay, Chloe!" Mavis hollered breathlessly. "We're perfectly safe."

That told me that they couldn't see Isobel and were unaware of how close they were to real danger. They were fascinated by what was happening around them, because there was no feasible explanation. This was probably a life-changing moment in their nonexistent careers as paranormal investigators, and they were loath to let it go. I shook my head vehemently.

"You don't understand! Please listen!"

The bloated corpse continued to float eerily alongside them. Her eyes were closed and her lids blue with cold. Her face was a frozen mask. Water lilies were scattered around her, and some had caught in the loops of hair that fanned out in the water like an ink stain.

I was up to my knees in the water now, urging them back. I squatted, trying to get a better view between breaks in the mist. I wanted to scream the truth at them, but I didn't know what effect that might have. I didn't want to frighten Rory any more than he already was. Panic could only make his situation worse. I just needed them to reach the riverbank before the creature in the water did something unexpected.

"Alex, where are you?" I cried helplessly. That was a serious mistake. The ghost heard me and reacted instantly. Isobel's eyes flew open. She rolled over so that her face was submerged with only her dark, crazed eyes lurking above the surface. She looked directly at me.

Then she sank out of view. For a moment, I thought she'd gone, until I saw her head appear beside Rory. He was bundled up next to May in his quilted blue parka, chewing the inside of his lip, a habit he had when he was nervous.

I plunged into the frigid lake, but it was too late. A bony hand emerged from the water, skin wrinkled and puckered, fingers laced with algae. All my worst fears were realized when it reached up and gripped the side of the paddleboat.

# CHAPTER SEVENTEEN

"Rory! Watch out!" I screamed. But there was no way he could see what I saw, a dead hand slowly inching toward him. I watched, helpless, as it finally closed over his wrist. Rory let out a shudder without knowing why. A look of surprise crossed his face when he tried to pull his hand away and couldn't. It was held in a viselike grip.

The Hunt sisters looked around in bewilderment as Isobel began to haul Rory out of the boat. Mavis lunged for him, wrapping both sinewy arms around his waist and using her body as an anchor. But the supernatural force was too strong for her to resist. Both women shrieked in tandem when my brother was pulled over the side into the lake. Until that moment, the water had been strangely still. Now it started to churn violently. Rory struggled until he disappeared completely from view and all that remained was his beanie, bobbing on the water.

If I hadn't known about Isobel I'd have thought I was watching a scene from *Jaws*. Rory thrashed and fought his way back to the surface. What scared me the most was that he wasn't calling for help; he was too busy struggling for air. I swam toward him as fast as I could, but he was too far away; I wouldn't reach him in time. How long did it take for someone to drown? Was it three minutes or five? His heavy jacket was quickly absorbing water, weighing him down. His arms flailed uselessly against his invisible assailant. With a strangled splutter, he went under again.

All of this happened really fast, but it felt like it was playing out in slow motion. I was a reasonably good swimmer but cold and shock slowed me down. It had always been my job to look out for Rory. His slight build, plethora of allergies and preference for chess over football had earned him a life of torment at school. I was his safe port. I was the one who confronted the bullies and warned them not to mess with my kid brother. I couldn't let him down now. But I felt like I was like swimming against the tide, encountering invisible resistance.

Just when I thought I couldn't compel my arms to swim another stroke, I heard something crashing through the scrub around us. A blurry figure sailed past me, arcing through the air to dive into the wintry lake. It was Joe. He'd chased after me, no doubt worried I'd come to harm. I could tell he was a strong swimmer by the way his arms sliced through the water. It didn't take him long to reach Rory. Once he did, he expertly grabbed hold of my brother from behind, a calculated move, because Rory's panic might otherwise have dragged them both under. Joe managed to wrap an arm around my brother's neck to keep his head above water.

There was a short lull of silence, but it felt eerie. I didn't dare allow myself to relax. Then the water started churning again. Suddenly, a wall of it rose freakishly in front of

the boys. It hovered in midair for a moment before cascading down over their heads. Joe looked stunned but was
quick-thinking enough to brace himself as they were both
dragged under again. When they emerged, I saw his eyes
darting fiercely around in search of some unseen foe. But he
wouldn't find her. I watched in horror as Joe's gaze began to
grow distant. He stared into space, eyes unfocused, oblivious now to the turbulence around him. My heart somer-
saulted as I realized that Isobel had gotten to him. His body
was starting to slacken. Rory began to slip from his grasp.
Within a minute or two they would both drown. There was
only one thing left to do.

"Alex," I screamed. "Help us!"

The words were barely spoken when he appeared as a vision on horseback on the opposite side of the lake. He was
wearing the long fawn coat I'd seen once before and his
golden hair was swept boldly away from his face. He dis-
mounted and stood at the water's edge. But why did he look
so calm? Why wasn't he disrobing and going in after them?
Instead he simply called out "Isobel!" in a commanding voice
that seemed to echo for miles.

Isobel's head emerged from the water like a siren, an ecstatic light in her eyes. He kept his gaze fixed on her as if
the rest of us didn't exist.

"Isobel," he repeated, extending an arm. "Come to me."

I watched her grisly form rise from the water as she
mouthed his name. *Alexander.* Like a sleepwalker, she moved
across the water toward him.

"Make haste, my love," Alex continued. "The day is almost done."

It must have made her recall some long-lost memory, because a flicker of a smile crossed her face. The deranged look was gone now, and she moved toward Alex as if under a spell. Her hair was bedraggled, her garments sodden, and water rolled off her in tiny rivulets. She was a sight to startle even the dead, but Alex looked deep into her eyes as if she were the most beautiful creature he'd ever beheld. He swung gracefully back onto his horse and reached down a hand to her. She clasped it eagerly and in one swift movement he hoisted her up. She leaned tenderly against him. It was strange how completely transformed she was in his presence. I started to realize that what Isobel really wanted wasn't revenge, and it wasn't my heart on a platter, like I'd first assumed. All she wanted was Alexander Reade, and she wanted him for the rest of eternity. It was really that simple.

"I knew you'd come back," she murmured into his neck, her voice carrying all the way over to me. Even though I was filled with relief that my brother was now safe, I couldn't help the pang that rippled through me, seeing the phantom horse with its ghost riders turn and vanish into the trees. Alex had come to my rescue but, yet again, it left me feeling utterly empty.

Now the worst was over, Joe tucked Rory under his arm and swam back toward the boat. Mavis and May helped them back in and then rowed at manic speed to the dock. I dragged myself through the reeds and collapsed onto the grassy bank. I should have been shaking from cold, but I was too numb to feel anything. I couldn't shake the image of Alex and Isobel. We had all escaped unharmed, so why did it feel like she'd just won another round?

I hadn't known Isobel for very long, but I could tell that she was relentless, the sort of person who wouldn't give up

until she got what she wanted. She hadn't stopped torment-
ing me from the moment I arrived. And she wasn't about to
run out of steam anytime soon. Maybe there was only one
way to truly be free—leave and never look back. I dragged
myself off the ground, tasting the bitterness of defeat. I'd
been delusional to think I was here on a mission to unearth
the secrets of Grange Hall and learn to harness my gift rather
than be controlled by it. Those objectives might have driven
me before, but now that the safety of my family was in jeop-
ardy, that motivation had been extinguished.

What just happened to Rory changed everything. The
dead had power, and they couldn't be bargained with. They
lived by their own rules and were accountable to no one.
Eating humble pie might not be a Kennedy trait, but maybe
it was time for me to admit I'd taken on more than I could
handle. I was no closer to finding answers, and maybe it was
time to stop looking. Maybe this place would always belong
to the dead.

Mavis and May tethered the boat to an old gray post and
we all rallied around Rory.

"Hold up. Give him a chance to catch his breath," Joe
urged, ushering back the sisters to give my ashen-faced
brother some room. I knelt beside Rory and held his head
while he coughed up water. He was shivering violently.

"We need to get back to the house," Mavis said, stating
the obvious.

"As quickly as possible," May concurred.

I looked around at the rapidly fading light and was forced
to agree. If we didn't move soon, we'd be stumbling our way
back in the dark. But it was more than the fading light that
was making the women anxious. They might not be the best

ghost whisperers in town, but they knew when something sinister was at work.

Rory's teeth were chattering so loudly, they sounded like castanets. Joe managed to liberate him from the waterlogged parka, tossing it over a log. He ignored the lancing cold that must have been cutting through him.

"Do you think you can walk?" Joe asked.

Rory managed a nod. We helped him to his feet, supporting him on either side. Purplish shadows ringed his big brown eyes, and he reminded me of a defenseless fawn cornered by a predator he didn't recognize.

The sisters surprised me with their agility. They sped ahead so that by the time we reached Grange Hall, Harry and Gran had already been alerted to the situation. They were waiting for us at the bottom of the front steps, worry etched all over their faces. Harry bundled Rory in a thick wool blanket as Gran ushered him inside. Miss Grimes scurried past us like a field mouse in her perennial black, running a hot bath and searching for clean pajamas. I felt terrible thinking it, but I was glad to hand the responsibility for Rory over to someone else. This was all too much for me.

After Grandma Fee ordered Rory to bed with a bowl of hot soup and a grilled-cheese sandwich, she called the rest of us into the kitchen so we could have *a little talk* without being overheard. We all filed in like errant children into the principal's office.

"All right." She folded her arms and looked at each of us in turn. "Which one of you would care to explain just what happened out there?"

"It all happened so fast," I said, but Gran was having none of that.

"Chloe, I'm on the verge of calling your father. I just need the facts first."

"Why not leave Dad out of this?" I suggested with a sigh. "What would you tell him anyway?"

"I don't know, as I wasn't actually there. Perhaps someone would be kind enough to enlighten me?"

I exchanged glances with Mavis and May. Our eyes locked for only a second, but it was long enough for me to see they knew what we'd been up against. It was also long enough for us to reach a tacit agreement. There was nothing we could offer Grandma Fee that would make her feel better. She was looking for something she could grab hold of, a formula to explain the inexplicable. We couldn't give her that, so nobody said a word. Gran pursed her lips. "Really? None of you has anything to say?"

I scratched my head and feigned a look of confusion. "I think they lost control of the boat."

"Chloe," she said sternly. "There hasn't been a single boating accident during the whole time Grange Hall has been in operation. Now my grandson nearly drowns, and that's all you have to say?"

"We're so sorry, Mrs. Kennedy," Joe said. "He was in the boat one minute and in the water the next."

I could see what Joe was doing, sticking to the bare, incontrovertible facts. That was what Gran had asked for. The sisters nodded in confirmation of Joe's story.

"He must have been doing something silly," Gran pressed. "Like standing up or rocking the boat."

"He wasn't."

"Something pulled me under," said a small voice from the doorway. We all turned to see Rory, who had crept downstairs. He stood in his flannel pajamas looking so earnest, it was hard not to believe him.

"Rory!" I jumped in as quickly as I could. "You shouldn't be out of bed. If there's something you need, I'll get it for you."

"Wait!" Grandma Fee put a silencing hand on my shoulder. "What did you just say, Rory? What do you mean *something* pulled you in?"

"He probably has a fever." I tried to brush it off.

"No," my brother protested. "It's the truth." Gran stared at him, speechless.

"What he means is that a freak current sprang up out of nowhere," Mavis interrupted. "I've never seen anything like it."

"In our little lake?" Gran looked dubious. "That would have to be some current. Is that what it felt like to you, Rory?"

"Nope." Rory shook his head adamantly. "I told you… something grabbed me."

He held up his wrist, and we all leaned in to see angry red blotches like rope burns across his pale skin. Grandma Fee snatched up his hand.

"What in the world…?"

"He probably just scraped it trying to get back in the boat," I said desperately, flashing my brother a look that said *For the love of God, shut up.* There was no way of telling Gran the truth without opening a Pandora's box.

Rory looked a sorry sight. His fluffy hair, sticking upright, made him look like a sad, underweight teddy bear.

May made a clucking sound with her tongue. "Poor little dear, he's had quite a shock."

"It wanted to kill me...." Rory mumbled.

"Honestly, I have no clue what happened out there," Joe said, turning to my grandmother. "But maybe the first thing would be to get Rory checked out by a doctor?"

It was the right thing to say, because it spurred Gran into action. "You're right, Joe. I'll call Dr. Garland right away. Chloe, take your brother back to bed."

She bustled out of the room. I tucked Rory under my arm, and he looked up with eyes like orbs.

"I'm not lying," he said meekly. "There really was something in the water. What if it comes back and tries to get me again?"

I blinked away the tears that sprang into my eyes and gave a smile so forced I thought my face might crack.

"There's nothing here that can hurt you. I promise," I said, even though it was an assurance I was in no position to give. "In the meantime, stay away from the lake, okay?"

"Okay," Rory agreed. "Can I have some pizza now?"

# CHAPTER EIGHTEEN

Dr. Garland wanted Rory's breathing monitored overnight, so I took the first shift and stayed up watching until he fell asleep. Exhausted by the ordeal, he didn't take long. There was a tiny crease between his brows, as if he was trying to figure out a math problem in his dreams. I went back to my bedroom as soon as I heard Gran coming down the hall to relieve me, but not before pocketing the bottle of pills Dr. Garland had left behind in case Rory needed them to sleep. He wasn't the only one with anxiety tonight.

It turned out I was the one too shaken to rest. My body was beat, but the wheels in my head refused to stop spinning. I pulled the bottle out of my pocket, unscrewed its safety cap and shook a small blue pill into the palm of my hand. It looked harmless enough.

"Just this once," I told myself and tossed it back with a glass of water.

I waited a few minutes, but didn't feel any different. I decided they must be weak and gulped down another. Ten minutes later, I could barely keep my eyes open. My thoughts were slipping and sliding around in my head, falling out before I had a chance to catch them. I heard a soft tap at my bedroom door, and a minute later, I was conscious of someone leaning over me. When I opened my eyes I was looking into a pair of limpid green eyes like saucers, so clear and innocent they could have belonged to a child.

"Hey, Joe," I mumbled.

"Hey, Chloe," he replied. "Just wanted to say good-night and make sure you're okay."

"You know you have eyes like a dragon," I answered.

"What?"

"It's a good thing. Dragons are our friends."

Joe glanced at the bottle of pills on my nightstand. "*Right.* Are you feeling okay?"

"Yes," I said happily, snuggling under the covers. "My head is full of empty bottles of wine."

Joe picked up the tablets. "How many of these did you take?"

"Just two," I said, hearing myself slur my words.

"I'm assuming you don't take medication often?"

I stretched, locking my hands above my head. "Not unless it's vegan!"

Joe smothered a smile. "All right." He tucked the duvet around me. "I'm going to let you rest now."

"I can see your colors." I winked at him whilst waving a hand in front of his face. "All your colors, like a rainbow."

He took my hand and gently guided it back under the covers. Then he sat down beside me, his eyes looking like prisms of light. I felt like I was in a hot-air balloon and he was lifting me up with his presence. I really could see colors radiating from him, spilling in all directions, like an explosion of pastel paint. It made me feel happy. And I hadn't felt happy in a long time.

"I can see your colors, too, Chloe," Joe replied. "They're very bright."

"Are you sure?" I murmured. "Are you sure I'm not full of darkness?"

"No." He slid down beside me. He closed his eyes, and somehow, I felt I could trust him implicitly. "The darkness doesn't control you. Remember that."

"Okay," I replied sleepily.

Joe hesitated a moment. "Now may not be the right time to bring this up...but who's Alex?"

"What?" I felt a little bolt of panic run through me.

"Today by the lake," Joe pressed on. "You asked someone named Alex to help us. Who is that?"

I stayed silent. There was really no acceptable answer to that question.

"He's a ghost, isn't he?"

I would never have admitted it under normal circumstances but Joe had caught me with my guard down.

"Yep," I whispered. "He sure is."

"I see." Joe's tone was impossible to read.

"You remind me of him," I said with a sigh. "With one little difference, of course—you're alive!"

Joe frowned. There must have been a hundred questions he could have fired off at this point, but he didn't.

"I don't want to remind you of someone," he said eventually. "When you look at me, I want you to see *me*, not a shadow of someone else."

Somehow, his words made perfect sense in that moment. "Don't lose your rainbow, Joe," I said. "Promise you won't?"

"I promise."

By the time I woke up, it was nine in the morning, which meant I'd slept for twelve hours straight. Joe was long gone. Thankfully, the pills had worn off, but I still vaguely remembered snippets of our conversation. I rolled over and groaned. How would I ever be able to face him again? I cringed as I remembered ranting on about rainbows, but I knew that wasn't the worst of it. I'd told him about Alex, and that wasn't something I could just laugh off or take back.

I was busy trying to think of a rational way to explain myself when I heard a light tap at the door.

"Hello?" I called out cautiously. The door opened a crack and Mavis's childlike face appeared.

"Is it okay if we come in? We'd never dream of intruding like this, but after yesterday there's something we want to talk to you about."

Technically, they weren't even supposed to be up here, but I guessed what had happened had broken down some barriers. I waved them in. I was curious to hear what they had to say. They stood awkwardly before speaking. May came right out with it.

"She's more powerful than we thought," she said bluntly. I frowned and rubbed my eyes. Had I heard that right?

"Excuse me?"

"There's no need to keep up the charade, Chloe. We know you can see her."

That woke me up well and truly. I opened my mouth to protest, but it seemed pointless to deny what they already

knew. Part of me was secretly relieved to finally have someone to confide in.

"How long have you guys known?"

"From the day we first met you," said Mavis, as if the answer was obvious.

"What? How?"

"The EMF was going crazy. At first we thought there was
something haunting the dining hall. Then we realized…it
was reacting to *you*."

"Well, that makes no sense," I objected. "I'm not a ghost."

"No, but supernatural energy surrounds you," May explained. "You reek of it, so to speak."

"What's that supposed to mean?"

"It means you're half in, half out," said Mavis. "You're
caught between this world and theirs."

"Are you trying to say I'm half-dead?" I demanded. Part
of me thought I had to be dreaming this conversation.

"Of course not." May pressed her lips together. "But you
need to tread carefully, my dear. It's a fine line."

"Don't frighten the girl!" Mavis flapped her hands. "We
have bigger problems to deal with."

I narrowed my eyes. I didn't like where this was headed.
"What do you mean *we?*" I asked suspiciously. Looking back
on it, the question was redundant; the threat that loomed af-
fected all of us now.

"We knew the spirit was unpredictable." May shook her
head sadly. "But we never expected things to get so out of
control."

"Wait, how much do you know about Isobel Reade?"

"Ah, we suspected it was her! We know very little—only

what we've been able to access through village archives. But we've known about her presence here for quite some time."

I could barely process this information. The supernatural world was not one to tamper with. What if the Hunt sisters were just messing around with psychic toys they'd bought on eBay? What if they had no idea what they were actually doing? But then again, what if they did? Maybe if we joined forces they could help me rid Grange Hall of Isobel's malevolent presence once and for all. For the first time in my life, I had potential allies, only I wasn't sure how to feel about that.

"So have you seen her or not?"

"No, but you have." May folded her hands. "And that's all that counts."

I let out a long, whistling breath. "I didn't think anyone would believe me. So I've never told the truth, except to my mom."

"There are times when the truth does more damage than good." Mavis smiled. "But we may have an idea."

"To get rid of Isobel?" I asked eagerly.

"We can't get rid of her, dear." May enunciated each word as if I were hard of hearing. "But we might be able to slow her down. Show her who's boss, so to speak. Let's meet back here at midnight."

"Hold on!" They hadn't explained anything. "What's the idea?"

"We're just conducting a little experiment. This spirit has to be handled carefully. It's volatile.... It went after your brother today and drowned that little boy in 1961."

My mind flashed back to the article. I remembered it in perfect detail.

"I haven't forgotten. Why did they call Grange Hall a Women's Home?" I asked.

"Because your grandmother's home wasn't always a bed-and-breakfast," Mavis replied. "After World War II it was bought by the Anglican Church and turned into a home for unwed mothers."

"Unwed mothers had to live in a home?" I could hardly believe it.

"Social mores were very different then," May said. "Unwed mothers were hidden away until they gave birth, and their babies were put up for adoption. Then they could be rehabilitated, returned into respectable society and made *marriageable*."

"That's ridiculous," I said. "Who thinks that way?"

"This was a while ago, remember," Mavis qualified. "People were less tolerant than they are now. They'd lock the girls up in a room and leave them totally alone throughout delivery. They weren't allowed out until the baby was born. Can you imagine, going through that alone?"

"No, but how does it relate to the little boy?" I asked quickly.

"Oh yes!" Mavis came back to the topic under discussion. "Well, we've checked local records and it seems that in 1955, Benjamin's mother showed up here. She was only sixteen years old at the time. But once her child was born, she refused to give the baby up." I was genuinely listening now. "To avoid being cast out onto the street, the girl took on the job of housekeeper. She earned her keep and was allowed to live here with her son. Even after he died, she remained at Grange Hall. It was the only home she ever knew."

"When did she leave?" I asked. Mavis gave me a level stare.

"My dear, she didn't."

"Excuse me?" I wasn't following their logic at all.

"She's here still—she came with the place. I don't think your grandmother had the heart to turn her away." I froze as another piece of the puzzle clicked into place.

"Miss Grimes," I breathed.

"Exactly," May said and checked her watch. "Now we really must be going."

"Where?" I asked.

"To make necessary preparations, but we'll be back at midnight as planned. Make sure to wait for us."

"Why midnight?" I called after them as they almost ran out the door.

"Surely you know the answer to that, Chloe?"

I returned them a blank face.

"Why, it's the witching hour, of course."

"That's not a real thing," I muttered under my breath. Or was it? Maybe I needed to get up to speed.

They scurried out of the room, leaving me more confused than ever. Climbing out of bed, I shut the door firmly behind them. I couldn't shake the image of sixteen-year-old Miss Grimes showing up here with no one in the world to help her. She was probably scared and alone, with all her possessions in one suitcase, knowing her life was over before it had even begun.

Then I thought about my brother and how close I'd come to losing him so soon after Mom and how Isobel would keep on taking lives that didn't belong to her, as carelessly as plucking daisies from the earth. A switch flicked inside me.

My body was racked with despair so strong I couldn't stay upright. I buckled and curled up on the floor with my arms wrapped around my knees and my cheek pressed against the boards. The pain was like lashings to the heart.

"Get up," I told myself out loud, fixing my gaze on the baseboard at eye level. "Pull yourself together, Chloe."

What did that expression even mean? I wondered. It wasn't like you could gather all the damaged parts of yourself and superglue them back together. I felt like glass that had shattered into splinters and shards. Nothing short of a miracle could make me whole again.

I was lost in my own thoughts when I heard someone speak.

"Stay there as long as you like."

I raised my head to see Alex sitting at the rolltop desk, the sun revealing strands of copper in his hair. He didn't seem concerned or unsure how to act despite finding me in the throes of a meltdown. I'd never had one in front of anyone before, but somehow it felt okay. Alex didn't offer some meaningless platitude or tell me he knew what I was going through. He was just there.

"I… I'm sorry," I hiccuped.

"Never apologize for feeling things," he replied. "It's what makes you human."

"I just don't know what to do without her," I said between ragged breaths.

"I know, darling," Alex said softly. "I know."

A moment later, his shimmering form crossed the room and knelt down beside me. I shuddered, feeling invisible fingers trace down my cheeks. The sensation was not dissimilar to cool running water. The touch was too familiar now to startle me. In fact, it had the opposite, soothing effect.

"Alex?" I whispered, my voice thick with tiredness and pent-up emotion. "My little brother almost died today."

"But he didn't," Alex replied. "We caught him in time."

"What if you hadn't come? What would've happened then?"

"I'll always come, Chloe."

"How can I be sure of that?"

"Grange Hall is my home and my prison," he replied. "I see everything that happens, and I *will* know if you're in trouble."

I pressed my face into my hands. "We can't keep doing this. One way or another, it has to end."

A forlorn expression came into Alex's blue eyes. I waited for him to say something but he didn't.

"Mavis and May think they can help. I don't know what they have in mind, but it better work."

"There's only one thing that will work for certain," he said finally.

I felt my chin lift involuntarily. A spark of hope ignited in my belly. "What is it? Tell me!"

"You have to go home." His words sank into me like stones. He didn't meet my gaze, and I felt like the world was falling away beneath me.

"What?" It was a struggle to get the words out. "You don't mean that."

Alex bowed his head. "It's the only way I can think to keep you safe."

"But I don't want to leave," I blurted.

"I don't think we have a choice now." He was merely articulating the same conclusion I'd come to myself as I watched

Rory's trembling frame being lifted out of the boat. So why was it so hard to accept coming from Alex?

I was still shaking my head, unwilling to believe he wasn't joking. "I'm not going anywhere!"

"Chloe, listen!" He pressed his fingertips together, as if in prayer. "Until today, I thought I could keep Isobel in check. But I don't know how much longer I can control her."

"If I leave, she wins." I clenched my jaw.

Alex sighed audibly. "It's not about winning or losing. If you leave, you and Rory will have your lives back. You were never going to stay at Grange Hall indefinitely. You have a life to get back to."

I wasn't ready to contemplate that thought yet. My home in America—in fact, the entire world outside Grange Hall— seemed so far away now. It was as if my whole life was now contained in this house and its grounds. I wasn't even sure I would remember how to place an order at Coffee Bean or navigate traffic on the 405. Even if it was the smartest thing to do, I couldn't leave yet. I couldn't let Isobel drive me away. Maybe I could orchestrate things so that Rory went home without me, even though he'd complain vociferously and feel betrayed.

"Why does Isobel hate me so much?" I asked, trying to steer the conversation away from departures. "I know she's jealous of our friendship, but there has to be more to it."

"The dead never stop envying the living, Chloe," Alex replied. "That's a fact."

"Why?"

"Life may be unpredictable and sometimes painful, but once you die, you realize how precious it was. It's normal to feel anger or sadness or despair, but that doesn't detract from the value of living. Who in their right mind would choose death over life? Isobel hates you because you can feel the sun on your skin and the earth under your feet. When she looks at you, she is reminded of all that she's lost."

"I guess that makes sense." I looked up slowly. "But why harm Miss Grimes's son? It was Isobel, wasn't it?"

"I don't know why she took that little boy," Alex said heavily. "There's no explanation other than revenge."

"But Benjamin was from a different time."

"I've never known revenge to be rational, have you?"

"Couldn't you reason with her? Make her understand she has to stop?" I looked at Alex pleadingly.

"Isobel and I ran out of things to say to one another many years ago. I would talk to her if I thought she had any humanity left. The woman I loved died a long time ago. The thing that remains…that's just a monster."

"There's something else…" I shook my head, trying to zero in on the thought skating around in my brain.

"What?" Alex asked.

"I sometimes get the feeling that… No, it sounds too ridiculous."

"Say it."

"That maybe I'm not the only one who's afraid," I said tentatively. "Maybe Isobel is afraid, too. But I don't know why."

Alex reached over and touched my cheek with the pad of his thumb, like he was wiping away invisible tears. It lifted my sadness and replaced it with an entirely different sensation, one I couldn't quite describe. "It pains me," he whispered. "Knowing the upheaval I've brought into your life."

"Don't worry." I gave a faint smile. "My life was pretty boring before you came along."

Alex's face looked pinched. Even in death, I could see that he felt everything acutely. "I will not allow you to be placed in danger. You have dreams to realize, a future to look forward to. I have nothing but sadness and memories to offer."

"Then tell me one thing." My voice was hushed. I desperately wanted to touch the arc of his cheekbones and wind my fingers in his hair. "Why am I happier when you're around?"

"I am nothing but a phantom," he answered, sadness hanging over his elegant features like a shroud.

"No, you're not!" I exclaimed. "You're here, you're talking to me. I could reach out and touch you…."

"Yes, but this is *all* there will ever be." Alex squeezed his eyes tight shut. When he opened them, they seemed brighter. "Don't you want to marry someday, have children?"

"I don't care about that," I scoffed. I edged closer, so that we were almost nose to nose. "All I know is that I'm sad almost all the time. My mom's gone and I'll never see her again. But when I'm with you, it's somehow easier to breathe."

Normally I'd be cringing after going out on a limb like that, but I didn't care anymore. I wanted Alex to know everything…to know *me* inside and out. He watched me, his expression inscrutable.

"Perhaps," he murmured, "it's because I carry enough sadness for the both of us."

"Do I make you happy?" I asked.

"You are so full of life," Alex said simply. "How could anyone be unhappy around you?"

Without thinking I slipped a hand around the back of his neck, amazed to find I could make contact. He didn't pull away, and it ignited a tickling sensation that rippled across the surface of my skin. Goose bumps rose on my bare arms.

Alex's face was so close to mine, but I could hear only my own breathing. Our foreheads touched. My touch seemed to solidify him and infuse his body with warmth. We spent a long time like that, just gazing at each other. I didn't want the moment to end. When he finally moved, I felt his lips graze mine. They were warm! Just as they did, the grandfather clock in the foyer floors below reliably chimed the hour.

*Midnight.*

# CHAPTER NINETEEN

Alex vanished on cue, leaving me clutching the empty air. There was no reason for him to go, but I supposed it was habit now. It would be weird, talking to people with him standing right beside me, knowing they could never see what I saw.

A moment later, Mavis and May stole silently into my bedroom, holding lit candles, which lent a ghoulish aspect to their appearance. I was reminded of the weird sisters in *Macbeth,* except I hoped these girls had better intentions. Then I noticed they were wearing bunny slippers and fleecy pink robes. If that wasn't enough to kill the mood, I didn't know what was. I sat up quickly and tried to compose myself.

"Hi," I said as casually as I could.

"Good, you're still up."

May had a burlap bag tucked under her arm. Without saying a word, she headed straight for the window, where she dipped into the bag and began scattering white powder in a line across the windowsill like some kind of medieval herbalist. Meanwhile, Mavis withdrew a leather pouch and a stoneware bowl. I watched her reach into her pocket for matches.

"What the heck are you doing?" I hissed.

May tossed me a look over her shoulder, as if gravely injured by my doubt in their abilities.

"Trying to stall your vengeful spirit," she replied.

"With spells?" I slipped off the end of the bed to get a closer look and dipped a finger into the white granular powder. I touched it to my tongue. "Salt?"

Mavis pulled a container of herbs from their neverending bag of tricks.

"You really think salt and a few herbs are going to keep Isobel away?"

"Hardly," Mavis scoffed. "We're just trying to distract her."

"Umm…" I tried to think of a tactful way to word this. "Do you ladies have anything that will have a more *lasting* effect?"

May looked at me and sighed. "Chloe, we're talking about the invisible world here, another dimension. It's hard enough to catch glimpses of those that dwell in it, let alone try to control them."

Any glimmer of hope I'd placed in their expertise vanished like smoke. I felt them plummet in my estimation.

"Then why are you even here?"

"It's not as hopeless as you think," May answered, reading my face. "There are other things we can try later."

"Later?" I asked bitterly. "You mean before or after Isobel realizes what we're up to and takes us all out?"

"Listen," Mavis said. "Before we can deal with this haunting effectively, we need more information about the woman in question. Otherwise, we're just taking stabs in the dark."

"What do you need to know?" I asked as Mavis struck a match and held it to the little dried bundle. The room was immediately infused with the acrid scent of burning herbs. She walked around, allowing the smoke to waft into every corner of the room. I looked on, mystified.

"Where and how she died would be a good start," suggested May.

Suddenly, I was aware of how little I actually knew about Isobel besides the random flashes I'd been offered. She had shown me only what she wanted me to see. When it came to concrete facts, I had zip.

"I don't know," I said, crestfallen.

"The lake. She drowned herself there in 1853." The voice came from behind me. I swiveled my head to see Alex. He was sitting in his usual place by the window, legs crossed and arms folded, his face unreadable. "The anniversary of her death is exactly a week from today."

He nodded, prompting me to share the information. The Hunt sisters showed no awareness of his presence. How could they be so oblivious? To me, Alex seemed to fill the room. I could hear the soft tapping of his foot on the bare boards. I could even catch notes of his scent in the air.

"Why?" I stammered.

"Why what?" Mavis looked at me intently. "Are you all right, dear? You seem distracted."

"I'm sorry. I'm fine." I snapped to attention. "I just remembered. I do know how she died. She drowned herself in the lake in December of 1853."

May narrowed her eyes. "Did she tell you that?"

"I just know, all right?" I snapped. "What else?"

"Did she have any weaknesses in life? Anything that might prove useful."

There was only one weakness I could think of, and he was

sitting a few feet away, regarding the women with an expression of curiosity mingled with a vague distaste. I glanced at him questioningly and he shook his head.

"She's wasn't the weak type," I told them.

"Don't be silly, Chloe. She was human once. All humans have weaknesses."

"Vanity," Alex said in a low voice. "She was always very vain and proud."

"Vanity," I parroted.

They both drew sharp intakes of breath, like I'd just made the revelation of the decade. They were drama queens; there was no question about that.

"What makes you say that?" May asked.

"Umm… I've met her, remember?"

They glanced at one another, a spark in their eyes. "How very interesting," Mavis said.

"Sure, but is it useful?"

"It might be. Do you know how old she was when she died?"

"Twenty-two," Alex answered promptly. I obediently relayed the information. Then suddenly, his forehead creased and he doubled over, like he'd just taken a punch.

"Are you all right?" I was immediately on my feet.

The Hunt sisters watched, openmouthed. Alex's gaze flickered across the room, until it fell on the smoking bundle of herbs. I picked them up, burning my fingers.

"What *is* this?" I asked.

"It's a concoction of myrrh, mandrake and lavender," said May. "It's a well-known remedy to repel spirits that dates back to the Middle Ages." She gestured toward the window. "Salt does the same trick."

I dropped the smoldering herbs on the floor and ground them under the heel of my shoe. "Not cool," I told them. "Not all spirits need to be repelled."

Mavis raised an eyebrow. "You should never let the dead call the shots, dear. It lets them think they're in control. No offense to your friend..."

"What?" I spluttered, taken aback by her blasé attitude. "You can see him?" Alex lifted his almost-translucent blue eyes and fixed his gaze on the Hunt sisters.

"No, but we can feel the cold spot in the room. Are you at liberty to share his name?" I looked to him for approval, and he gave a small shrug as if to say it was inconsequential to him.

"Alexander Reade."

"Well, please let Alexander know that we only want to help."

"He can hear you," I replied. "He's sitting right over there."

Both of their faces lit up, ecstatic smiles stretching across their faces. May even reached up to fix her hair, like she was worried about making a good impression. I got the feeling that in all their years of research, this was the moment they'd been waiting for. They both gingerly took a few steps back toward the door, as if they didn't want to do or say anything that might chase him away.

"Do you think he might manifest himself to us?" May asked hesitantly.

I looked back at Alex, who shook his head. "I couldn't even if I wanted to," he answered. "They don't have the sight."

"Sorry, guys." I shrugged. "No can do." A violent rap

on the window drew everyone's attention. I spun around. "Oh no…"

"What is it?" May asked nervously. "What was that noise?"

She might have been invisible to them, but Alex and I could both see her all too clearly. Isobel hovered outside the window, only inches away from us. Muddied hands clawed at the glass with a grating noise, like chalk scraping down a blackboard. Alex was on his feet in an instant.

"Tell your friends to leave," he instructed. "It's not safe."

"You guys need to get out of here," I said urgently. "Go. Now." They both fixed me with a resolute stare.

"Do you know how long we've waited for this?" May said. "We're not going anywhere."

"Fine," I said, exasperated. "But if she gets in, don't say I didn't warn you." Mavis gave a wicked little smile.

"But she can't get in, can she?"

From outside, I heard an anguished howl like a wounded wolf. Maybe the sisters were right. Alex watched as an insubstantial Isobel threw herself against the glass again and again in mounting frustration. Slowly but surely it began to crack.

"Oh crap…" I muttered, but Mavis and May remained unperturbed.

"Stand your ground, Chloe." May squeezed my shoulder. "She can't get in. *Trust* us."

I glanced at Alex. He, too, was unconvinced, tensed for a fight. I didn't blame him. We'd gone up against Isobel before with disastrous consequences. She was a madwoman, vicious and unscrupulous. Finally, with a deep groan, all the glass panes of the window shattered, sprinkling fragments across the floorboards. I ducked instinctively. When I looked up, Isobel remained outside, locked behind some invisible barrier.

Like Peter Pan when he tried to return home, the window was barred to her. In her rage, she pushed a hand through broken glass, and rivulets of phantom blood poured down her arm before she vanished with a final incensed shriek.

"She's gone," I said breathlessly. "I don't believe it."

Alex cautiously approached and laid a hand on the windowsill. There was an immediate sizzling noise, like meat on a barbecue, followed by a shower of sparks. He moaned in obvious pain and his outline seemed to blur at the edges.

"Oh my God!" I rushed forward, but this time, my hands went right through him.

"Rock salt," he told me through gritted teeth. "It really does work."

"Are you okay?"

"I will be," he said. "But I need to go now." He faded away without another word, leaving a thin layer of blue vapor in the air.

Speechless, I turned back to Mavis and May, looking at them with new understanding. Was that the beginnings of admiration stirring in my chest?

"Is Alex gonna be okay?"

"He'll be fine. The effect is temporary."

"Well," I said, "I guess you guys do know what you're talking about. I'm sorry I wasn't more supportive."

"Your skepticism was entirely warranted," Mavis replied. "You had no reason to believe in us before, but perhaps now we can work together?"

"I think that might be the best idea I've heard so far," I said slowly.

"Then we're a team!" May trilled, blinking rapidly, as if she couldn't contain herself. Sometimes she reminded me of those fluffy lap dogs that got so excited, they trembled all over and ran in circles. "Us against them!"

"Against *her,*" I corrected. "And it won't be easy."

"Don't you worry, dear." She gave a sly grin. "We're tougher than we look." She walked over and linked hands with Mavis and me. "We're ready for you, Isobel Reade! Let's get this show on the road."

# CHAPTER TWENTY

The following day I was woken by the sound of banging and voices carrying up to my room from the front garden. I looked at my smashed window and tried to think of an excuse that Gran wouldn't see right through. Nothing plausible came to mind. I decided to think on it as I pulled on my jeans and a floppy gray sweater and padded downstairs to see what all the commotion was about. I found Grandma Fee in the foyer directing a group of men in lumber jackets as they traipsed inside lugging trestle tables.

"What's going on?" I asked.

"Honestly, Chloe," she scolded. "Do you listen to anything I say? I've told you a dozen times we're hosting the Bearwood Winter Ball."

"That's tonight?" I asked incredulously. "I thought it was weeks away."

"That's because you don't listen. Oh, that reminds me... one of our servers has fallen ill."

*"Servants?"* I repeated incredulously.

"No, dear, like a waitress. I told them you wouldn't mind stepping in."

"What?" She had my full attention now. "Why would you do that? You've totally ruined my plan for the evening."

Grandma Fee raised an eyebrow. "That being?"

"To hide in my room and wait for everyone to leave."

"Don't be so antisocial," she reprimanded. "It's just for one night. The proceeds go to charity, you know."

There was no point arguing. I slipped past her out into the yard, where I found a crew of workmen erecting an enormous white marquee strung with thousands of fairy lights. Strings of the glowing, pea-size nodules hung from the roof, transforming the tent into a glittering ice cave. I spotted Rory, trailing after one of the men, watching in fascination. He was soaking in every detail while he could. Once the festivities started, he'd be banished upstairs, where, in Grandma Fee's words, "he wouldn't get underfoot."

She appeared at my elbow with a satisfied smile on her face, checking items off a very extensive to-do list.

"Not half-bad, is it?" she said. "Wait until you see the ballroom."

She was right. The ballroom had been decorated from floor to ceiling in silver and frosty white. The ground was covered in a layer of snowflakes that, when I bent to touch them, were soft and downy beneath my fingers. Clusters of glitter-covered helium balloons adorned the tables, and chiffon swathed the chandelier so that it cast a soft, moon-blue light around the room. Tree branches that had been spray-painted silver were arranged around the outskirts of the room so that it felt as if you were stepping into an enchanted wood. A giant floral arrangement of white roses formed the centerpiece for the long banquet table. It was hard not to be entranced by the wintry landscape. For a moment I felt like Cinderella, wishing I had a gown I could wear to the ball.

Grange Hall was suddenly a different place. There was newfound buoyancy in the air, created by the babble of voices and the hum of activity. Rays of winter sunlight poured through the tall windows, and with the smell of pastries and freshly brewed coffee drifting in from the dining hall, I almost felt safe and cozy. At times like this it was hard to believe the house had so much darkness buried within its walls. But as I made my way through the foyer to see if Joe had arrived, something brought me up short.

*She stands no more than a few feet away, looking nothing like her usual formidable self. In fact she looks as vulnerable as a startled deer caught in a trap. Her puffy-sleeved dress is plastered to her shoulders, and her hair has come loose from its braid and tangled at her neck. She cringes as a wind springs up and whips across her face. She's shivering, soaked to the bone.*

*"Can you help me?" she implores and takes a step forward, water squelching from her shoes. Isobel's face is sallow and haggard now, her beauty mysteriously erased. She doesn't seem to recognize me as she holds out a dirty bundle. I make no move to take it. "Why aren't you listening?" Her voice is choked. "Run and fetch the doctor, Becky. There's no time to lose!"*

*She's mistaken me for one of the housemaids. "Go quickly! Do you hear me?" Her tear-streaked face is a mask of distress. "My baby, Becky! He's not breathing!"*

*Before the vision ends I catch a fleeting glimpse, inside the blanket, of an infant. He's blue-faced and as still as stone.*

★ ★ ★

For the remainder of the day, there was no space in my head for anything but the vision. I felt stiff and cold inside every time I thought about it. Isobel once had a child? Why didn't Alex tell me? What was his name? Who was the father? And how had that little baby wound up dead in his mother's arms? Faces were racing through my mind: my own mother, Benjamin Grimes, the lifeless infant, Alex, Carter and Isobel's decomposing face, until they all blurred into one.

I knew what was happening here. So many significant people in my life right now were ghosts. The dead were taking over. How had I let this happen? There was only one thing they all had in common—they'd departed the earth before their time. Did that mean I was next? Was that why they'd come to me…because…because… I couldn't breathe.

"Chloe!" A voice brought the panic attack to a halt. I looked up to find a big-haired woman in a salmon suit inspecting me carefully.

"Hi," I said awkwardly. "Do I know you?"

"I'm Pamela," she declared. "Head of the PTA. Your grandmother said you're going to be filling in for Lucy? Silly girl went and got food poisoning last night. Some people never think of anyone but themselves!"

"Right…"

"I've put you on drinks duty tonight. Now, I know you're from Los Angeles, but please keep in mind that all drinks are strictly nonalcoholic."

What the hell was that supposed to mean? A snide remark was on the tip of my tongue, but I swallowed it back, knowing how important this night was to Grandma Fee.

The bossy woman steered me into the ballroom and

pointed to a huge silver punch bowl. Rows and rows of crystal tumblers were lined up behind it.

"You'll find all the supplies you need in the kitchen." She spoke very slowly and carefully, as if the directions were incredibly complicated. "All you need to do is serve the drinks and let me know immediately if you notice any sneaky flask-action. Do you think you can handle that?"

I forced myself to give my most reassuring smile. "I think I can manage."

"Good," she replied. "You had better get dressed. The girls will be arriving soon from Mulberry College."

"Don't the couples come together?"

"No," she said. "It's tradition for the boys and girls to arrive separately."

"I wouldn't know about that," I told her sweetly. "We don't have many traditions in California…except alcoholism, of course."

She flashed me a dirty look and marched off in search of someone else to harass.

I went to my room to get ready for the ball, throwing together the closest thing I could find to an outfit a waitress might wear—black skinny jeans and a stark-white shirt. Then, figuring I might as well commit to the part, I gathered my hair up into a tight ponytail. Through the window I could see the Mulberry girls starting to arrive. Long, white limousines were pulling into the driveway. When the first batch of girls emerged, they were all dressed in flowing floor-length white gowns, like debutantes. They'd gone all-out with ribbons and pearls woven into their hair and elbow-length satin gloves. Some were even carrying fans and dance cards as if they'd stepped right out of a Jane Austen novel. The Bearwood boys looked equally classy when they showed up in tuxedos, their hair neatly waxed and combed.

I ran into Mavis and May on the stairs, heading up to their bedroom.

"You're not staying for the show?" I asked.

"Oh no, we've got work to do," May replied. "Spirits don't hunt themselves, you know, dear."

"Wait, you're not going to do anything tonight, are you?" I asked nervously. "Gran will freak out if something goes wrong."

"We're just writing up notes for our blog," Mavis assured me. "It's called *Ghosts and Grits*."

"*Grits?*"

"Yes, we like to include recipes in case our readers get bored. You should check it out sometime."

"I'll be sure to do that," I replied.

"Very good," Mavis said happily. "And don't worry about tonight. Isobel will never show her face with this many people around." They patted me on the shoulder and padded up the vast staircase.

As I made my way into the foyer, I felt suddenly self-conscious. I didn't belong here and it was painfully obvious. Tonight was like a scene from *Pride and Prejudice* and I was the modern California girl, sticking out like a sore thumb. When I reached the foot of the stairs, a flash went off in my face. I blinked away the purple dots to see a reporter snapping pictures like crazy. I assumed he was from the local newspaper. No offense to Grandma Fee, but it probably wasn't so newsworthy by the *Daily Telegraph* standards.

"Doesn't Mrs. Rochester look striking?" I overheard one of the mothers ask. I looked up to see a woman who, by her demeanor, could only be the headmistress standing in the tiled foyer. She shook hands and welcomed each student by name. She was a tall woman in billowing black taffeta, her dark hair styled in a pompadour sweep. Her face was severe, and I was glad the principal of my school in California usually walked around in his jeans and sneakers, cracking jokes. The girls curtsied before Mrs. Rochester, and the boys gave a formal bow before moving into the ballroom. Everything was a blur of polished shoes, bow ties and gowns sweeping the floor. As the couples filed in, I ducked ahead of them to take my place at the drinks table. I was almost nervous about my assigned task. I felt as if spilling so much as a drop might shatter this evening's perfection.

"Hey, you." I turned upon hearing a familiar voice behind me. I almost didn't recognize Joe in his tux. I was so used to seeing him in old shirts and worn cowboy boots and smelling of hay. Tonight, with his hair combed and his cuff links glinting in the light, he looked every inch the polished English gentleman. With his hair pushed away from his face, his eyes were an even more startling shade of green.

"Not a bad effort," I said, taking him in. "You scrub up okay."

"Why, thank you," he replied as a girl materialized at his side. "This is my date, Amelia."

Amelia was beautiful in a wood-nymph kind of way. From one look at her, I could tell she was one of those well-connected girls with an apple-pie family who'd probably never seen a therapist in her life. She looked a whole lot less complicated than me. I couldn't help envying her a little. Just for once, I'd like to know what it felt like to worry about ordinary things like finding the perfect dress to wear to the ball.

"Isn't this wonderful?" Amelia's eyes shone and she could barely contain her excitement. Her flaxen hair had been arranged into two large coils away from her face, which made me think of Princess Leia, except for the little silver stars woven deftly into a glittering headband. "I've been waiting for this night all year."

"Well," I said, reaching over and pouring her a glass of punch, "enjoy yourself."

As Amelia moved off to talk to some friends, Joe caught my arm. He lowered his voice and leaned in close. "You know she's just my date for tonight, right?"

"What are you talking about?" I said lightly. "You don't owe me any explanation, Joe. This is your school ball. Have fun."

"I just don't want you to think…" He trailed off as he struggled to find the right words. "I don't want you to get the wrong idea."

"Don't be silly!" I laughed. "I'm not thinking anything."

His face fell, and I mentally kicked myself for sounding like I didn't care. I hadn't meant it to come out like *that*. I liked Joe, but it wasn't like I owned him. We definitely weren't together, so he shouldn't feel bad about bringing another girl to the dance. Especially after I'd rejected his invitation. Twice.

"Okay," he said, backing away from me as if I had the plague. "I get it."

"Joe, wait. That isn't what I…" I began, but he was already moving away. I wanted to go after him, but a drinks line was already starting to form. Behind me the caterers were wheeling out a lavish array of finger food. There were platters heaped with deviled eggs, crustless sandwiches filled with a funny pink paste, mini meringues in an assortment of pastel colors and something called kilted sausages that I worked out were really just sausages wrapped in bacon. I served drinks mechanically as I was swept away by smooth notes of the jazz band's saxophone. For the first time in weeks, I allowed my mind to switch off and my body to take over.

Hours passed, even though it felt like minutes. I was too entranced by the dazzling couples gliding across the dance floor to keep track of the time. I saw Joe and Amelia swaying to the beat of the music. She was leaning her head on his shoulder, but his gaze was distant, his thoughts clearly elsewhere. Their bodies moved awkwardly, not in sync at all. My gaze traveled to the other couples. Body language was telling, and I entertained myself by picking out who was in love and who was suffering through small talk.

Just as the band struck up a waltz, a girl on the dance floor stumbled over her own hem, splashing the cherry punch across her white dress like a bloodstain. Her eyes immediately welled up with tears. I hurried over to her.

"Hey, it's all right," I said. "The restroom is right down the hall. I'll get something to clean that up."

I steered her through the crush of bodies and ducked into the kitchen in search of something absorbent. The idea that the most anticipated night of the year could be so easily ruined for someone bothered me.

The kitchen was full of replacement food platters and stacks of glasses, but at that moment, all the servers were tending to refreshments, so I found myself alone.

"Where's your dress?" I jumped in alarm and almost hit my head on the side of a cabinet.

"Alex! What are you doing here?"

"Just observing," he replied innocently. "Is that allowed?"

I pointed a warning finger at him. "Nothing can go wrong tonight," I said. "It's very important to my grandmother that this ball goes smoothly."

"I'm not in the habit of causing spectacles at social gatherings, Miss Kennedy," Alex replied. "I simply wanted to see you." He moved out of the shadows and walked up to me, stopping just short of his nose brushing against mine. "And I wanted to tell you that, even minus a gown, you are still the most captivating woman in that room."

I blushed like a schoolgirl. "You shouldn't say stuff like that."

"Why not?"

"I'm not used to it."

"You must learn to accept compliments graciously when they're offered," Alex answered, but his eyes were smiling. "I have a question to ask you."

"Yes?" I replied, breathless in spite of myself.

"Would you care to dance?"

"What?" I burst out laughing. "How would that work?"

Alex shrugged. "Same as every other couple here."

"Right, I get it." I rolled my eyes. "You want everyone in there to laugh at the crazy waitress, waltzing with herself?"

His vivid blue eyes filled with gentle amusement. "Who said anything about *in there?*"

"Where, then?" I was intrigued and followed his line of vision out the window to the twinkling garden. "Really?" I asked, feeling a fluttering in my chest. "You think we could?"

"Why not?" Alex replied. "I know the perfect place. Meet me outside in five minutes."

Before I could protest, he was gone. I ducked back into the ballroom and delivered a damp dishcloth to the girl with the spilled drink. Then I told Pamela I needed to use the restroom. She grudgingly agreed to fill in for me for a few minutes, as if highly irritated to discover I had bodily functions. As discreetly as possible I wove my way through the crowd and slipped out into the crisp, clear night.

As soon as I ran down the front steps, Alex emerged from behind a tree trunk wound with silver lights. He silently motioned for me to follow him down a winding path to the fringe of the forest. It was far enough from the house not to draw attention from any guests who'd wandered out for a breath of fresh air. But the music still floated down to reach us. Alex offered me his arm. Something about the simple gesture filled me with a burning happiness that seemed to course through my veins.

"May I have the pleasure of this dance?" He gave a formal bow.

"You may," I said. In hindsight, it wasn't the smartest thing to do, but I was too intoxicated by the night to consider consequences. I gave a small curtsey that wasn't exactly easy to execute in tight pants.

"Sorry if my attire isn't appropriate."

"On the contrary," he said. "Your attire is perfect...and practical."

"Thank you. As you can see, it took weeks of planning."

"And yet looks so effortless."

The lighthearted banter put me at ease. It was something we hadn't had the opportunity to do much of till now, as we were usually preoccupied with matters of survival. But tonight, for the first time, I wasn't consumed by fear. Isobel's omnipresent threat seemed to fade away. Alex, too, seemed uncharacteristically carefree. When I took his arm, he became completely solid beneath my touch. Tonight he didn't feel like he could fade away in an instant. Tonight he felt real. He reached out his hand and with a flick of my wrist I released my hair, letting it fall around my shoulders. We heard the muted strains of the band as they finished their song. A moment later, a slow ballad started up. Alex wound an arm around my waist and drew me closer. I let out a soft gasp as his body pressed against mine. It was cool in a comforting way, like when you scalded your hand and ran it under water. His touch always brought me relief, as though he was soothing my body, which felt like it was on fire right now.

I realized something then. I'd never learned how to dance. It hadn't exactly been a priority on the high-school curriculum in California.

"I've never done this before," I said, in case he had high expectations.

"Just follow my lead."

I shuffled my feet awkwardly, and Alex smirked. But he was a patient teacher, guiding me with his hands while I followed the rhythm of his body. I leaned my head against his shoulder, relishing the fact that I was actually able to do that. Above us was a blanket of glittering stars. I gasped when the first snowflakes began to fall. It felt as if they had been orchestrated for our benefit alone. They were like white petals dropping out of the sky and catching in Alex's hair.

The pace of the dance quickened and he lifted me off the ground, spinning me in a graceful arc. What would this look like to an impartial observer? I didn't know, and right now, I didn't care. He placed me down just as the song came to an end. I leaned against the tree to catch my breath. I wasn't tired; I was exhilarated by the experience. Alex joined me, pressing his back against the trunk and turning his head to look at me.

"And you say you've never danced before."

"I must be a quick learner."

"The light in your eyes is back," he observed softly.

"Isn't it always there?"

"No. Usually you look haunted."

"I am haunted." I smiled. "But I'm learning to live with that."

Alex tilted his head up to the sky. "I meant haunted by your own past, by memories, by grief. All that weighs a person down. But right now, in this moment, you are free of it all. That freedom may be short-lived, but it's beautiful to watch."

I couldn't help it now. I had to find a way to kiss him. The anticipation had been building for too long. When were we going to have a setting more perfect than this one? I checked quickly that no one was in sight before impulsively taking his face in my hands. Without thinking about it, I brought my lips up to meet his. He'd never felt more alive to me than at that moment. His energy flowed into me like cold, sweet bubbles. As I kissed him, I saw flashes from the happiest moments of his life. I saw him as a boy, reading at the base of a weeping willow. I saw him laughing and riding bareback in the rain. I saw him swimming in the lake with his dog and lying in a hammock with his sketchbook. The kiss was exactly as I'd dreamed it would be. It took my breath away. But most amazingly of all, I felt like I was shifting through different dimensions. I opened my eyes and saw the lights of Grange Hall, but behind Alex was an even more dazzling white light. Shadowy figures passed in and out of it. Was I looking at the past? If I was, I felt like I was part of it and floating as if I weighed nothing at all. I was utterly lost in him.

Alex pulled away first. I had to lean against the tree to steady myself. Kissing him had almost given me an out-of-body experience.

"Are you happy right now?" he whispered.

"Do you really have to ask?" I closed my eyes to savor the moment and to sear it into my memory.

We stood wrapped in a cocoon of silence until a piercing scream shattered the perfect stillness of the night.

# CHAPTER TWENTY-ONE

I saw the lights in the ballroom flicker and then go out, leaving only a few candles burning weakly. A gale started up, strong enough to shatter the glass in the French doors.

"No way," I whispered, aghast at what we might have unleashed. "She wouldn't dare. Not tonight." I started to run back toward the house, but Alex grabbed ahold of me.

"Chloe, you can't go in there. We don't know what's happening."

"Whatever it is, I'm pretty sure it's my fault!"

"I can't let you put yourself in harm's way."

"I don't have a choice, Alex," I said. "I can't just stand here and watch."

"Wait here. I'll go. What do you think you can do?"

I struggled to free myself from his grasp. "I don't know, but please let me go!"

His hands were already starting to fade, until he couldn't hold me anymore. I slipped easily away and sprinted toward the house. There was nothing Alex could do but follow, calling out after me.

"Chloe! Stop! Please listen to me!"

But I wasn't listening. I refused to let those kids get hurt because of me. This was supposed to be their night. Besides, my little brother was in there, and Grandma Fee.

At the entrance to the ballroom, we both froze. In front of us lay a scene of utter disarray. Glasses and cutlery hurtled around the room in a sight as surreal as a special-effects movie. Students panicked. Those whose common sense hadn't completely abandoned them ducked frantically for cover. I watched a knife cartwheel past a girl, leaving a long gash across her cheek. She paled as her blood dripped onto her white dress. Plates flew through the air like artillery, smashing against walls. A silver candlestick spinning out of control slammed into the back of a boy's head. He dropped like a stone, out cold. Mrs. Rochester stood speechless on a platform where the band was now cowering, their instruments abandoned. Her perfect hair had collapsed and her face was as white as a sheet as she tried to process what was happening around her.

"What should we do?" I shouted at Alex over the clamor.

His eyes were full of both anger and helplessness. I could see he wanted to step in and help out but what could he do? I noticed Miss Grimes peeking in from another entrance, like a rabbit caught in the headlights. Shielding my head with my arms, I inched my way around the edge of the room.

"Chloe, where are you going?" I heard Alex's voice behind me, but I didn't stop until I reached Miss Grimes.

"This is your fault." I was taken aback, hearing her voice for the first time. It was higher in pitch than I'd expected and hoarse as if it hadn't been used in a hundred years. "You made *her* angry, didn't you?"

I gaped at her for a moment, unsure what to say. "We didn't mean to!"

"*We?*" she hissed. "You and the dead are one and the same, are you?"

"That's not true! I just…"

Miss Grimes shook her head. "Whatever happens here is on your hands."

"Just tell me what to do!" I cried. She looked dumfounded by my question.

"Do? What is there to do? No one can stop her." She glowered at me before retreating to the safety of the kitchen.

I ducked just in time to miss a crystal vase that flew through Alex's chest and shattered against the wall behind us.

"I'll find Isobel," he said. "I'll stop her."

He was gone before I could answer. I watched as an on-slaught of flying silverware knocked over a candelabra in its path. The lit candles that toppled set the linen tablecloths alight. I needed to get these kids out of here before things spiraled further out of control. I spotted Joe shielding Amelia with his body as he guided her to safety under a table.

Gran appeared in the doorway. Poor Gran. My heart sank, seeing the devastation on her face as she watched Wistings's charity event of the year fall apart before her eyes. Her standing in the community rested on this. I knew she'd put every ounce of energy into making this night a success. She didn't deserve this. The photographers, there to make sure the event made it into the society pages of the local press, were now snapping photos of the wreckage that would surely end up online and splashed across the front page.

Isobel was out of control. Going after me was one thing, but this was a random act of violence against innocent people who didn't deserve her wrath. So much effort had gone into this night and seeing it trashed like this was too much to stand. At that moment I was filled with so much rage I could have punched the nearest wall. I could feel a resolution stirring in me, one of those moments of total clarity. I couldn't run from Isobel anymore. I had to face her and one way or another put an end to this.

I saw Joe dodging his way across the room like he was running through a minefield. He took hold of my elbow and shouted into my ear, "Help me get everyone out of here!"

It helped to have a specific task. I ran into the fray, grabbing people and trying to make myself heard over the tears and the shouting. No one was paying any attention. I took hold of the girl closest to me and pushed her toward the exit.

"Go!" I told her. "You need to get outside as fast as you can." She looked at me, terror stricken, too paralyzed to move.

"You'll be safer outside," I said and watched as comprehension dawned. She clutched the sleeve of her date and tugged him toward the doors.

"Come on!" I rounded up as many as I could, herding them as you might sheep. They started spilling out into the cold night, where they stood shivering in huddles. The ballroom was emptying, but not fast enough. Anything could happen.

That was when I heard it.

From above my head came a deep, shuddering groan that sounded as if it was coming from the very bowels of the house.

I looked up to see fragments of plaster rain down on my face as the colossal chandelier was rapidly dislodged from the ceiling. Voices urged me to move, to run. But all I could do was stand and stare at the mass of rattling crystal rushing toward me.

Something heavy thudded into my side, shoving me out of the way. I skidded across the polished boards and landed on my back. Seconds later, glass and metal exploded onto the floor, shards flying everywhere. The remaining guests dropped to the floor, covering their faces.

Winded, I stared up at the balloons bobbing on the ceiling. I moved my arms and legs tentatively. Nothing felt broken. I was confused, but I wasn't hurt. How was that possible? What had just happened? People began to gravitate toward the damage. It reminded me of passing a nasty car wreck— nobody could resist slowing down to inspect the damage.

Why weren't they running? I wondered through the fog in my head. They were all standing around the wreckage, girls covering their mouths, hushed and horrified whispers flying around the room. Still flat on my back, I tried to look through the press of bodies, but I couldn't see much. I struggled to my feet and stood unsteadily before making my way over to see what was holding everyone's attention.

I realized someone was trapped under the pile of twisted metal and broken glass, one leg bent at an odd angle. The massive lead crystal chandelier must have been at least five feet in diameter and had pinned the boy's body to the floor. One of its bronze arms had punctured his neck, and blood was spurting from the wound so profusely, I thought an artery must have been severed. A sick feeling spread through me like a poison as I recognized the thatch of dark hair and the carved ring on the middle finger. Joe had thrown me out of the way, risking his life to spare mine.

Mrs. Rochester was shaking and looked ready to pass out. She closed her eyes tightly, as if praying that when she opened them again, there would be no destruction and no students bleeding in front of her.

I pushed my way over to where Joe was lying, a crumpled heap on the floor. Close-up, the chunk of metal wedged in his neck looked much worse. His face was a mess of cuts and bruises. I wanted to do something but I was too scared to even touch him. I knelt down, sweeping away the glass around his head. What had Isobel done?

"Joe?" I cried, hot tears muffling my words. "Can you hear me? Oh God, somebody call 911!"

I panicked for a moment, realizing nobody here knew what that meant. What was the emergency number in England? I didn't know! But I felt my chest loosen a little when I saw that people had already started dialing.

Alex reappeared at my side. His gaze traveled over Joe's broken body, taking in the situation. "Help him," I whimpered.

"*You* have to help him, Chloe," Alex said.

"This is my fault," I choked. "If I hadn't kissed you in the garden, I never would have made her angry."

The onlookers glanced uncertainly at one another, probably wondering who the hell I was talking to. But I didn't care. They could throw me in the loony bin if they wanted. At least then nobody else would get hurt.

"Chloe?"

"How could I have been so thoughtless?"

"Don't do this now," Alex commanded. "Right now your friend needs you. You have to be strong for him."

"What can I do?" I asked helplessly.

"First you have to be calm. Are you calm?"

I took a deep breath and exhaled shakily. "Okay, yes."

"Don't attempt to remove the metal," Alex instructed. "Just try to control the blood flow."

"How?" I looked down at Joe, painfully aware that his life was hanging in the balance. I'd never seen so much blood before. It was pooling around him like a rich mantle. How long did it take for a person to bleed out?

"Locate the source of the bleeding and apply pressure around it." Alex's voice was low and quick.

"I'm scared to touch him! What if I make it worse?"

"Trust me," he said. "I trained for the military before becoming a painter and a disgrace to my family."

"But…"

"Hurry! Before he suffers any more blood loss."

"I need something to use as a bandage!" I cried out to the nearest person. Someone shoved a wad of clean napkins into my hand. I fought back a wave of dizziness as I bent closer to the grisly wound so that I could locate the exact spot the blood was spurting from. I covered it with the fabric and used the tips of my fingers to gently apply pressure, careful to avoid contact with the metal spike in case I pushed it in farther. Within seconds, blood covered my fingers. I wiped them hastily on my shirt, leaving a crimson handprint on the crisp white fabric. I discovered that blood had a distinct coppery smell.

The spectators watched on, clutching one another in silence. The only sound was the occasional choked sob. The greatest casualty of all was lying in front of us, and the knowledge that I had brought this fate on him was almost too much to bear. Why hadn't I realized this would happen the moment I kissed Alex? Had I thought Isobel wouldn't see? She saw everything. The truth was, I'd been too caught up in the moment to use common sense. And so had Alex. The worst part was that all this destruction had been intended for me and me alone. But Joe had stepped in at the last minute, sabotaging Isobel's plan and taking the brunt of her wrath.

Joe's eyelids fluttered and he momentarily regained consciousness. A soft moan escaped his lips.

"Joe!" I resisted the urge to hug him. "Can you hear me?"

He blinked and seemed to have difficulty focusing his eyes. "Chloe?" His voice was unchanged, despite everything that had happened. "Are you okay?"

His concern for me at such a time was almost my undoing. "I'm fine." I refused to let my voice crack. I didn't want him to see how afraid I was. If I could convince both of us that everything would be all right, then maybe it would be. Wasn't that the idea behind positive thinking? "You're going to be fine," I said, willing myself to believe it. "Don't try to move. Help is on the way." I attempted a smile to show him there was no need to worry, although the sight of his broken body and the sticky blood between my fingers told a different story. "Does it hurt?"

"Actually, I can't feel a thing," he said. "But I'm glad you're here."

Before I could respond, his head lolled and he lapsed into unconsciousness again. I stayed by his side, eyes locked on the shallow rise and fall of his chest until I heard the sound of sirens screaming up the driveway. It was a relief to see the paramedics walk in and take charge, but I wished they'd move faster. They ushered everyone out of the way calmly.

The chandelier was so heavy, it took both of them plus the assistance of several strong guys to shift it.

"Never seen anything like this," one of them muttered as he bent over Joe, checking his vitals. "Blood pressure's falling. Let's get him out of here."

Quickly but carefully they maneuvered Joe onto a stretcher. As they did, the silver chain slipped from inside his shirt. I caught it right before it hit the ground and turned the dog tag over in my hand. The inscription read: It Will Be Golden and Eternal. I didn't know why, but the words brought a surge of emotion rushing forth. I gritted my teeth to fend off the tears. Now wasn't the time to fall apart.

As they wheeled him outside, I saw a crowd gathered on the lawn. The incandescent fairy lights had fallen to the ground and were being trampled underfoot. The billowing canopy that had reminded me of a dream castle was now a ruin of shredded canvas. Overwrought parents were beginning to arrive in their prestigious cars. I caught sight of Mrs. Rochester surrounded by an angry mob, a barrage of questions and accusations flying like daggers. In those few minutes, I heard the words *lawyers* and *lawsuit* more times than I could count.

I glanced over my shoulder to see Rory standing in the doorway of the house, tucked under Grandma Fee's arm. He looked so lost I felt my heart snap in two. Joe was like the big brother he'd never had. How much more loss could the poor kid handle? Grandma Fee was talking rapidly under her breath into the phone, but her eyes were fixed on Joe's body. I knew how fond she was of him.

"Are you family?" I realized the paramedic was talking to

me. Through all the commotion, I had somehow managed to stick by Joe's side.

"Yes," I lied without hesitation. I wasn't going to abandon him now. "I'm his sister."

He helped me into the back of the ambulance and slammed the doors behind us. Through the glass panel, I caught sight of a lone figure, standing at the edge of the fray. It was Alex, head bowed and shoulders slumped. I knew what he was thinking, because I was thinking the exact same thing.

There was no fight left in us after tonight, no need for further strategies.

It was over. Isobel had won.

# CHAPTER TWENTY-TWO

Joe was still unconscious when we got to the hospital. I clambered out of the ambulance to find his ashen-faced parents hovering outside emergency.

"Joe!" His mother stepped forward, both hands flying to her mouth when she saw him. I noticed his father had eyes the exact same shade of chartreuse green. He was battling to keep his emotions in check. The paramedics didn't give them a second glance, wheeling Joe straight into the E.R. without time for explanations.

"Mr. and Mrs. Parrish?" I said tentatively. "You don't know me, but my name is Chloe Kennedy and—"

"Of course we know you," his father replied before I could finish. "Joe never stops talking about you."

"Really?" I felt a pang in my chest and a surge of guilt that threatened to drag me under. Joe's mother smiled through her tears.

"You must be very special."

I sat with Joe's parents in the waiting room for what seemed like hours. I couldn't block the memories that crept up on me of the last time I'd been in a hospital. My world had crumpled around me then like it was made of paper. The same sense of impending doom engulfed me now, but I focused on emptying my mind of all negative thoughts. *He's going to be okay. He's going to be okay.* I repeated the mantra over and over in my head. I even tried praying to the man upstairs. I wasn't sure he existed, but I wanted to cover all my bases.

Before long, the waiting room began to fill with parents and injured kids. There was a girl with a broken elbow, a boy with a nasty contusion across his face and a multitude of others with cut lips, sprains and fractures. In the stark surrounds of the hospital, the dresses that had looked dazzling only hours earlier were now dirty and bedraggled. The small county hospital with its meager night staff was not equipped to deal with the sudden influx of injuries. One of the fathers was pacing like a caged lion. He approached the nurses' station.

"When is someone going to see to my daughter?" the man demanded, and a chorus of parents joined in to express their combined outrage. The overwhelmed nurse shrank back at her desk.

"We're doing everything we can," she said meekly.

When Joe's doctor finally emerged, I was the first to leap to my feet.

"How is he?" Mrs. Parrish clasped her hands together like she was praying.

The doctor tucked his clipboard under one arm and straightened his tie. I realized I'd been nervously chewing the inside of my lip because it felt rough and ragged now. "Your son has a severed artery, several broken ribs and a punctured lung," the doctor told us.

"What does that mean?" Mr. Parrish's voice was wiped of all emotion.

"He's going to need surgery," the doctor replied. "But if all goes well, he should make a full recovery."

Mrs. Parrish expressed her relief by letting out a sound like a strangled bird and collapsing against her husband.

Even though I knew Joe was in good hands, I couldn't bring myself to leave the hospital. They didn't want to move him, so they called in a surgeon from a city hospital. It was a four-hour procedure to repair the damage. When they brought him back to the ward, I hovered outside, keeping vigil. We weren't allowed to see him yet, not until his condition was stable enough. I used the hospital pay phone to call Gran and make sure she was okay. I'd never heard her sound more despondent. She said they were busy cleaning up and Harry would come to collect me in a few hours.

I didn't feel right leaving my family unattended with Isobel on the loose, but at the same time, I couldn't abandon Joe. I could see him through the little pane of glass in the door. He looked so vulnerable, hooked up to a plethora of tubes and monitors. For some reason, my thoughts kept returning to the horses at Grange Hall. Joe was the only one who worked in the stables and nobody could calm the horses the way he did. Who would tend to them with him gone?

Around 2:00 a.m. I went to get a drink from the vending machine. An unearthly quiet hung over the corridors. The clink of the coins as I dropped them into the slot seemed exaggeratedly loud. In my peripheral vision, I caught sight of a figure sitting in the now-empty waiting room. I knew it was Alex by the way he held himself, stiff and upright with the straight fall of gold across his face. I glanced around, but there was nobody in sight except a lone nurse at the end of the hall, engrossed in a mountain of paperwork. I walked over and slid quietly into the seat next to him.

"Alex, how did you get here?"

"I had to see you."

"But I thought you couldn't leave Grange Hall."

"I can only haunt the places I was connected to in life," he replied, neglecting to elaborate further. "How's your friend?"

"He's not in great shape, but I think he's going to be okay."

Alex didn't seem to take comfort from my words. "This could have been averted."

"I know," I said, fixing my eyes on the ground. "I didn't think about the consequences."

"I came to you, Chloe," he replied. "I am the one to blame."

"We shouldn't beat ourselves up," I said. "Isobel's the crazy one here. We didn't actually do anything wrong."

I reached out to take his hand, but to my surprise, he rose from his seat, intentionally putting distance between us. The hurt I felt must have been obvious.

"Chloe, I came because I must speak with you." I didn't like the ominous ring in his voice. It sounded like the nineteenth-century version of *we need to talk*.

"I'm listening," I said apprehensively.

"What happened tonight changes everything," Alex said. "Surely you must know that."

"Changes everything how?" I asked, but I knew what was coming.

"I have no choice, Chloe," he said. "My presence has brought only grief to you and your loved ones."

"None of this is your fault."

"We will have to agree to disagree on that point," he said. "But I know one thing…it is within my power to prevent more harm from occurring. It would be unbelievably self-ish of me not to do so."

"What are you saying?"

"I have to disappear from your life." There was a resolution in his voice I'd never heard before. "You must not look for me or ask me to return. That will only make things harder for both of us." He could see the heartbreak in my eyes, but he struggled on.

"Where will you go?"

"You need not concern yourself with that, Chloe. Just know that it's the right thing to do. Perhaps this is my chance to redeem past mistakes."

"But I thought we were…" I couldn't find the words to finish. How could he walk away so easily?

"What?" He turned his eyes up to the ceiling and his tone became harsh. "What could we possibly be? Forget me, Chloe."

"I can't." I heard my voice crack.

"It will get easier with time. You'll see."

"Why are you saying all this now?" I burst out. "I know things are bad, but why can't we keep fighting? We don't have to give up." I'd considered doing the same thing myself on plenty of occasions, just throwing in the towel and walking away from it all. But now that the idea was about to become reality, I couldn't go through with it.

"Listen." Alex leaned forward and locked his fingers together. "When you touched me last night, something happened. For those brief moments, I felt alive again."

I inched closer to him, challenging his decision. "And that's bad because…"

"Because I'm *not* alive. Nothing can ever change that."

By now I was feeling pretty strung out. Too much had happened in one night. I didn't have the reserves to cope with any more stress and my patience was wearing thin.

"You know what I think?" I snapped. "I think you want to run away because deep down you prefer your twisted relationship with Isobel!"

Through the doors, I saw the nurse glance up, alerted by my raised voice. I dropped it a few octaves. "I think you never got over her. You don't want to move on. You *like* your tortured existence."

Alex fixed me with a solemn stare. "Nothing could be further from the truth."

"Then prove it!" I cried. "Don't bail on me now. Stay so we can deal with this together."

For a moment I thought I'd gotten through to him. He looked almost on the verge of changing his mind. But then he dropped his gaze and shook his head. I read the message loud and clear: he was walking away, and whatever bond I believed held us together had broken. After tonight, I would never see him again.

"Chloe, you have a whole life to live. Mine is a half-life, lurking in shadows, trapped by the past. I have nothing but an illusion to offer. I won't ruin the life of someone I love."

*Love.* Had I heard right? Had Alex just admitted to loving me? Did it really matter either way? It was still going to be followed by a devastating blow.

"Goodbye, Chloe," he said. "I hope you'll think of me fondly from time to time."

"Alex, wait! Please don't go!" But he was already fragmenting before my eyes, leaving only the scent of rain in the woods and a slight shimmer on the plastic seat.

I couldn't believe what had just happened. If I never saw Alexander Reade again, there wasn't a thing I could do about it. I was entirely at his mercy. I stood up, blinded by tears, and kicked over a chair. The nurse from the station appeared in the doorway, frowning.

"Is everything okay in here?"

"Sorry." I wiped my eyes on the back of my sleeve. "Just clumsy, I guess."

"That's okay." She smiled sympathetically. "I know you kids have had a rough night. But on the upside, your brother is stable now. He's going to be fine. You can see him if you like."

I followed the nurse back to Joe's room, where I found him staring blearily at the television blaring above his head.

"You're awake!" I cried.

"Indoor voice, dear," the nurse told me as she jotted notes on her clipboard. Joe turned his neck and for a split second he looked at me without recognition. I felt my stomach plummet. Then his cracked lips broke into a smile.

"Chloe…" His voice was uneven from the meds. "You came!"

"I never left," I answered. "How do you feel?"

"Better, now that I've seen you."

"Did you hear the good news?" I asked. "You're going to be all right." Joe tried to shake his head but immediately grimaced from the stiches in his neck. "Careful," I warned. "That's going to hurt for a while. You need to take care of yourself."

"I just wish I knew what happened. Feels like I got run over by a bus. Was I?"

"You don't remember anything?" I couldn't believe it. "Joe, a chandelier fell on you."

"Really?" His eyes widened. *"Cool."*

"No, not cool," I replied. "You could have been killed."

"But I'm still alive…which essentially makes me Batman."

I couldn't stop myself from smiling. "Pretty much." I winked.

"So how did that happen?"

My smile froze on my face. How much should I tell him? He was still weak and hopped up on pain meds. Would he even remember this conversation tomorrow?

"Don't worry about that," I said. "You just focus on getting better."

"Thanks for being here, Chloe." Joe's eyelids were already drooping.

I fished his necklace from my pocket, where I'd put it for safekeeping, and cupped his head in my hands, gingerly slipping it over the bandages. Then I leaned down and kissed him on the forehead. "Where else would I be?"

About an hour later, Harry came to take me back to Grange Hall. Snow had fallen overnight and my waitress outfit offered next to nothing in terms of warmth. I slid gratefully into the heated leather seat and watched the hospital recede through the tinted window.

"How's Gran doing?"

"You know her," Harry replied. "Nothing can knock that woman down."

"Have they worked out what happened yet?" I asked tentatively.

"They're saying it was some sort of freak wind." He rolled his eyes.

"You don't sound convinced."

"Well, for a freak wind, it was pretty selective," he replied. "It looks like a bomb went off in the ballroom, but the rest of the house escaped untouched. That doesn't add up."

"Weird," I agreed flatly.

We pulled into the driveway of Grange Hall, and I saw that the cleanup operation was already under way. A group of volunteers was scattered across the lawn, picking up bits of broken crockery and sweeping paths that were littered with glass and plaster. A Dumpster had been delivered, and it was filling quickly with rubble and furniture broken beyond repair. I'd never seen my grandmother in jeans and a sweatshirt before. A scarf covered her hair as she crouched on the porch, holding a dustpan and brush. Rory appeared as I stepped out of the car. He was gnawing at a hangnail, and I sensed he couldn't bring himself to ask the question on his mind.

"He's going to be fine." I watched his face flood with relief. "You can go visit him in a few days."

"I wish there was something we could do to make him feel better," Rory said.

"There is," I replied. "We can take good care of the horses while he's away. They'll need fresh food and water, and Joe taught you how to muck out the stalls, didn't he?" My brother nodded. "Come on." I put an arm around him. "They need you."

We walked in silence through the snow to the stables. The horses must have known something wasn't right, because they seemed unsettled, whinnying and kicking their hind legs. Rory tried to pet Cinnamon's nose, but she snorted and turned her face away.

"They miss Joe." He sighed. "I thought he was going to leave us...like Mom did. Why do people always leave us, Chloe?"

I felt the prickle of tears threatening to spill. "Not because they want to, Rory," I said. "They don't always have a choice."

"Sometimes I worry that I did something..." He wouldn't look at me as he drew outlines in the dust with the toe of his shoe. "Something bad...like maybe it's my fault."

I walked over and put my arms around him. It had been a while since I'd hugged my brother, and at first neither of us knew what to do. Then Rory turned around and buried his face in my shirt. I knew he was crying, because I could feel his tears seeping through the fabric.

"It's not your fault." I cupped his head in my hands. "Not even a little bit."

"You won't leave, will you, Chloe?" His voice was muffled.

"Never," I said truthfully. "We have to stick together. We're a team, you and I."

"Chloe?"

"Yeah?"

"I love you."

"I know." I leaned down to kiss his wet cheek. "I love you, too, Rory, and no matter what happens I'm always going to be your big sister. I'm always going to take care of you. Remember that."

# CHAPTER TWENTY-THREE

True to his word, Alex stayed away, while I wavered between indignation and longing. Every night I went to sleep and woke thinking I saw him in his usual position, standing thoughtfully by the window. But it always turned out to be the light playing tricks on me. Still, I didn't believe he could seriously stay away. I spent a good part of each day imagining our reunion. The scenario I liked best was Alex appearing from behind a tree in his long, black coat. He would stand there, the way he had the day I first met him, only this time no words would be needed. We would simply gravitate toward each other until we were close enough to collapse into an effortless embrace. When it didn't happen, I was left contemplating a future where I could never be quite sure that he'd ever existed.

With Joe in the hospital and Alex MIA, things were quieter than usual at Grange Hall. The ballroom was still in a state of ruin, but it was too close to Christmas to call in tradesmen to fix it. So Grandma Fee simply locked the door and made it item Number 1 on next year's to-do list. She'd been in touch with my father, who was taking the next available flight out. I'd overheard her on the phone to him:

"You have to come, David," she'd insisted. "Because Rory almost drowned a few days ago, and Chloe's behaving more bizarrely than ever. I hear her at night talking to someone in her bedroom. She can't be on her cell—there's no service here. *Yes,* I know this was my idea. *No,* I'm not saying I was wrong. I'm saying the children need their father."

Maybe she was right. I'd expected my stay at Grange Hall to be mind-numbingly boring. But in reality, there'd never been more chaos in my life. As a result, I was seriously lacking in Christmas spirit this year. It had always been my third-favorite holiday, behind Thanksgiving and Halloween, but I just wasn't in the mood to be festive. Grange Hall was the perfect setting, with the snow and the smell of pine needles permeating the air and the sprigs of mistletoe Gran planted around the house. But after everything that had happened, the halls felt cold and cheerless.

Isobel and the visions disappeared along with Alex's departure. It occurred to me that that was what she'd wanted all along. He had guessed the sacrifice he needed to make to finally appease her. I felt like the butt of some cruel, supernatural joke, where everyone had anticipated the outcome except me.

One morning I wrapped myself in a fleecy throw and took my copy of *Madame Bovary* to the library. I tucked myself into the window seat, where my breath made patches on the frosty glass. I was on the last few chapters, and things weren't looking good for Emma B. But she had taught me one thing—passion wasn't sustainable. It would just suck you dry and exhaust you. Maybe I'd turned into a cynic before my time, but at least cynics didn't wind up brokenhearted. I tried to focus on the page before me, but my gaze kept traveling to the window.

Outside, the trees looked like huge robed figures, reaching out their arms to me. My mind couldn't help spiraling back in time, envisioning Alex and Isobel all those years ago when they were carefree and in love. Now, it seemed, they would remain together for the rest of eternity. I still had so much to say to Alex, but I'd never get the chance. It wasn't right. I slammed the book shut and tossed it aside.

There was a vast mahogany desk in the center of the room, in front of the ladder that reached the uppermost shelves. I rummaged around in the drawers until I found what I was looking for, an old notebook, pages discolored from age, and a fountain pen. It was fitting, I thought sourly...stuck in the past, just like Alex. I took a seat determinedly in the wingback leather chair and began to write. The words poured out of me, without any need to stop or reflect. I could feel the pent-up emotions inside me itching for release.

*Dear Alex,*

*I'm writing you this letter knowing that you'll never get to read it. I suppose it's more for me than it is for you. But I need some sort of closure, something to set my mind at ease, although I don't even remember what that feels like anymore.*

*Who knows, maybe you can see me right now...maybe you're standing behind me, reading every word over my shoulder. I guess I'll never know. But the thoughts in my head feel so tangled and confused—if I don't write them down I might implode. So here goes...*

*You just left me. How could you do that? You probably think it was brave and self-sacrificing, but it was exactly the opposite. You took the easy way out. Staying and fighting for what we had would have taken real strength. I know you were trying to protect us all from Isobel, and maybe you succeeded. But you left me open to a whole other kind of hurt. Broken bones I can deal with, but when you left, you broke my spirit and no doctor can heal that. Maybe you just didn't feel as strongly as I did. But why show up in my life if you had no intention of staying? You just appeared one day and became a fixture in my life. You were my ally, my friend, my confidant. Then you took it all away without any warning. That night in the hospital when you said you loved me. Did you really mean that? You can't have, because if you truly care for someone, you don't bail when things get tough. I can only conclude that you never cared about me at all. Maybe I was just a fleeting distraction. Maybe I was the only person in over a hundred years you could speak to and your emotions got mixed up and confused. But what you're doing right now? That isn't love.*

*The worst part is this...what I feel for you is so hard to describe. You woke something in me that I never knew existed. You might be dead, but when I was with you, I never felt more alive. You were like a phantom that showed up in the night and painted my world in color. Then I woke up, never certain if you were really there. Maybe you never were. Maybe all this has been a figment of my imagination. Maybe I'm really a patient in a psych ward and this is just a fantasy I've created in my head. Maybe I never left America. Maybe my name isn't even Chloe. Okay...this train of thought isn't helping.*

*The point of this letter is that I'm never going to forget you, Alex. I'm never going to get over you. I see your face every time I close my eyes. I'm sorry you're trapped and unhappy, and maybe it's selfish of me to want to keep you here. I want you to be free from pain, free from Isobel, free from the past that's haunted you all these years. And maybe you'll never be free if you remain at Grange Hall. Maybe this is the end for you and me, but I want you to know that I think you're extraordinary, and not just as an artist, even though I know you have mad skills in that department (that means you kick butt...sorry, that means you're very accomplished... I heard that watching* Pride and Prejudice *with my mom) But, Alex... you're extraordinary simply at being you. There's so much light in your eyes and I'll remember the way you used to look at me forever. Love, Chloe x*

I felt better after I was finished writing, even though my leg had gone to sleep and my fingers were cramping up. I hadn't written anything this long by hand since the fifth grade. I wasn't entirely sure what to do with the letter. I was half tempted to leave it out in the hope that Alex might stumble across it, but I knew I couldn't risk it falling into the wrong hands. Instead I took it upstairs and hid it in the bottom drawer of my dresser.

"Chloe?" There came a tap at my bedroom door, and Grandma Fee tiptoed in like she was walking on eggshells. She could tell something wasn't right with me, but she assumed my depression was the result of Joe's injuries. "How are you feeling?"

"Fine," I replied, not even bothering to feign enthusiasm.

"What an unfortunate time for all this to happen," she said, settling down on the end of the bed and smoothing out a loose thread on the duvet. "I know you and Rory have been through a lot, and it's your birthday in a couple of days."

"What?" I couldn't believe I'd forgotten my own birthday. She was right. I was only a few days shy of eighteen. "I guess I don't feel much like celebrating."

"Nonsense," she scoffed. "It's not every day a girl becomes a woman."

I smiled weakly. "Actually, I've never felt more like a kid."

Grandma Fee patted my knee. "I'll let you in on a little secret, Chloe. No one ever really grows up. We just get better at pretending."

"I'm sorry about your ballroom, Gran," I blurted. "I know how much you loved it."

"Don't be silly," she told me. "Buildings can be repaired. It's people we have to take care of."

"I just feel so...guilty."

"Listen to me." Grandma Fee wagged a finger in front of my face. "Bad things happen every day, but the world doesn't stop turning. You keep your head down, and you weather the storm. That's what we Kennedys do."

She enveloped me in a hug, and for a moment I felt like I was back in my mother's arms. Then I realized the touch of her hands was too cool...the embrace was too bony...the scent was different. We broke apart and she left the room, leaving me feeling even emptier than before.

To distract myself, I picked up *Madame Bovary* again. I knew I had to finish it before the start of semester. By now the town's moneylender had seized her house due to unpaid debts, and her last resort was to run away with a lover who'd already lost interest in her. So she was pretty much screwed. I could relate to that. I found my place in the text but had barely started reading when a sound like pounding hooves outside distracted me. I tossed the book aside and ran to the window.

*Two horses gallop up to the house, their hooves kicking up gravel, their coats luminous with sweat. Isobel wears a sumptuous green riding outfit and rides a powerful black stallion, his tail lashing the air. Alex is right behind her. Both are breathless. The waning light and descending mist suggest it's evening. Alex is wearing a ruffled shirt, and his burnished gold hair is pulled back in its usual ponytail. Isobel jumps down without waiting for his assistance and turns her flushed face up to the sky to catch the first drops of rain.*

*Immediately a servant, bent and hoary, emerges from the side of the house. He wears brown breeches and a rough shirt that looks like it was made out of a hessian sack. He shuffles over to them, takes the reins in his callused hands and begins to lead the horses away.*

*"Isaac!" Isobel calls after him. The man stops in his tracks. "Has the master returned?" Her tone is imperious like she knows the power she has and enjoys wielding it. She's brazen and makes no attempt to conceal the fact that she has spent the day alone with Alex.*

*The servant gives her a sidelong glance and shrugs. His disdain for her rings loud and clear; he doesn't even try to hide it. "Yes, madam."*

*She purses her lips superciliously. "And where, pray, is he?"*

*"Passed out on his bedroom floor in a pool of vomit." Isaac takes some delight in conveying this piece of information. He shows no loyalty to Carter. I notice the backs of his hands are covered in scars and there's a piece of his left ear missing.*

*Isobel looks disgusted, either by the servant's manner or the picture he's just painted of her husband.*

*"Tend to the horses," she commands in a contemptuous voice. "Then tell Becky to serve supper in the library."*

*"Right away, madam." Isaac gives a short bow as Isobel sweeps past him into the house.*

*Alex gives his horse a final stroke and moves to follow her, but Isaac coughs as if he has something to say. "Master Reade?"*

*On the front steps, Alex turns to face him. "What it is, Isaac?" His manner is kind, in sharp contrast to Isobel's air of superiority. Alex addresses Isaac as a man, as a human being; Isobel treated him like chattel created to do her bidding.*

*"I don't wish to speak out of turn, master." Isaac removes his cap and twists it in his hands.*

*Alex takes a step closer to him. "Please, speak freely. What is amiss?"*

*Isaac leans in and spits out the words quickly, as if in fear of the repercussions should he be overheard. "You're a good man," he says. "Everybody says so. But she will bring darkness upon this house!"*

*"I beg your pardon?" Discomfort flits across Alex's face.*

*"She's a Jezebel!" he says forcefully. "You mark my words, Master Reade. Be on your guard. That woman will be your undoing."*

As the vision freed me from its hold, I sank down in the window seat. The quivering knees and sweaty palms...it was getting old. I couldn't do this anymore. Each episode left me dizzy and disoriented and more confused than ever.

"You've won, Isobel," I said suddenly, turning my face up toward the ceiling because I didn't know where else to look. "Are you happy now?"

I was met with echoing silence, but I knew she could hear

me. "I'm leaving," I yelled out. "Going back to California. Grange Hall will be yours again. You got what you wanted, so just...just leave me alone."

I wasn't naive enough to believe she'd listen. But a girl can hope, right?

# CHAPTER TWENTY-FOUR

Dad arrived on the afternoon of my birthday. Even though it was freezing, Rory and I waited on the porch, bouncing from foot to foot to stay warm. As soon as the gates opened and we caught a glimpse of the car, we bounded down the steps so fast we almost toppled over each other.

The moment he stepped out of the passenger seat, I could see that my dad had changed. The changes were subtle, obvious only to those who knew him best. He'd lost weight, and his jeans hung loose on his hips. He hadn't cut his hair or shaved in weeks, and his beard had grown in thick and fast. There were a few more creases around his eyes than I remembered, but he seemed to be in one piece. Rory didn't waste any time. He flung himself at Dad the moment he dropped his bag.

"Dad! I've missed you! How was the flight? Did you watch any good movies? How's Darcy? Did you know I can ride a horse now?"

"Steady on, buddy." Dad squeezed him tight. "Sounds like you've got a lot to tell me."

Grandma Fee, who was never too forthcoming with her emotions, gave him a formal peck on the cheek. "Good flight, darling? Come in out of the cold now," she said, her silver bob swinging like a pendulum as she bustled us back to the house.

Miss Grimes appeared in the hallway to collect Dad's bags.

"Hello, Edna," he said. "It's good to see you again. You haven't changed a bit."

She didn't answer. She just kept her eyes downcast and nodded her head like a cracked old doll.

Dad turned to Gran. "You've done a fantastic job with the place. Angie would have loved this," he said, echoing Rory's first thought upon our arrival.

His first reference to Mom since her passing took us by surprise. But I realized it marked a turning point. Wasn't it high time we all started talking about her? Why try to bury her memory and act like she never existed? She wouldn't have wanted that.

"She would have hated this weather, though," I said. "I barely saw her in anything but flip-flops."

Dad smiled, and I knew he was remembering the way she would complain whenever she had to wear heels to a business event.

We left him to shower and freshen up before Harry brought the car around for my birthday dinner. I hadn't given much thought to the fact that I'd turned eighteen today. I knew it was supposed to be a milestone, an official transition into the world of adulthood, when you leave your carefree childish ways behind you. But my childhood had been far from carefree. So today felt like just another day...another typical day in the unconventional life of Chloe Kennedy.

Before he headed upstairs, my dad stopped, one hand on the banister.

"I have something for you, Chloe," he said. "I know I'm supposed to wait till dinner to give you your present but…" He withdrew a little velvet pouch from his coat pocket. "Happy birthday, sweetheart." He placed it delicately in my hand.

I opened the drawstrings to find an antique Baltic amber pendant suspended from a silver ball chain. The pendant was flecked with rich swirling colors, held in place by little silver claws.

"This belonged to your mother."

"Really?" I held it gingerly in my palm. "How come I've never seen it before?"

"She was saving it to give you on your eighteenth birthday." Dad smiled thoughtfully. "It's a family heirloom passed down from her great-grandmother."

Receiving one last gift from my mother was a privilege I'd never expected. My grip on the pendant tightened.

"I love it," I said, slipping the chain over my head. "I'm never going to take it off."

The amber felt like it was pulsing against my chest, like it had a heartbeat of its own. I could feel my mother's energy inside it, as if a little part of her had been captured and preserved. I knew now that I would carry her with me always.

Since Dad had gotten the ball rolling, other presents came out. Gran gave me a matching designer wallet and purse I'd had my eye on for a while, while Rory had clumsily wrapped up a new perfume that smelled like cotton candy. I didn't know when he'd had time to go shopping, but I rewarded him with a big kiss on the cheek, and he squirmed with obvious embarrassment.

"Thank you, guys," I said. "This is really awesome."

Rory could tell I was starting to get misty-eyed. "Yeah, yeah, Chloe." He nudged me. "We know. Now let's go eat. I'm starving."

Gran took us to the village pub called the George and Dragon, where I was allowed to have my first Pimm's Cup. It tasted light and fruity, so the buzz of alcohol crept up on me out of the blue. But it did make me feel more carefree than I had in a long while. Was I actually enjoying myself? I wondered. I'd forgotten what that felt like.

When we got home, Grandma Fee even had a fluffy cream cake waiting for me in the kitchen, slathered all over with a sparkly pink frosting like I used to have when I was a child. The sight of it was strangely comforting. We cut the cake and drank hot chocolate in front of the roaring fire until I was yawning and ready to climb into bed. It hadn't been the eighteenth-birthday extravaganza Sam and Natalie might have planned, but it had been perfect in its own strange way.

I opened my door to find the Hunt sisters sitting comfortably on my bed. Mavis had her nose in a book, while knitting needles clattered in May's hands. I guessed she was supposed to be making a scarf, but it looked more like an elephant trunk.

"Do make yourselves at home…." I said lightly, resenting the intrusion after the first decent evening I'd had in a while. I wasn't in the mood for their schemes.

"Thank you, dear," replied May obtusely. "As you can see, we have."

"What's going on?"

"We've had an idea," Mavis announced.

"Seriously?" I burst out. "Look, I don't think we need any more ideas. I haven't seen anything in a while. Maybe we could drop the whole thing now?"

Nonplussed, May looked at me over the top of her knitting. "Are you always this irritable?"

"I just want to go to bed."

"That's all very well and good," May said pertly. "But we made a pact, and now we need your help."

"You guys must be crazy," I said, pulling off my shoes. "The solution is simple—stay out of Isobel's way. You've seen what she's capable of."

"Just hear us out." Mavis's face was alight. "Then you can decide whether you want to be involved or not."

"Fine. But make it quick."

"We want to make contact with the ghost of Benjamin Grimes."

I was brought up short. "Why?"

"If anyone can help us, he can. He might know something we don't."

"*Right...*" I gave them a caustic thumbs-up. "Good luck with that."

I decided these women were too naive. They just didn't know when to back off. But I wasn't going to let myself be dragged in. Alex was gone, and I'd closed the door on the ghosts of Grange Hall. There was no way I was going out of my way to draw Isobel's attention. As far as I could see, you didn't go poking a bear unless you had a death wish.

"It's not about luck, Chloe, and you know it. You have a vital role to play."

Damn it. How had I known this was coming?

"What role is that?"

"Well, on a practical level, we need a minimum of three people to hold a séance," announced May. She sounded matter-of-fact. "It won't work without you."

I had to wonder whether this information had been freshly looked up on the internet. I let out a long sigh.

"Isn't there someone else who can help you? It's my birthday."

"Happy birthday, dear!" Mavis exclaimed.

"Thanks," I said. "And what better way to celebrate than a chat with a dead child?"

"But it's not just any chat," May explained. "We think we may have figured out the missing piece of the puzzle. But we need the séance to confirm our suspicions."

"Your suspicions being?"

She tossed aside her knitting needles. "No séance will work without a medium present.... We think the medium might be you."

I let out a short, brash laugh and sidestepped them on my way to the door. I would sleep in Rory's room if it was the only way out of this. "Sorry, ladies, you've got the wrong person. I'm not interested in communicating with the other side anymore."

Mavis held up one knobby finger. "Just do this one last thing for us, Chloe. The séance won't work without you. If you help us out tonight, we'll never bother you again."

"Is that a promise?"

"Cross our hearts," she said, laying a hand over her breast. "You'll never see us again."

"Fine," I grudgingly agreed. The idea of having them off

my back was just too tempting. "Let's just get this over with. Then I never want to hear another word about ghosts again!"

If I was expecting the séance to involve a Ouija board and an upturned sherry glass, I was sorely disappointed. I met Mavis and May in the dining hall after the rest of the household went to bed and found nothing but three candles dribbling wax onto the table.

"This is it?" I asked doubtfully. "I was expecting more of a show."

"Not necessary." Mavis beckoned me over. "A true medium needs only their presence in a room."

"So no pendulum or blood sacrifice?"

"You've watched too many bad television shows. Although——" May frowned and glanced around the room "——perhaps a little offering wouldn't go astray." Her eye fell on a glass jar of Grandma Fee's lemon shortbreads. She took them from the sideboard and repositioned them in the center of the table. I blinked incredulously at her.

"You're not seriously offering cookies to a ghost."

She shrugged. "It's the gesture that really counts."

"Are you sure he'll even come? What if he's having an awesome time on the other side and doesn't want to be disturbed?"

"He'll come," Mavis assured me. "Just think back to the manner in which he died. Those spirits never fully cross over. They're never at peace."

"Okay...whatever." The room felt hot and stuffy. I settled at the table while Mavis opened the window a crack and let the icy wind in. The candlelight flickered and cast ghoulish shadows on the wallpaper. I joined hands with the sisters to create a circle, and May told me to close my eyes.

"You have to summon him, Chloe," she said.

I tensed up. "Why me? You're the experts. I don't know what to say."

"Listen to the voice in your head," Mavis encouraged. "Then you'll know."

I took a deep breath and cleared my thoughts. I tried to picture the face of the little boy in the photograph. I remembered his eyes and imagined myself staring directly into them. Then, as clear as day, the words appeared in my mind.

"Benjamin Grimes, we invite you into our circle. Come forward. Be guided by the light. Do not be afraid. If you can hear me, make your presence known to us." I was surprised at myself. Where had that come from? It hadn't even felt like me speaking.

For a moment everything was still. Then May's eyelids drooped and her chin slumped onto her chest. Was she really falling asleep right now? I gave her hand a warning squeeze, but she didn't respond. Then suddenly her head flew up and her eyes opened, staring fixedly into space. When she spoke, the piping voice of a child rang out.

"Mummy! Where's my mummy?"

I looked at Mavis, too horror stricken to speak.

"Benjamin?" she asked softly. "Is that you?"

"Mummy?" he asked frantically.

"I'm not your mother," Mavis replied. "But I know of her. She still lives here. She misses you terribly."

"Can I see her?" the voice asked hopefully. It was a pretty eerie thing to witness, the voice of a five-year-old boy speaking through the mouth of a woman with a face as wrinkled as a walnut. Ordinarily I would have concluded that May was faking it, but tonight the idea didn't even cross my mind. If I closed my eyes, I was convinced the boy was standing right next to me.

"Not right now," Mavis said. "She's sleeping. But you can help her…by helping us." The spirit was quiet as he waited for her to elaborate. "Can you tell what happened on the day you *left us*?"

"I followed the beautiful lady into the woods," Benjamin said.

"Was that the first time you saw the lady?"

"No, I used to see her everywhere," the voice replied. "The lady and the men."

"What men?"

"The two that were fighting over her." Mavis looked confused, but I knew exactly what Benjamin was talking about.

"Why did the lady want to hurt you?" I threw in.

"I went too far," the ghost child said. "I lost my way. She told me she would take me home."

"But she didn't, did she?" I whispered.

"No." The voice was growing increasingly agitated. "She took me out in a boat…on the river. Then she turned it over. I didn't know how to swim. I want to see my mummy now!" May's body jerked violently, and I imagined the little boy Benjamin stamping his foot.

"Okay," I said, trying to placate him. "Just tell me one more thing. Did the lady say anything to you?"

"She said she was sorry she had to take me."

"But *why* did she have to take you, Benjamin?" I pressed. "Tell me." I felt like I was picking away at a lock that was about to spring open.

"Because I knew things."

"Who told you that?"

"She did. She called it a gift." Shivers started shooting up my spine. I'd hated that word for as long as I could remember. Alex had called it a gift, too. It was anything but.

"Did she tell you what that means?"

"She said the ones with the gift knew too much. She said I belonged to two worlds and she was worried I would hurt her. I promised I wouldn't, but she didn't believe me. She said there were very few others like me." The ghost child felt silent, and May kicked her legs in her chair like she'd been suddenly distracted

"Can I play now? Tell Mummy I put away my toys like I was supposed to." The ghost seemed to have no inkling of how much time had passed.

"Benjamin," I said softly, "if you see your mother now, you might not recognize her..." I wasn't sure how much I should reveal, but the words spilled out anyway. "You've been gone for over fifty years."

May went rigid, and a sound halfway between a moan and a cry of surprise escaped her thin lips. The candles died on the spot and the window slammed shut. She slumped forward onto the table and was still for several seconds before she lifted her head with a gasp.

"What happened?" she asked, blinking red-rimmed eyes.

"What an astounding thing! I can hardly believe it. The boy spoke through you! It was as if he was right here in the room. Do you remember any of it?" Mavis was rapturous, but May shook her head, disappointed to have missed the most definitive moment of their careers. Mavis fixed her gaze on me. "Chloe, you heard what he said?"

"Yeah, I heard."

"Isobel believed the boy had the power to harm her. It's as we suspected."

"How?" I asked. "Gift or no gift, *how* could he have possibly hurt her?"

"Well…" Mavis thought for a moment. "During our research over the years, we've learned that ghosts can be destroyed by making them relive the pain of their past. Now the past is buried until someone comes along who can unearth it and use it against them, if they know how. I'm not sure whether Benjamin Grimes understood his own power or not, but the important thing is that Isobel did. She saw him as a threat…and perhaps a reminder of what she'd lost. Maybe that's why she had to dispose of him."

I desperately tried to piece things together in my head. "But if Isobel didn't want people to know about her past, why would she show me all those visions?"

"Aah!" Mavis grabbed my arm. "Perhaps Isobel was not the one controlling the visions. The power of the medium was controlling her, forcing the past to resurface, forcing her to relive it."

"*What?* So that would mean…" I faltered. "She didn't want me to see them, after all?"

"Of course not!" Mavis cried. "She's afraid of you. That's why she's been trying to scare you away."

"But what could I do to her?" I asked weakly.

May's eyes shone. "You can do a great deal. More than all of us combined."

I fixed my eyes on the floor as the new information sank in, like a wave of nausea crashing down on me.

"Chloe," Mavis whispered. "You and Benjamin are the same..."

I couldn't stand hearing it spoken aloud.

"No!" I shouted, jumping up and backing instinctively toward the door. "Don't say that. I didn't want any of this!"

"It isn't something you choose," May replied, her misty eyes full of understanding for my plight. "It's a gift you're born with."

"It's not a gift!" I shouted at them. "Was it a gift for Benjamin Grimes? Look how he wound up!"

Mavis stretched her hands toward me. "But you're not like him. Benjamin was an easy target. You're older and wiser, and you have us here to help you. We thought we were at Isobel's mercy, but don't you see? You're running this show, Chloe. You're the only one who can control her...who can stop her."

"I doubt that. She seems pretty indestructible to me."

"I mean, you can make her cross over. Isobel doesn't want to leave this place, but once she does she won't be able to get back."

I couldn't believe it, the idea that I might possess the ability to destroy Isobel forever and break the curse that had haunted Grange Hall. All this time I'd thought she hated me for loving Alex. But she'd been trying to protect herself. She didn't want to leave this place, and she'd known all along that I had the power to make her.

"Right!" May pushed her glasses up her nose. "We can't sit around now twiddling our thumbs! We know what we have to do."

"Um...no, we don't," I objected. "There's no rule book

for this. No seven-step procedure for disposing of unwanted ghosts. What the hell do we do from here?"

"We have to confront Isobel," Mavis answered simply. "She's going to come after you the moment she realizes you've learned your true identity."

I sighed. "I wish you wouldn't make this sound so much like a B-grade horror movie."

"Sorry." She shrugged. "But we don't have a choice now. We have to find her before she finds you."

"Yeah, I get it," I said in a dull voice. "It's her or me. One of us is going to have to go."

# CHAPTER TWENTY-FIVE

I agreed to meet Mavis and May in the foyer ten minutes later. I'd headed upstairs after the birthday celebrations barely able to keep my eyes open. Now the adrenaline coursing through my veins was enough to put all my senses on red alert.

Despite their attempts to reassure me, I couldn't help being plagued by doubt. Did these women *really* know what they were talking about? They'd damn well better. I was entrusting them with my life…all our lives, in fact.

I found them already waiting for me with their childlike enthusiasm, bundled up as if they were embarking on a trip to Antarctica.

"Are you sure about this?" I hesitated. "How do you even know where to find Isobel?"

"We're not completely useless, you know!" May said. "We have a few tricks up our sleeve." She winked at me, but her levity didn't offer much comfort.

"What does that mean?" I asked.

"It means try having a little faith, dear."

"We're not taking that MEF thing again, are we? It seemed pretty useless."

"That's an *EMF* detector," Mavis corrected. "And it works perfectly well."

"Fine," I said. "Assuming you're right and we do find Isobel, what then?"

"We're hoping your gift will guide us when the time comes."

"Um…what?" I struggled to keep my voice down. "I thought you had a foolproof plan!"

May gave me a faint smile. "What on earth gave you that idea?"

Mavis nudged her sister. "Did you remember to bring a torch?"

"I think so." May looked suddenly flustered.

"Well, we won't get far without one, so you had better check!"

I tapped my foot impatiently as May knelt to rummage through her bag. The delay wasn't helping my nerves. The faster we got this over with, the better. I didn't need time to dwell on all the possible outcomes and change my mind.

Through the open door, I heard a soft rustling of plumage nearby and turned to see a horned owl perched in the old oak. Its eyes were the color of lemons and its white chest reflected the moonlight. It watched me without blinking. I was pretty sure the look was intended to say, *Turn back, girlie. It's not too late.* There was something hypnotic about the bird's eyes. Light seemed to spill from them and engulf me. I felt the all-too-familiar sensation of being sucked through space and time. I tried to resist, but it was like trying to swim against the current. *Not now,* I thought. *Please, not now.* But of course, it happened anyway.

*I stand in the foyer of Grange Hall as it once was. Carter is there, lingering at the library door, his ear pressed against it and his fingers twitching on the handle. A gamut of emotions cross his face, but finally an expression that can only be described as unmitigated rage dominates. I'm so close to him I can smell the cigar smoke and whiskey on his breath. His forehead is filmed with sweat and a vein throbs at his temple. His body is taut as a bowstring and ready to snap. It's obvious what has him so riled. I, too, can hear the feverish whispers coming from inside the room. Then, while Carter remains locked behind the barrier, the door becomes permeable to me and, as if in a dream, I'm able to pass right through it.*

*Isobel and Alexander are no longer distinct individuals but a tangle of limbs on a velvet chaise. I've never seen them like this, so hungry for one other. Alexander claws at the lace collar of her gown, revealing the smooth skin beneath. He buries his face in her swanlike neck and drinks her in like a parched man who's just found water. Isobel moans softly and her whole body vibrates in response to his touch.*

*"I've missed you," she says ardently.*

*"I'm obsessed with you," he whispers back.*

*"Make love to me, Alexander," she moans. "As if there's only the two of us left in the world."*

*As if by magic the door becomes transparent. Through it I can see that Carter's face has settled into an eerie sort of mask. His skin is a mottled shade of purple, and I wonder if he's forgotten to breathe. For a moment, I think he's about to burst in on the lovers, but instead, he backs away with the stealth of a cat.*

*I don't know why, but I decide to follow him. He climbs the stairs one step at a time as if he needs to gather his thoughts. When he* reaches the second floor, he stops outside a door. For a moment he sways unsteadily and leans his forehead against the wood. Then he turns the handle and slips inside. I follow him into a nursery decorated in various shades of blue with a frieze of dancing bears around the walls.

The window is half-open and I can hear the distant hum of cicadas outside. Carter moves methodically across the room and shuts it firmly. The sun is setting. As it drops behind the line of the horizon, it sets the sky on fire. There's something too brash, too violent in the merging of colors.

The nursery is charming, with a rocking horse stationed by the window and an open trunk bursting with toys. They're the kind you don't see anymore: a mechanical bear with cymbals attached to its paws, a miniature train set and carved wooden soldiers. In the crib, a baby sleeps. He's the most angelic thing I've ever laid eyes on. I can see Alex in his sleeping face. He has the same symmetry in his fine features, and if he opened his eyes I imagine they would be the same pure shade of cornflower blue.

Carter walks over to the crib and studies the sleeping child. For a moment he doesn't move, then he reaches in his hand and adjusts the blanket away from its tiny pink face. His sways on his feet and his expression turns stony as he picks up a lacy pillow. He inhales the scent, eyes ringed with red from liquor and sleeplessness.

For a moment, I actually think he's going to put it under the baby's head. But he doesn't. Instead he clenches his jaw, closes his eyes and brings it down over the child's face. His hand is flat and broad as he presses down on the pillow, grinding his teeth with the lunacy that's overtaken him.

It's not hard to smother a sleeping baby. Minimal effort is required. There's no struggle, no muffled sounds. This could be a scene from a movie, only it's real and there's nothing I can do about it. I can't *change the past, and I can't save the child being murdered in front of my eyes. I feel dizzy, and a heaving sensation rises in my stomach. I seriously hope I faint, because I can't watch any more. I clamp my shaking hands over my mouth to stop from screaming.*

"Come along, Chloe!" a familiar voice called out.

"Hold on just a second!" I sagged against a balustrade and waited for the vision to release me from its hold. Relief washed over me as I transitioned back to the present. Mavis and May watched me with concern from the porch.

"What's wrong? Are you unwell?"

"I'm fine," I croaked, knowing the image of that child, sleeping peacefully just seconds before his death, would never be erased from my mind.

While the rest of Grange Hall slept, the three of us walked silently into the dark night. A crater-faced moon hung in the sky as we made our way to the lake. There had been a light fall of snow, and the grass crunched underfoot, loud enough to announce our arrival to anyone listening. Otherwise, the night was soundless. Not even the rustle of the wind in the treetops could be heard. We passed a stone angel in the garden, hands folded over her chest, eyes turned heavenward. As we approached, the statue began to tremble, then lurched slowly forward as if it were drunk. The Hunt sisters didn't seem to notice, but I took it as a clear warning. Trouble lay ahead, and we should turn back. But it was too late now.

"If all goes well tonight, Chloe, ghosts will never trouble Grange Hall again," May told me. She looked as excited as a Girl Scout on her first camping trip, but my mind immediately conjured Alex's face. Isobel was one thing, but I didn't want to send him away. Pathetic as it might seem, I was still holding out hope of seeing him again.

"Not all spirits are bad," I muttered.

"But Isobel is," Mavis said. "And it's up to us to stop her."

"Is all this really necessary?" I asked. "What if I just go back to California? Then I and my special *gift* will be out of her way."

"That's true," Mavis agreed. "But do you really want to leave Grange Hall at her mercy? Sooner or later another medium will come along. What if it's another child, like Benjamin?"

I really couldn't argue with that. Isobel was capable of anything. Conscience alone compelled me to act.

"You're right," I said glumly. "It's just that..." I couldn't finish the sentence, but they seemed to read my thoughts anyway. Maybe they'd known all along.

Mavis put a ringed hand on my shoulder. "He's not really here, you know, dear."

My lip trembled and I swallowed the rising lump in my throat. "I know that."

"Nothing good can come from loving a ghost."

"But he hasn't crossed over yet," I objected. "And he doesn't want to." Even I knew I was feebly grasping at straws.

"That makes no difference." Mavis's eyes were kind but firm. "He can never give you what you need. I'm sorry, Chloe."

I looked away. I couldn't think about Alex for too long without feeling my chest tighten up and my eyes begin to smart.

"You need to be strong now," May said, her voice full of resolve. "For everyone. You might not be able to bring Alexander Reade back from the dead…but you can stop others from joining him."

In the darkness, the walk through the wood seemed to take longer than I remembered. Thoughts of Alex relentlessly pounded my brain. I found it hard to believe he could abandon me at a time like this. Didn't he care what happened to me? I found myself wishing I could wipe him from my memory. I wanted to go back to my first day at Grange Hall and never wander into those woods where I'd found him.

Soon the lake came into view. Mist snaked around my ankles like a thousand clammy hands. The water looked like a vast ink stain, stretching before us.

"Can you see anything?" May asked tensely. I could feel the air around me beginning to electrify. We all felt it.

"She's coming," Mavis answered.

It felt strange to be openly seeking out Isobel when I'd spent all my time at Grange Hall trying to avoid her. Now we were calling her out to play. It was like putting yourself in the path of a wild dog; all your instincts tell you to run like hell, but you decide to stand your ground. I didn't feel particularly courageous; my legs were like jelly and I had to clench my jaw to keep my teeth from chattering. Already I knew we were being watched. I looked out at the calm surface of the brackish water. It was too quiet, even if it was after midnight. The silence itself weighed down the air. Our frosty breaths filtered out like wreaths of smoke.

"Maybe she won't show," I said, but we all knew it was wishful thinking.

"Ghosts are creatures of routine," Mavis replied. "She'll come."

My feet were already taking involuntary steps backward. "I don't think we should go through with this. I have a bad feeling…"

The sisters converged around me like members of a support group. "You can do this, Chloe. Isobel may be stronger than us, but she's not stronger than you. You have so much untapped potential. Don't back out now…."

But I wasn't listening to them anymore. I heard her laughter before I saw her. The air around us became glacial, and the dew on my coat hardened into droplets. There was a rustling sound in the reeds before I caught sight of her white dress silhouetted against the trunk of a weeping willow. She had her arms wound around its girth as if she was playing a game of hide-and-seek. The leaves swirled in an eddy around her ankles. Isobel's eyes were bright, her chin lifted in the same self-assured pose I'd come to recognize as her own. Her black hair was hanging free and wild. I'd never seen anyone look so beautiful and so wild at the same time.

"I see her," I whispered, and I heard the women draw breath in tandem.

"Stay calm, Chloe," May urged. "Remember—fear is your biggest enemy."

But I couldn't stay calm. This was it. The final showdown. I took a hesitant step forward, my mouth dry and my palms clammy.

"It's just you and me now, Isobel," I called out.

Her lip curled in a smile. At the same time I felt invisible vines wrap around me, drawing me toward the footbridge that led to the other side of the lake. I realized that must be Isobel's side. I'd always seen her there.

Then something happened I wasn't expecting. The world

on the other side of the lake seemed to shift, its color leaching, and everything solid crumbled to dust. I found myself looking into a shadow world, a pale imitation of life, like a poor mirror image. Isobel stood silently, waiting for me. The phantom ropes dragged me onto the bridge, and I heard May's voice behind me.

"Chloe, no! Don't cross over," she called out. "You must stay with us. You might not find your way back!"

I heard the hammer of footsteps behind me and turned around, but Mavis and May were gone.

*I'm no longer by the lake but back at the house. The polished staircase gleams in the lamplight. The world seems unsteady, like I'm watching footage taped by a cameraman whose hands are shaking.*

*Carter charges past with a wolfish glint in his eyes and a crazed grin on his face. He's disheveled, his jacket missing and his shirt untucked. He lurches, and I know the whiskey has long taken effect. He grabs hold of the banister to steady himself, but there's an unshakable resolve in his eyes. I'm afraid for anyone who encounters him like this. Isaac sticks his head through the kitchen door, but after taking one look at his master, he retreats.*

*In my dreamlike state I'm able to speed past Carter, guided by an unknown force. I know where I'm going—back to the library, where Alexander and Isobel are still absorbed in one another, completely ignorant of what has just transpired. Part of me thinks I might be able to issue some kind of warning and change the course of history for Grange Hall.*

*I find the lovers where I left them. Their passion spent, they lie with their limbs entwined, talking lazily about nothing in particular. Ornaments from a nearby side table have toppled to the floor.*

*No one has bothered to retrieve them. They're too lost in one another to notice.*

"Hey!" *I scream at the top of my lungs.* "You have to get out of here!"

*Alex smiles dreamily, oblivious to my presence.* "Do you know what I'm thinking, my love?" *he asks, his fingers tangled in her hair.*

*Isobel lifts her head from his shoulder and looks at him curiously.* "Tell me," *she whispers.*

"We should go to Italy." *He lowers his lips to her forehead.* "Like Percy Shelley and Mary. She was only seventeen and he was already married, but love overcame all their impediments."

*Isobel casts her eyes up to the chandelier and sighs.* "What a wildly romantic story."

"We shall take James, of course." *It takes me a moment to realize he's talking about their son, who's lying lifeless in his crib upstairs.*

"Do you really think we could?" *I watch Isobel's face change as the idea takes root in her imagination.*

"Of course." *He smiles.* "We would finally be free." *Their combined laughter ripples around the room.*

"When do you expect Carter back?" *Alexander's tone turns sober, but Isobel only stretches languidly.*

"Not for days, my love. He's in London on business. Don't fret. Shall I ring for tea?"

"In a moment. Let me look at you awhile longer."

*Through the transparent door, I see Carter steady himself, preparing to launch like a missile into the library. One arm is positioned oddly behind his back, as if he's shielding something. He's a strong, broad-shouldered man, and it takes only a second for him to ram open the door.*

*Instantly the room becomes charged with adrenaline.*

"Carter!" *Isobel springs to her feet and her face drains of color.*

*Alexander's expression is less fearful and more resigned, as if he knows ahead of time the fate that awaits them all. Carter looks like a raging bull, cheeks burning with fury. His eyes travel over the scene before him. His wife and younger brother are both still in a state of undress. There is no denying what has transpired here...no excuses...no way out. They are both trapped. No one speaks, and yet the silence is deafening. It roars in my ears. Finally, Carter lets out a muffled growl. Isobel is the first to find her voice.*

*"This was my doing!" she cries. "Punish me, but do not blame Alexander for my indiscretion."*

*Carter gives his wife a passing glance, something between loathing and indifference. "Oh, I've no doubt who the instigator was," he replies. The lack of emotion in his voice is chilling. I feel my stomach plummet. Alex pushes Isobel behind him, refusing to let her bear the brunt of Carter's wrath. I don't blame him; the look in Carter's eyes is one of a madman. "You are both fools," he hisses, "to think you can mock me like this. Under my own roof! Is this how you repay my generosity, brother?"*

*"We did not intend for this to happen," Alex begins, but his voice falters, as though he doesn't feel he has any right to defend himself. Carter throws back his head and roars with a demented sound.*

*"Your intention is noted. But you shall both pay the price for this." Isobel rushes to Carter's side and falls to her knees.*

*"Please!" she implores. "I beg you to forgive us."*

*Carter reaches down and seizes a fistful of her hair, dragging her to her feet.*

*"Don't touch her!" Alexander runs to her aid, but before he can reach her, I catch a glimpse of something polished appearing from behind Carter's back. A second later he's pointing the barrel of a Colt Dragoon Revolver at his brother's chest. I'm not sure how I*

know the name of the gun. I just do. And I know that's its sleek and powerful and deadly.

Isobel screams, her eyes filled with panic. The words spill out and ricochet around the room. "I beg you, don't hurt him. I'll do anything you ask!"

Carter looks down at her as if he thinks he might be contaminated by her touch.

"It's too late for that, my darling." He throws her roughly aside, and she crashes into the fireplace. Soot stains her hands and tears stream down her cheeks. "You were a whore when I married you, and you're still a whore today."

"I'm so sorry," Isobel sobs. I'm not sure whether the words are meant for Carter or Alexander or both.

"I took you in," Carter roars. "You were penniless with nothing but your looks to recommend you. I gave you a life of luxury, and this is the thanks I get."

"Listen to me…" Alexander begins, trying to reason with him. "Please try to…" He falls silent when Carter cocks the gun. Keeping it pointed firmly at his brother, Carter stalks over to Isobel, his boots heavy on the plush rug. "What a fine example you have set for our son," he sneers. "I had hoped he would take after me. But today I learned that only the blood of an adulterous harlot and a coward ran through his veins."

Isobel stops midsob at his use of the past tense. A hideous realization grips her. She lets out a strangled sound and, wide-eyed with terror, pushes past Carter and bolts upstairs.

The two brothers stand facing one another until an earsplitting shriek from the nursery shatters the silence. Alex seems to fold at the waist like all the stuffing has been knocked out of him. When he looks up again, his eyes are bright with unshed tears. All he cares about in the world has been lost.

*Without warning, the vision steers me back to the nursery, where Isobel is on her knees clasping a bundle of blankets to her chest and rocking back and forth in silent lamentation.*

*When the gunshot sounds downstairs, her mouth opens in a silent agonized scream. She doesn't need to see his body to know that Alex, too, is dead.*

# CHAPTER TWENTY-SIX

Released from the vision, I fell to my knees on the footbridge, panting for air. Isobel still hovered on the other side of the river. The backdrop didn't look real, like a charcoal sketch that could disintegrate at any moment. I realized the Hunt sisters were right—I was looking directly into another dimension, into the spirit realm. Like the legendary River Styx, the lake separated the world of the living from the world of the dead. Isobel's voice called out to me, as silky as a siren's.

"Come with me, Chloe," she said. "It's so peaceful here."

My mind was cloudy and my vision seemed to tunnel, blocking out Mavis and May as they called my name. On Isobel's side of the river, the clouds rolled away and a resplendent light broke through, bathing everything in a dreamy bronze sheen. Isobel was no longer a chilling phantom; she was beautiful, even serene in her glittering golden world. I couldn't stop the idea from sprouting in my mind like a weed. Maybe there was a place where all self-doubt and suffering could end. Maybe I was being offered an escape from the desolation and hardship that life brought with it. Isobel was showing me the way. All I had to do was follow her. I felt my feet start to move, inching closer.

"You can rest here, Chloe," her fluty voice affirmed. "Nothing will ever trouble you again. You can be with the one you love. She's waiting for you."

Behind me, the bridge was beginning to fall apart, crumbling like powder and pushing me forward into the brilliant light. I could hear the voices of the Hunt sisters somewhere, but I didn't know what they were saying and I wasn't really listening. I was ready to follow Isobel into the blissful white. I stretched out my hand, and just as our fingers were about to lock—

"Wait!" a voice cried out, and Alex's figure appeared on the riverbank. He was side by side with his former love, and yet there was so much distance between them. His luminous blue eyes were full of dread, but through my trance, I couldn't work out why. "Chloe, don't take her hand!"

"Alex!" I was so overjoyed to see him all I could think about was joining him. "I'm coming with you! I'm choosing peace."

"You're choosing death," he replied. "This is an illusion. With every step, your life ebbs away, and soon you will be trapped in the shadows with us forever."

"But I want an eternity with you," I said and watched an expression of triumph spread across Isobel's face.

"Of course you do," she crooned. "There is no heartache or loneliness in our world."

"There is *only* heartache and loneliness!" Alex cried. "Don't listen to her, Chloe! If you cross over, you won't be able to get back! You'll be trapped there forever! She wants you dead, Chloe! She wants to see you throw your life away."

He moved forward like a flash and succeeded in snapping the connection between our fingertips. I reeled back, feeling as if someone had thumped me in the chest. At the same time Isobel let out an incensed screech.

"Go back!" Alex yelled, but I couldn't. It was happening again. The world was shifting before my eyes as I was caught in the throes of another vision. The transition happened so fast this time, it made my head reel. But the setting didn't change; it was the same place…only different.

*It's dawn and the sun fights weakly to break through the canopy of dense cloud. The river seems younger, fresher somehow, and I realize it's because the weeds haven't started to emerge and the dock isn't yet wasting away. Isobel wanders along the riverbank, unaware that her hem trails inches deep in mud. She walks aimlessly, clutching a bundle to her chest. It's the body of her infant son. She doesn't seem distraught anymore, just dazed and distant. There are leaves caught in her hair and scratches along her arms as though she has rushed here full pelt through the woods, crashing into the scrub along her way. Her face is smudged and tearstained as she looks vacantly around for someone to help her. But there is no one left. Alex is already dead, slumped on the library floor, and although I can't see it, I know Carter is swinging from a tree on the end of a noose. The servants have fled in alarm and the house is empty. Isobel has nothing to live for anymore and no one to turn to. She is completely alone.*

*There's desperation in her movements as she slumps, defeated, on a slope and gingerly places the little lifeless body beside her. She's still rocking rhythmically back and forth as if to soothe the pain. Then she does something unexpected. On her hands and knees, she begins scrabbling in the dirt, grabbing handfuls of stones. She stuffs them into every pocket of her elaborate dress, into her soft leather riding boots, her bodice and her hooped petticoat, weighing herself down. Then, cradling her dead child in her arms, she moves like a sleepwalker toward the water. She's humming a lullaby, a tune I recognize, as it used to trail after me in the corridors of Grange Hall.*

> *"Lullaby and good-night, thy mother's delight*
> *Bright angels beside my darling abide."*

*Isobel stops singing and bends to kiss her baby's stone-cold cheek. She's hit by a fresh wash of distress and shakes her head vehemently, muttering under her breath. She looks down into the swathe of fabric and then shakes it fiercely. But there is no response, no cry of life. She squeezes her eyes shut, trying to will the truth away, but when she looks again, nothing has changed. Her body convulses with tearless sobs. The sound she makes is so alarming I want to cover my ears. She doesn't sound human anymore; she sounds like a wild animal. Even though Isobel Reade has done her utmost to torment me since my arrival, it's impossible for me to hate her in this pitiful state.*

*Suddenly she is silent as she looks out at the glassy water. For the first time, the unbearable anguish in her eyes fades, replaced by a strange kind of acceptance.*

*The reeds rustle as she pushes through them to the water's edge. It must be cold, but she doesn't even shiver. It's as if all her senses have shut down. This can't be happening. I watch dumbstruck as she wades into the black lake up to her waist and doesn't stop. The stones and the heavy fabric of her dress drag her down to her watery grave. With her child still clutched in her arms, Isobel sinks below the water. I expect a struggle, but only a few bubbles appear on the surface of the lake, and she's gone.*

*I turn away as the baby's blue blanket drifts to the surface and floats away, carried by the gentle ripples of the water.*

★ ★ ★

As the vision faded, the past and the present seemed to merge. Now Isobel's ghost was standing right in front of me. Any sympathy I felt for her was snuffed out by the ferocious look in her eyes. I had no time to escape or even back away as the ghost rushed forward, her face contorted in a vitriolic mask. There was nothing I could do to stop what happened next.

Her spirit invaded my body like a million tiny electrical currents. The alien presence made me feel like I was literally being split in two. I wanted to scratch and tear at myself, but I knew I couldn't get her out. Already I could feel the ghost sapping my energy, siphoning away my life force. Sharing a body with the dead was enervating, and I was losing the battle fast. Alex watched on, horror scrawled over his face. His body was braced as if he wanted to run forward, but there was no point now. Isobel was beyond his reach. How could he stop her without hurting me? For minutes the internal tug-of-war continued, and I was certain I would never come out of this alive.

"Let her be!" his tortured cry rang out. "Isobel, stop!"

"You always knew this was how it would end." The voice of Isobel spoke through me. It was alarming to feel my mouth move and know that I wasn't controlling it.

"Haven't we seen enough death?" Alex implored. "Do not force an innocent girl into the same fate. Even you are not that cruel. This is your chance for redemption. Take it!"

"She's not innocent," Isobel hissed. "She will destroy us both."

I felt myself struggle to the surface for a brief moment.

"Alex!" I managed to croak out before Isobel beat me down and resumed control once again.

I screamed as I felt my internal organs shift, but the scream quickly morphed into a maniacal laugh. Isobel forced my body to the ground, pressing my face into the mud. My arms and legs thrashed as I struggled with myself. I couldn't tell anymore which movements were my own and which belonged to her. I could feel myself edging closer to the shadow world. There was a strong swallowing sensation, like I was headed toward a whirlpool, but I couldn't command my legs to stop moving. I tried to send messages to my brain, but the interference blocked them. The shadow world whispered to me, voices from the beyond calling out. Some were crying, some moaning. The light had waned now, and I was looking into a skeletal land that looked as if it were made from nothing but dust and bones. I was right on the fringe, on the verge of taking the final step. A host of spirit beings appeared, hovering above the ground, their faces wasted and reedy arms extended in welcome. Something was happening. I could feel my spirit starting to detach, leaving my body behind, an empty vessel.

An indistinct figure appeared in my path, glowing with a soft light. The outline of a woman emerged, her face rubbed out like on a news show when they try to protect the identity of a witness. I could see that she was wearing flowing clothes, and her dark curly hair hung lose around her shoulders. I recognized that hair. I saw it every day on my little brother.

"Mom?" I whispered.

The vision grew clearer, her face coming into focus until there she was, standing right in front of me like it was just another ordinary day. She was wearing her favorite blue sweater,

and it was the only speck of color in the gray wasteland behind her. I was gripped with a sudden fear. I didn't want the
vision to end. I couldn't lose my mother a second time.

"Surrender." Isobel's taunt rang in my ears. "And you shall
never be separated from her again."

I stood and took a decisive step forward, longing to run
into my mother's arms.

"Chloe, wait." She held up her hands and smiled at me
like I was a child again. "This isn't what I want for you."

"Mom…" I heard my voice crack. "I miss you so much.
Why did you have to leave?"

"My time was up," she said. "I'm sorry, Chloe. I never
wanted to go."

"Then let me come with you."

"No, my darling." She shook her head. "Your life is just
beginning."

I hugged myself, trying to keep from falling apart. "It's
too hard without you," I whispered. "I can't do it."

"You've always been strong," she replied. "Even when you
were just a little girl. You told those ghosts to leave, and they
did. You can do it again."

I could feel her presence now, like a protective shield
around me, an unexpected ally. But my mom was not a spirit
in torment. She didn't belong here. She had already passed on
to the next life, and I knew she wouldn't be able to stay for
long. I might never get another opportunity to see or speak
to her again. Right now she was so close, within reach. But
it couldn't last.

"Don't you want me with you?" The hot tears I'd been
holding back sprang forth now to course down my cheeks.

"I want you to *live*, Chloe," she said. "Remember all your

dreams? I want to see them realized, every last one. One day we'll be together again. But not today."

"When, Mom?" I whispered. I was so reluctant to let her go; I wanted to grab her and hang on for dear life.

"When it's time," she answered. "You're going to do great things with your life. I've always known you would. And I'll be watching. Just remember who you are and make me proud, okay?" She was already starting to fade.

"Okay," I said, then added as a desperate afterthought, "I love you! I don't think I said that enough."

"I know you do." She smiled. "I love you, too, my darling girl. I'm always with you."

"Wait! How will I know if I'm making the right decisions?"

Mom smiled as if she had total confidence in me. It was the same smile that had gotten me through countless challenges in life so far. I felt bolstered by it.

"You'll know because they'll be yours."

Then, just like that, she was gone. But the power of her presence remained behind like a healing aura. I felt my strength return and slowly swell inside me like a tidal wave. I closed my eyes and took control of my body. Every inch of it belonged to me and me alone. I was going to live, because that was what my mom would have wanted. This wasn't just about me anymore. I needed to live for my father, for my little brother and for Grandma Fee. I was choosing life and closing the door on the world of the dead, locking them back where they belonged. I wouldn't let my mother down. With a sound like splitting wood, Isobel was evicted from my body. The ghost flew out and landed on the riverbank. She looked up at me, this time with genuine bafflement in her eyes.

"It's not possible," she gasped.

"You have to go," I told her brazenly. "You can't stay here."

She snarled at me, but I stood my ground. I remembered my mother taking my hand when I was six years old and imparting these words: *They only exist if you allow them to exist, Chloe.* I knew what I had to do then. I had to lock Isobel out of my head and at the same time lock her out of this world.

"I'm not afraid of you," I said. I could feel my mind starting to close already, pushing against her, forcing her out. She could only hold on as long as I did. If I didn't believe in her, she had nothing to cling to. My whole body contracted with the effort, but it was working. I was literally willing her into nonexistence.

I realized something then. Mom had been right all along. I saw ghosts only because my mind was open to them, always wondering when the next one might appear. But a closed mind is like a closed door. They cannot get in.

"You don't really exist," I told her. "You're dead."

*Dead.* The word seemed to echo, bouncing off the trees and hitting Isobel in the chest. She let out a harrowing wail and the shadow world began to shrink around her. I could see an expression of pure relief flood Alex's face. I didn't want to let him go, but there was no way around it. It seemed as if a portal was opening before me like a vortex and the memories of the past were being sucked back into it. I saw Carter, noose in hand. I saw the infant James swaddled in his blanket. I saw Alex's sketchbook and Becky the maid and Benjamin in his boat as they all flew past me and vanished into the twister of gray light. Then it was Isobel's turn. She stretched her arms up to the sky and opened her mouth in a pitiful howl as she was engulfed and torn away from the house she had haunted for more than one hundred and fifty years.

*"No!"* Her scream reverberated through the woods long after she was gone.

There was only one person left.

"I'm so sorry," I whispered as Alex in turn began to blur at the edges. He was still the most devastatingly beautiful vision I'd ever seen. I longed to run to him, but his form was transparent now, glowing and intangible. He had been so real to me; now I felt like I was watching him die. I didn't know if he could hear me, but there was something I needed to say.

"You'll never know how much you meant to me."

His eyes didn't leave mine as he raised one hand in a final farewell. Then he, too, surrendered to the light. It swallowed him up...and Alexander Reade was gone. The churning vortex disappeared with a crack and I was left staring at an ordinary lake.

I turned back to the world of the living, where the Hunt sisters were waiting for me. But my legs didn't seem to be working properly. All my energy had been leached from the internal battle. The last thing I saw was May's beaming face and the sisters running to catch me before I hit the ground.

There was only one thought left in my head. *It's over now.*

# CHAPTER TWENTY-SEVEN

The next few days passed in a blur as I tried to piece together what had actually happened at the lake. When I woke in my bed, with Grandma Fee and members of the household standing over me, I had no recollection of the events that had transpired. But it started to come back to me in disjointed flashes, like a dream. One thing was certain: Grange Hall was a different place now. The presence of the ghosts could no longer be felt in its walls and arbors. Even the sisters confirmed their EMF reader was now picking up zero activity. Alex and Isobel were gone.

The one image that kept coming back to me was Alex's brilliant eyes as he was wrenched away into the afterlife. We hadn't even gotten a proper goodbye.

Alex was now a part of my past. I would think of him incessantly over the next few months, but then it would inevitably begin to taper off. Eventually he would be nothing but a distant memory recalled fondly from time to time. I had no physical record of our time together, and there weren't any photographs or mementos to keep his memory alive. I wondered whether there would come a time when I'd try to conjure his face in my mind but it would be blurry.

Christmas had crept up on us and was now only days away. It was going to be a low-key family affair, just the way we wanted it. I didn't feel like we had much to celebrate. Even the expulsion of the ghosts wasn't the victory it should have been. If truth were told—and I hated to admit this—the house felt kind of empty without them. The Hunt sisters had spent the past few days parading around, proud as peacocks because the Baton Rouge Paranormal Society was going to publish their paper entitled "The Haunted Homes of Rural England." They seemed to think it would kick-start their careers as professional ghost busters, and I pretended to be happy for them. They were leaving soon, to spend the remainder of the holidays with their families.

"Don't be down in the dumps, Chloe," Mavis told me on her last day as I watched her pack a small suitcase with precision. "You've got your whole life ahead of you."

"I've heard that before," I said. "But coming from you… I might actually believe it."

"You better." She winked at me.

"I guess I'm just confused. I discovered that I have this… *gift,* but I still don't know what I'm supposed to do with it. Is my whole life going to change now?"

"You make it sound like you have a disease, dear." May laughed. "You don't need to have all the answers. Things will become clear in time. You might end up devoting your life to communing with the dead, or you might choose to ignore them for the rest of your days."

"It's up to you." Mavis patted my shoulder. "Your gift will change your life if you *want* it to. Besides, the future tends to take care of itself. All we can do is deal with the here and now. That keeps us busy enough, don't you think?"

Eccentric as they were, I was going to miss the Hunt sisters and their quirky routine. But I would take their advice and focus on leading a normal life—well, as normal as possible, for someone like me. I was starting to realize that maybe it was okay to be me. Maybe I didn't need to spend my days wishing I could be like everyone else. I'd been created this way for a reason. Perhaps that reason wasn't entirely apparent yet, but I believed that someday it would all make sense.

If the saga with Isobel had taught me anything, it was that holding grudges didn't pay off. If I died tomorrow, would I want to go out bitter and full of resentment? It was hardly worth it. If you had no peace of mind in life, you would have no peace in death.

I left the Hunt sisters to their packing and went downstairs, where Rory and Dad were engaged in a chess battle in the library. Things were starting to take on a semblance of normality, and it felt almost like a family vacation from my childhood.

In the kitchen, I found who I was looking for. Miss Grimes was stooped over the counter, stuffing a turkey for Christmas dinner. Usually, I went out of my way to avoid her, but today I walked right over.

"Do you need any help?" She glanced at me suspiciously, as if my offer was some kind of trap. "I know you don't like me very much," I went on. She fixed her eyes on the bird determinedly and hunched over as if trying to will me away. "But I have a message for you."

I paused a moment, searching for the right words. She had to be in her eighties, and I didn't want to startle her into a heart attack. Wouldn't that just be the icing on top of a perfect visit? But there was really only one way to say this. "Benjamin wants you to know he's okay…and that he loves you."

Miss Grimes dropped her fork with a clatter. Her knotted hands clutched the countertop as she turned slowly to face me, eyes nearly bugging out of her withered old face. I always used to think she was scary, with her straggly hair and stale smell. But today she just looked sad, like someone who had lost her reason for living a long time ago and was just going through the motions while she waited for death.

"He doesn't blame you," I said. "Nobody does." Then I walked out of the kitchen, leaving her gaping after me.

Out in the garden I found an unexpected burst of sunshine and stopped to savor the feel of it on my skin. I saw Gran bossily directing Harry, who was staggering under the weight of an enormous Christmas tree. The clean scent of pine was already wafting over to me. The porch was strung with lights and a silver wreath adorned the front door.

"Classy," I commented when Gran reached me.

"We like to keep things understated around here," she replied with a wink. "Not like you Americans with your flashing reindeer and Santa Claus popping out of every chimney."

*"Americans,"* I agreed, smothering a smile. "So I was thinking I might go see Joe. It won't be much of a Christmas for him, stuck in a hospital bed."

Gran didn't say anything at first; she just dug around in the pocket of her tailored pants. Then she tossed me something. I caught it midair and opened my palm to find the keys to her Mercedes.

"Seriously?" I asked. "You're letting me drive your car? What if I wreck it or get a parking fine or something?"

"You're all grown up now, Chloe," she answered. "I think you can handle yourself."

I didn't know what to say. Coming from Grandma Fee, this was a big deal. It was her way of telling me we were equals now. The adult/child relationship had been dissolved.

"Thanks." I smiled at her. "I won't mess up."

I found Joe lying in bed, flipping aimlessly through a sports magazine. "How's the patient today?" I asked as I pushed open the door.

"Thank God." He let out a low whistling breath. "I'm literally dying of boredom."

"Better than dying from a chandelier."

"Nope," he said as I settled in the chair by the bed. "The chandelier would have been faster."

"You just need to kill some time," I replied jovially. "Are you a fan of knitting?"

"Shut up." He rolled his eyes. "I start rehab tomorrow. I can't wait to get back on a horse."

"How about you get back on your feet first," I teased.

"It'll be a while," Joe said resignedly. "They said two months at least. Looks like I'll be spending Christmas in here."

"Ugh." I sighed. "I'm so sorry. That really sucks."

"It's not so bad." He smiled. "The ladies down the hall are going to put on the over-sixties version of 'Jingle Bell Rock.' I feel pretty bad for everyone who's going to miss that."

I laughed. Trust Joe to be a good sport, even in the crappiest situation. But there was still something I needed to get off my chest. I twisted my hands nervously.

"You know, I never got a chance to say thank-you."

He turned his face slightly, hair rustling against the stiff pillow. "Don't mention it."

"No, really," I insisted. "Look what happened to you. You did that for me."

"Chloe…" His green eyes gazed up at me. "I'd do it a thousand times over. I'd rather be in here than see you in here. That would really break my heart."

Why did he have to go and say that? I had to sit very still for a minute to keep from choking up.

"I think you're the best friend in the world," I said eventually.

"Yeah, yeah, I know." Joe chuckled. "So how are you doing? How's all the…*stuff?*"

"I think it's over," I said.

"Really?" He raised his eyebrows. "How did that happen?"

"I wish I could tell you," I replied honestly. "It was so fast, I can barely remember anything. But I know they're gone… and they're not coming back."

Joe nodded thoughtfully. "I always believed you, you know?" he said. "I didn't always understand it, but I never doubted that you were telling the truth. You're really special, Chloe, and I…" He trailed off.

"You're not about to say you love me?" I asked teasingly, trying to lighten the mood. I didn't want this conversation to go somewhere we wouldn't be able to come back from.

Joe smiled. "You just think you're such hot stuff."

I gestured down at my sweatpants and Grandma Fee's sneakers that I'd borrowed from the shoe rack in the hall. "Um…have you seen me?" I said. "I'm in pretty high demand."

Joe laughed, but I could see his eyes becoming serious. "I don't say *I love you* that easily," he told me.

"Good," I replied. "Nobody should."

"But the thing is, Chloe…" He bit his lip. "I think I might be falling for you. I wouldn't take a chandelier for just anyone."

"How do you know that for sure?" I asked, partly out of genuine curiosity and partly because I wanted to avoid having to respond. "What do you think love really feels like?"

"I don't think love is just a feeling," Joe said. "I think it's a commitment. Lust is a feeling, and that's what hits you first. But you have to wait until it passes. Once it's gone, what are you left with? That's the real stuff, underneath." He looked to the ceiling. "When I get married one day, I want to be so committed to my wife that no matter what happens I'll never leave her. We might fight, she might cheat, we might sleep in separate rooms for a whole year. But I won't walk away. So when I tell a girl I love her, I'm going to really mean it."

"You're a rare individual, Joe Parrish," I told him. "Any girl would be lucky to have you."

"I want to be in your life, Chloe, wherever you are."

"I'd like that," I said.

I left the hospital that night thinking about what Joe had told me. I'd never heard words like that from any of the boys back home. They were all about beer pong and attempting to get your pants off at record speed. Joe really was one of the good guys…a good egg, as Grandma Fee would say. I'd miss Joe when I got back to California. I didn't want to forget him, and I promised myself we'd stay in touch. A precious friendship had blossomed between us, and if I hadn't fallen so hard for Alex, who knew where we might have ended up?

At Grange Hall, I found everyone in the sitting room, helping decorate the tree from a giant box of sparkling ornaments. I peeked inside and pulled out an item wrapped carefully in tissue paper. I unraveled it to reveal a lopsided angel made of wire and cotton wool.

"What's this?"

"Your father made that for our tree when he was five years old," Grandma Fee said proudly. "And one every year after that until he turned eighteen."

I smiled. "And here I was thinking you weren't the sentimental type. You kept them all?"

"Every last one."

I smirked at Dad. "You were very…um…creative?"

"Christmas isn't about having the best tree in town," Gran said. "It's about spending time with the people you love."

That gave me an idea. I decided right then that if Joe couldn't go home for Christmas, I would bring Christmas to him. I took Gran aside and outlined my master plan.

"You know something, Chloe?" she said when I was done. "I know we haven't always seen eye to eye, but I'm proud to call you my granddaughter."

On Christmas Eve we drove to the hospital together. I called Joe's family ahead of time and told them about my plan to make sure my visit didn't overlap with theirs. I was worried they'd shoot down the idea, but they jumped right on board. Gran went in first and convinced Joe to take a walk with her. We both knew he'd agree; he had trouble refusing her anything. I waited for the squeak of his wheelchair to disappear down the corridor before ducking in and getting to work. I wound tinsel around his monitor and hung a monogrammed stocking from the end of his bed. I propped a flashing reindeer that Gran had found in some bargain basement against a wall and plugged it in.

Joe's laptop lay open on the bed, an essay for school half-written on the screen. I slipped in a CD of cheesy Christmas carols and hit Play. I'd also packed a hamper full of weird British Christmas fare that I'd never eaten and probably wouldn't touch with a ten-foot pole—things like fruitcake and mince pies, roasted chestnuts and a thermos of something called mulled wine.

When Joe returned to the room, he found me waiting on his bed in a Santa hat with "Winter Wonderland" chiming in the background.

"Chloe!" His face cracked into the widest grin I'd ever seen. "What are you doing here?"

"Merry Christmas Eve, Joe. Did you think I was going to let you spend it alone?" He looked around the room, awestruck.

"You've gone to so much trouble."

"Oh pish posh," I said with a wink, thinking back to all the weird phrases I'd heard Grandma Fee use over the past few weeks.

"Did you just…" Joe beamed at me. "Who *are* you?"

"Just think of me as the friendly neighborhood Christmas elf." I winked and tossed him a matching hat. "Now, let the festivities begin."

I lay in bed that night feeling for the first time like I might be able to get my life back on track. All I needed to do was pretend that the past few weeks were nothing but a dream. They were starting to feel that way.

I shivered as a draft from the broken window blew into the room, lifting a slip of paper no bigger than a greeting card on my dresser and sending it floating to the floor. I swear it hadn't been there when I left this afternoon. I got up to shut the window and tugged on an extra sweater for warmth. Then I knelt down to retrieve the paper....

It was a charcoal portrait of a young woman with soft tendrils of hair swept to one side and knotted with a ribbon. The girl was looking over her shoulder as if the artist had caught her by surprise. She wore a long gown and loose curls framed her creamy cheeks. In one hand she twirled a parasol. Her features were graceful, eyes playful and full of life. It took me a moment to realize that the girl in the portrait was me. A hankering took hold of me for something I couldn't quite put my finger on. In the picture, I looked more comfortable than I was in my own skin. How was that even possible? Somehow, I felt like I'd been this girl before, and part of me wished I could melt into the page and live in her world.

There was a note scrawled in ink at the bottom. It was dated from two weeks ago:

*Happy Birthday, Chloe. May you live to see many more.*

It was a gift from Alex. So he hadn't forgotten my birthday. He must have been planning to give this to me, only he never got the chance. I pressed it to my chest. I wanted to keep it with me always, the only part of him I had left. But as the seconds ticked by and I looked out at the dark grounds of Grange Hall, I was reminded that Alexander Reade was gone forever and no amount of wishing would bring him back. Tomorrow I would spend Christmas with my family and then it would be time to go home.

I folded the picture and slipped it between the pages of *Madame Bovary*. There were so many emotions stirring in my chest and I couldn't allow them to surface. I thought about the iron vault in my mind, where I locked away everything that was painful. If I wanted to move on with my life, maybe that was where I'd need to bury my memories of Alex, file them away where they couldn't hurt me. But hard as I tried, I couldn't eject him from my thoughts. He'd left a handprint on my heart, and it beat faster every time I let myself think about him.

At least I finally had an answer to my question. Where did our loved ones go after death? They didn't go anywhere. They stayed right where you left them, because you carried them with you. They were a part of you, like a tattoo. Trying to forget them was like trying to forget you had legs.

I could put Alex's portrait of me away in a drawer where I wouldn't have to look at it, but what difference would that make? I'd only be burying the problem, not solving it. So I removed the picture from the pages of the book and smoothed it out carefully. I didn't want to forget it existed after all. This drawing was the only thing I had to remind myself that he was real and that our relationship had meant something before I'd lost him.

Although *lost* wasn't really the right word. He'd never been mine to keep.

# CHAPTER TWENTY-EIGHT

After the chilled air and rolling hills of rural England, coming home to dusty California was like an assault on the senses. The contrast was so sharp it was almost painful. Unlike the sleepy town of Wistings, my urban landscape was uninspiring. Even though I was back on home turf, I was suddenly aware of how bleak it was, with the thunderous roar of traffic in my ears and the indifferent glances from strangers. The prosaic city sprawled like an octopus with no sense of order or design. It swallowed you up and made you feel irrelevant.

Slipping back into my old life wouldn't come easily. I preferred the Chloe I was morphing into. The old me felt banal and shallow in comparison. Rory didn't look any happier, either, as he stared glumly out the car window. The cab that had picked us up from LAX smelled strongly of cigarette smoke masked with cheap cologne. On the skyline, smog made the skyscrapers hazy, like a grimy veil had been draped over everything. *Home sweet home,* I thought bitterly.

When I got back to the house, I knew something had changed. After the funeral, I'd felt my mother's presence everywhere. But she was gone now. Even her room was just a space filled with stuff. I barely even recognized my own bedroom when I walked into it. It didn't feel like it belonged to me anymore.

January rolled around so fast, it was time to go back to school before I knew it. On the first day of spring semester, I sat at the wheel of the burned-orange Volvo Mom had driven for ten years. It was mine now. It had been offered to me before, but I'd been holding out for my dream car, a black BMW with leather seats, a sunroof and less than fifty miles on the clock. But I didn't care about that anymore. The Volvo felt just right, and I imagined I could smell traces of Mom's perfume, like it had been preserved in the upholstery.

I didn't get out of the car right away. I decided to sit in the parking lot and wait till the last minute to get out. I couldn't keep my mind from traveling back to the last trip my mom and I had taken together in this car. It had been the day she died.

There was nothing remarkable about that day. It began like any other, the usual mad rush out the door, me trying to apply mascara in the car and Rory deliberately poking me in the side, just to be annoying. But when Sycamore High came into view, my mom didn't slow down.

"Mom! You drove right past the gate," I exclaimed.

"I did, didn't I?" She blinked like she was taking in her surroundings for the first time. "I just went blank for a minute." Her embarrassment made me soften my tone.

"*Someone* needs their morning coffee. Are you okay?"

"Of course, just sleep deprived." She massaged her temples with her fingertips.

"Maybe you need a spa day. You work way too hard."

"Maybe *we* could use a spa day." She grinned. "We haven't hung out just the two of us in a while." I knew she missed that. So did I, but life got in the way and somehow we never found the time.

"Let's do it," I said before she waved me out of the car.

I grabbed my backpack and watched her pull away from the curb, a little more cautiously than usual. "Be careful!" I called after her, but I didn't think she heard me.

That was the last time I saw her alive. I wished I'd said *I love you*. For a while after she died, I was tormented by the idea that I could have done more, like told her to go home or call my dad. It probably wouldn't have changed anything. And at least now I knew she wasn't as faraway as I thought.

Through the window, I watched the student body of Sycamore High arrive. There were plenty of parking spaces, but I'd chosen the one farthest from the entrance. I wanted my return to be as low-key as possible.

I turned my head briefly and saw Zac Green on the front steps, coming in from training. He'd been my crush for as long as I could remember. I half raised my hand in greeting. Zac smiled back and headed inside. I was distracted by the sound of French-manicured nails rapping urgently on my window. Sam and Natalie stood outside the car, examining the pumpkin color with expressions of deep concern. I opened the door to an onslaught of questions.

"Chloe! Where have you been? Why haven't you returned any of our calls?"

"Is everything okay? We thought they might have married you off to some lord with terrible teeth."

"Everything's fine, guys," I said with a laugh. "I've just been busy settling back in."

I looked at them properly as I got out of the car. They'd both dressed to the nines for the first day of the new semester. Sam was going through a vintage phase and wearing a pair of fringed cowboy boots, the sort of thing I'd never be able to pull off in a million years.

"I like your...shirt?" Natalie told me in a tone that made it perfectly clear what she thought of my shirt. I glanced down at my outfit. It was true, I hadn't put much effort into it. I was wearing a pair of jeans with a plain navy T-shirt and Converse.

I'd scraped my hair up in a ponytail, and the only makeup I'd bothered to apply was a dab of lip balm. Back at Grange Hall, I'd never felt the need to dress up. There was nobody to impress and no one's approval to win. But my friends, with their slavish devotion to fashion, couldn't keep the judgment out of their eyes.

"So did you meet Prince Harry?" Nat asked, to break the awkward silence.

"Sorry to disappoint you," I replied, and she looked genuinely crestfallen.

"Oh well, I'm sure London was awesome, right? What was the fashion like?"

"I wouldn't know," I replied. "I never left the village."

"The *village?*" she repeated. "Sounds like *Lord of the Rings* or something."

"Was there a guy?" Sam nudged me. "There had to be a guy."

"What?" I scoffed. "Of course not."

I'd never been a very good liar, and they saw right through me. "Who is he?" they squealed. "Tell us!"

"He's no one," I said emphatically.

"Aha!" Sam pointed a finger at me. "So he does exist."

I let out a long sigh. It was easier to offer them something than to let this tedious conversation continue. Part of me wanted to blurt out that I'd met a mystery man on horseback with eyes like jewels, but I didn't dare.

"His name is Joe," I said, and just to watch them freak out, I added, "He's related to the Duke of Canterbury." They both stopped walking and stared at me, mouths hanging open. "It's going to be a summer wedding and of course the Queen will be invited."

"You idiot!" Sam punched my arm. "We totally believed you."

We parted ways as we all headed to our first class of the semester. Being back at school was already starting to feel like a lot of effort. The corridors were buzzing with activity, and I kept my head down to avoid making eye contact. I'd grown accustomed to the peace and quiet of Grange Hall, and the flurry of animated conversation was overwhelming. I had Spanish first up, so I gathered my mountain of books and headed over early. The classroom felt foreign to me now. My mind kept flashing back to the misty, undulating hills of Wistings, the branches of the majestic willows sweeping the ground.

Memories and images keep spinning through my mind: Alex standing by the open window of my quaint little bedroom, the way it had felt when he'd become solid beneath my fingertips, the image of his figure shimmering and vanishing into the dark night.

"Hey." Someone touched my shoulder. I looked up, heart thumping. But it was only Zac Green again in his low-slung jeans and polo shirt that matched the exact shade of his eyes. He leaned against the desk, looking calm and unruffled as always. His straight blond hair had grown over the break, and he tucked a loose strand behind his ears.

"How was your Christmas?" I didn't answer for a moment and he took in my expression. "Is everything okay?"

"Yeah…" I shook myself. "Sorry, I thought you were someone else."

"You don't feel like you belong here anymore, do you?" Zac asked with uncharacteristic insight. He seemed different than the way I remembered him, not at all like the brawny jock I'd always pegged him to be. He was supposed to be one of the guys you could enjoy looking at but not get much satisfaction talking to. That was what Sam had always said, but then again, she wasn't exactly queen of intelligent conversation herself.

"I just…" I was taken by surprise at first, but then I figured there was no reason not to be honest. "I'm not really sure how I feel."

"One day at a time," Zac told me. "And every day it gets a little easier."

"When did you get so wise?"

"My little sister died when I was in ninth grade," he said.

My head shot up. Zac had come to Sycamore High in tenth grade, and I'd never spent enough time with him to know details about his past. I wondered how many people knew.

"I'm so sorry," I stammered. "I wish I'd known."

He waved a hand. "I'm not trying to make you feel bad, Chloe. I'm just saying if you ever need someone to talk to—" he gave an unassuming shrug of his broad shoulders "—I'm around."

With a gentle punch of camaraderie on the shoulder, he took a seat at the back of the room. Needless to say, I couldn't concentrate throughout the entire lesson. Luckily all the teachers had been briefed about my "situation" and knew better than to call on me for answers. Miss Lombardo barely even glanced in my direction, except to offer a brief, sympathetic smile that came across as completely patronizing despite her no-doubt good intentions.

I barely even registered the conjunctive verbs she'd written on the board. Isobel's haunting lullaby was playing in my head, mixed with the screams from the Winter Ball, the sound of Joe's heart monitor in the hospital and the cries of a long-dead baby. One corner of my mind was also trying to conjure the face of Zac's sister, but her features kept changing until she was a bizarre mix of Isobel and my mother and a stranger I didn't recognize.

Through the glass panel of the door, I caught a flash of a figure striding by in a dark coat, his tangle of golden hair falling over his eyes. But his posture was all wrong for a California teenager: too straight, too formal and way too familiar. But of course, when I blinked, he was gone. I had a feeling that was going to happen to me a lot over the next few months. I wasn't over Alex…not by a long shot, and even though he wasn't technically haunting me anymore, I knew I would be haunted by his memory for the rest of my life. I let out a shaky breath and bent determinedly over my notebook. The only way through this was to keep my head down and soldier on. What other choice did I have?

At lunch I met Sam and Natalie at my locker. They noticed my glum face immediately.

"You look miserable," Nat said. "Are you okay?"

I was tired of that question. The answer was a big fat no, a thousand times no. Nothing was okay. I wanted my ghost back. But how could I tell anyone that without seeming like a total freak? I'd sent him away, and now I would never see him again. It was my own fault and my own private torture to live with.

Even though my cheeks were stiff from trying to keep it together, I forced a smile that felt like it might collapse at any moment.

"I'm fine," I said, doing my utmost to sound casual.

"Good," said Sam as we pushed through the throng of students into the cafeteria. "Because we have news."

"Yeah?" I was only half listening, wondering how I could escape to the bathroom and cry. I just wanted to sit in a cubical with my head between my knees and wait for this day to be over.

"There's a new kid," Sam went on. "We saw him arrive this morning and, oh my God, Chloe, he's so gorgeous. Like something off The CW, don't you think, Nat?"

"I would say more ABC Family," she replied. "But yeah, he really had the whole tortured-artist thing going on."

That had to be the least exciting news I could possibly think of. This was a big school and new students arrived all the time. The girls would probably stalk him for a few weeks until the novelty wore off or they found some other network-star look-alike.

"He looks so cute and confused," Sam said dreamily.

"We're just gonna have to help him. Wonder where he's from. What was his name again?"

"Alex something..." Natalie replied, dumping a load of ranch on her salad. "Ray? Rich?"

"Reade!" Sam said triumphantly. "Yeah, that's it! Alexander Reade."

My tray crashed to the cafeteria floor.

★ ★ ★ ★ ★

# ACKNOWLEDGMENTS

Thank you, Momma, for being my best friend and the driving force behind everything I do. Nothing would be possible without you.

Thank you to the talented Natashya Wilson at Harlequin TEEN for being such a thorough editor and making me laugh through the pain with your comments!

Thank you, Pam van Hylckama Vlieg, for being a wonderful literary agent and a generally supercool human being.

Thank you, Mary Katherine Breland, for being my adopted sister and most enthusiastic fan.

Thank you, Clay Lafayette Mcleod III. You will always be on my wavelength. Don't lose your rainbow.

Thank you, Boo Radley. You're a little furry ball of happiness. I'm still convinced you're a human trapped inside a dog's body.

And finally, thank you, God, for your grace.

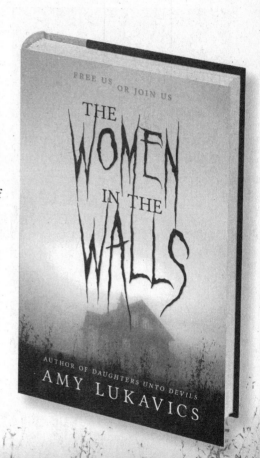

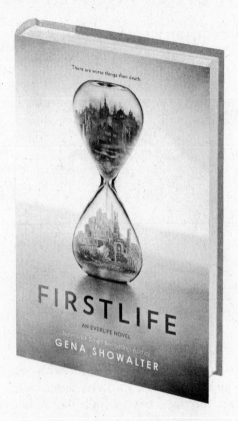

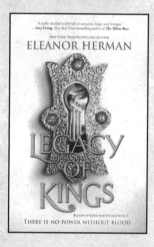
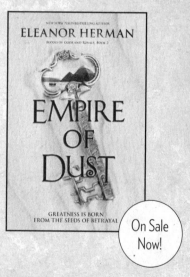